# THE NIGHTMARE GAME

Other books by Gillian Cross

*The Iron Way*
*Revolt at Ratcliffe's Rags*
*A Whisper of Lace*
*The Dark Behind the Curtain*
*Born of the Sun*
*On the Edge*
*Chartbreak*
*Roscoe's Leap*
*A Map of Nowhere*
*Wolf*
*The Great Elephant Chase*
*New World*
*Pictures in the Dark*
*Tightrope*
*Calling a Dead Man*

In this trilogy

*The Dark Ground*
*The Black Room*

For younger readers

*Twin and Super-Twin*
*The Demon Headmaster*
*The Prime Minister's Brain*
*The Revenge of the Demon Headmaster*
*The Demon Headmaster Strikes Again*
*The Demon Headmaster Takes Over*
*Facing the Demon Headmaster*
*Beware of the Demon Headmaster*

# THE NIGHTMARE GAME

GILLIAN CROSS

OXFORD
UNIVERSITY PRESS

**OXFORD**
UNIVERSITY PRESS

Great Clarendon Street, Oxford OX2 6DP

Oxford University Press is a department of the University of Oxford. It furthers the University's objective of excellence in research, scholarship, and education by publishing worldwide in

Oxford New York

Auckland Cape Town Dar es Salaam Hong Kong Karachi
Kuala Lumpur Madrid Melbourne Mexico City Nairobi
New Delhi Shanghai Taipei Toronto

With offices in

Argentina Austria Brazil Chile Czech Republic France Greece
Guatemala Hungary Italy Japan Poland Portugal Singapore
South Korea Switzerland Thailand Turkey Ukraine Vietnam



First published 2006



British Library Cataloguing in Publication Data
Data available

ISBN-13: 978-0-19-271975-1
ISBN-10: 0-19-271975-0

1 3 5 7 9 10 8 6 4 2

Typeset by Newgen Imaging Systems (P) Ltd., Chennai, India
Printed and bound in Great Britain by Mackays of Chatham Ltd, Chatham Kent

*For Helen*

*Whose story is it? Does it belong to Robert, who found himself suddenly, terrifyingly, smaller than a fingernail? He survived the dangerous journey back to his full size, but can he rescue the other tiny people, who saved his life by taking him into their cavern?*

*Or is the focus on Lorn, whose 'real' life was so appalling that she chose to be small for ever, leaving nothing behind? Now that she's safe in the cavern, she'll have to cope with her horrific memories of the past. Is that the core of the story?*

*What about Emma, Robert's sister? She dared to believe what he told her, and she wants to help the people in the cavern. But how will she react if it starts to get dangerous?*

*And then there's Tom. Is he simply a friend, supporting Robert, or is he somehow more important? Will he get drawn in deeper as the mystery unfolds?*

*It doesn't do to forget Lorn's father, either. Or her mother and brother. Or Cam and Zak, and the others in the cavern. No one is insignificant. All their lives are woven together, inextricably. Pull at one thread, to see it better, and the rest of the cloth shrinks and distorts, twisting out of shape.*

*How can any story tell the real truth? How is it even possible to start . . . ?*

Zak stroked the drum that lay in his lap, leaning back against the wall of the cavern and looking at the others as they settled into a circle. Their faces were hidden, except where the firelight caught them, and they were already silent and expectant. Waiting for the story to begin.

When everything was still, Zak tapped the drum-skin lightly and took a slow breath. 'Once upon a time,' he said, 'there was a man who kept his daughter in a hole in the ground.'

Lorn sat forward sharply, her eyes widening. *What are you doing? You can't make a story out of that.*

But he could. He was.

'The man had a wife and a son,' he said, 'and he loved them

well enough. But his daughter was the special one. She was more important than anything else in the whole wide world. Every morning he said to himself, "I'll bring her out of the hole tonight." But every evening, when he lifted off the lid and looked down at her—he couldn't do it.'

Bando burst out into one of his loud, incongruous laughs. 'She was too heavy to lift!'

'No, she wasn't heavy.' Gravely Zak shook his head. 'She wasn't heavy at all. She was as slender as a stalk of silkskin, as light as a moonbeam lying across the grass. He could have picked her up with one hand. But every time he saw her he thought, *She's too beautiful and fragile for the ugly, unkind world. If I take her out, greedy people will come and steal her away. She's safer where she is.* So every evening he put the lid back in its place and shut her away under the ground again.'

'Why did he do that?' Bando said, his simple, heavy face frowning and bewildered.

'Ssh!' Cam said impatiently.

She was trying to keep him in order, but for once her voice had no effect. She ran everything else that went on in the cavern, but Zak's stories were beyond her control. Zak had his own kind of authority and he used it now, ignoring Cam and weaving Bando's question into the story.

'The old man shut his daughter away because she was so precious to him. When he looked at her, all his troubles vanished. So he called her "Hope" and kept her away from the harsh, ugly world outside.'

Lorn felt herself grow hot and angry in the darkness. How could he know so much—and be so wrong? Stories were supposed to be made up, out of nothing, but this one was *real*. Somehow, Zak knew Hope's story—*her* story—and he was twisting it. She had been that poor, imprisoned girl, but not because a kind old man was keeping her safe. He'd locked her away in a deep, dark hole, because . . . because—

The words locked in her throat. She wanted to scream at Zak, to stop him before he said anything else, but she couldn't make a sound.

Zak leaned forward, lowering his voice. 'And then, one evening, three evil robbers came snooping around the old man's house.'

Bando caught his breath.

'They crept across the garden,' Zak whispered, 'and peered through the cracks in the shutters. They saw the old man lift the lid off the hole where he kept his daughter safe.'

Bando had his hands over his mouth now, and the others were totally silent. Everyone but Lorn was caught up in the story.

'The robbers crouched by the window,' Zak said softly. 'They watched the old man looking down at his beautiful daughter. They watched as he stretched out his hands to her, and they saw him hesitate. Then they saw him replace the lid and settle himself beside the fire to sleep. So, when he and his wife and his son were all asleep—'

This time, his pause was long and dramatic. At the other end of the cavern, the cold wind roared in the entrance tunnel. Outside, the nightbird called from the top of the bitternut tree. But they were distant, insubstantial sounds. Nothing was real except Zak's voice in the flickering shadows.

'When the poor old man was fast asleep,' he whispered, 'the robbers sneaked up to his door—and smashed the lock.'

His voice rose suddenly, in a great crescendo.

'They broke into the house and ripped the lid off the hole in the ground—AND THEY SNATCHED HIS DAUGHTER OUT AND STOLE HER AWAY!'

# MR WRONG NARRATES

# 1

They'd stolen Hope. Her secret room was uncovered, with its trapdoor tossed away to one side, and the space under the floor left gaping and exposed. She'd gone.

Warren stood on the edge of the hole, shivering in his pyjamas. The conservatory door was wide open, but he couldn't make the effort to close it and shut out the cold night air. He couldn't do anything except stare down into the shocking emptiness in front of him.

Hope should have been down there. All his life, he'd had a secret sister, hidden in her room under the floor. All his life, he'd known that he mustn't say anything about her. Mustn't even speak her name—*Hope Armstrong*—in case he gave her away to the rest of the world. Locked inside his head, the letters of that forbidden name had swirled around, making cryptic, hidden patterns. *Prongo Hamster. H. Poor-Garments. Grasp the moron.*

But none of those meant anything now. There was nothing left to hide.

His mother and father came running downstairs, pulling on the rest of their clothes. His father snatched up the car keys and his mother took the big torch from the hall table. Neither of them stopped to tell him where they were going. They hadn't told him anything.

But he knew. They were going after the kidnappers. They were going to find Hope and bring her back home, where she belonged, back to the secret room that kept her safe.

He heard the front door open and close. He heard the car start up, sliding out of the garage and down the close. It slipped away into the night, leaving him on his own, standing in the cold conservatory.

He shook his head from side to side, trying not to imagine Hope out there in the dark. She would be in an unfamiliar place, with people she didn't know. How could she understand what was going on? She'd be terrified.

He might have saved her, if only he'd yelled in time. The memory ran over and over in his head, repeating endlessly. He'd crept downstairs, because he couldn't sleep, and when he'd opened the kitchen door—there they were, carrying Hope out of the conservatory.

That was when he should have shouted. Bellowed, with all the breath in his lungs. *Dad! Wake up! They're stealing Hope!* If he'd done that, his father might have rescued her.

But he'd been afraid—because it was his fault. He'd seen the boys before. They'd been ready for him when he came off the school bus, yesterday, blocking the pavement and hassling him. Threatening terrible things unless he promised to turn off the burglar alarm. He hadn't even thought that they might be kidnappers, but he should have stood up to them. He should have realized—

*No.* He blocked out those thoughts. *It's not my fault. There were three of them, counting the girl. All bigger than me. And how could I have guessed what they were planning?*

But the accusing voice in his head didn't stop. To deaden it, he went into the kitchen to look for something to eat. There were no crisps left, but he made himself a sandwich, squirting mayonnaise on to the peanut butter and topping it with a slice of cheese. Chewing on the first mouthful, he went back to the conservatory and switched on the light.

It looked even more of a mess now that he could see properly. The wooden lid that should have been covering the secret entrance was lying upside down near the door. The carpet that went over it was rolled up in one corner. And the TV—which should have been standing on the carpet—was pushed to one side, with the screen facing the window.

It was still turned on, as usual. Warren let the sound wash over him and munched his sandwich, struggling to believe what had happened. His father had always said, *If people know Hope's there, they'll come and take her away.* But that had never seemed real, even though he'd heard it all his life. How could Hope go away? She belonged in her special room. He couldn't imagine her anywhere else.

But his father had been right all along. The kidnappers had found out about her and they'd sneaked in and snatched her away.

After a while, he remembered the photograph. He went into the study and turned on the computer, sorting through all the picture files until he found it.

It was one of the kidnappers. The tall one. They'd caught him snooping around, a few days ago. That must have been when he'd seen Hope, but they hadn't realized that. So they'd just taken a photo to scare him off. *If you come back, we'll call the police and show them your picture.*

That wasn't true, of course. They could never call the police, because of Hope. But the tall boy had no way of knowing that. He'd looked scared and furious as Warren's father tugged at his hair, dragging his head round to face the camera.

And there was the picture on the computer. Warren opened the file and stared at the wild, fierce eyes and the angry mouth, pulled sideways into a snarl. That was exactly how he'd looked. Cruel and savage, with a strong nose and dark, untidy hair.

The sort of person who could frighten you into doing anything.

The sky was still dark when the car came back. Warren heard it pull into the kerb and stop, with the engine idling. One of the doors slammed and footsteps came up the path.

Then the car started up again, driving back down the close and away.

His mother came in on her own, with her shoulders slumped and the torch in her hand, still switched on. She looked haggard and wretched.

'We couldn't catch them,' she said dully. Before Warren could ask. 'We chased them right across town, but they ran through all the back alleys.'

'But Hope can't run,' Warren said. 'She—'

'They dumped her into a supermarket trolley and pushed her away—like a bag of potatoes. She must have been so scared—' His mother broke off, pressing her lips together to stop them trembling.

'Dad will catch them,' Warren said quickly. 'He's got the car. He'll find them and bring her home.'

But his mother shook her head. Vaguely, as though she couldn't take in what he meant. 'I always thought it would be the police who came,' she said. 'Or maybe social workers. But they're just teenagers. What could they possibly want—?' Her mouth twisted suddenly and she sat down on the chair in the hall, covering her face with her hands.

'It's probably just a joke,' Warren said. Babbling desperately, to stop her bursting into tears. 'Why would they want to keep her? They'll probably bring her back after an hour or two. They're not going to take her to hospital—'

His mother was rigid, her face still hidden in her hands.

'Mum?' He dabbed nervously at her shoulder. 'We will get her back, won't we? You don't think she's really—going to die?'

His mother was crying silently into her hands. It took Warren a few moments to realize that he was crying too.

It was almost morning by the time the car came up the close again. It bumped on to the drive and stopped abruptly, as though the engine had failed.

Warren was asleep, with his head on the kitchen table. He was woken roughly, by the edge of the table ramming into his stomach as his mother pushed it away from her. She jumped up and ran into the hall while Warren was still struggling to catch his breath.

Without standing up, he saw her wrench the front door open, but it seemed a long time before anyone came through it. When his father finally walked into the house, Warren was so stunned that all he could do was stare.

It was like watching a different person. Someone who walked mechanically, looking blank and dazed. Over his shoulder, the car was just visible. It was parked carelessly, half on the drive and half on the grass, with the lights left on and the driver's door hanging open.

What had happened to him? He'd gone out full of energy and anger, determined to get Hope back. And once he'd decided to do something, he never gave up. It must have taken something shocking—something cataclysmic—to change him like this.

*Hope's dead already.* That was the worst thing Warren could imagine. *She's dead—and he's seen her body.*

He gripped the edge of the kitchen table, afraid to move. This was different from anything else in his life. There weren't any instructions about what to say, or how to behave. He was petrified.

His father walked straight down the hall and into the kitchen. For a second, he looked as though he was heading straight for the place where Warren was sitting. *It wasn't my fault,* said the panicky, terrified voice in Warren's head. *I didn't know—I didn't guess—*

But his father went straight past him without even a glance, heading into the utility room. Warren heard him open the cupboard where he kept his tools. And he still hadn't spoken.

Warren couldn't bear the tension any longer. 'Where's Hope?' he said. The words came out in a squeak. 'Where have they taken her? How can we get her back?'

His father answered without looking round. 'There's no hope,' Warren heard him say.

'We must be able to do *something,*' Warren muttered. Babbling again, to fill the silence. 'We have to get her back.'

His father shut the cupboard and turned round, with the big claw hammer in one hand and a jar of nails in the other.

'Weren't you listening?' he said. His eyes were cold. 'There is no such person as Hope. There never has been.'

Warren stared with his mouth open. His brain wouldn't make sense of the words. 'But—'

'You've never had a sister,' his father said harshly. 'Ask your friends. Ask anyone. You've always been an only child.'

He came back out through the kitchen, knocking his wife aside as though he hadn't even seen her. She watched him cross the hall and go into the living room. Then she looked round at Warren.

'I don't understand,' she said, in a scared, bewildered voice. 'What's he talking about?'

Warren didn't know what to say. He stared back at her, shaking his head stupidly.

And then the noises started.

They came from beyond the living room, from the conservatory. There was a dragging, scraping sound and then the unmistakable thump of a hammer against wood. Warren heard his mother catch her breath. She went straight out of the kitchen and across the hall.

When she reached the living room door, she gave a cry. Not loud, but full of pain. *I don't want to see,* Warren thought desperately. *Whatever it is, I don't want to see*. But he forced himself to stand up and follow her. She had stopped in the doorway, but he could see over her shoulder, across the living room and into the conservatory.

His father had dropped the wooden lid back into place, closing off the entrance to Hope's room. Now he was hammering nails in all around the edge, so that no one could open the trapdoor again.

Warren and his mother stood without a word, watching him hammer his way round the square. When the last nail was knocked down, he stood up and stepped aside, looking across at his wife.

'Put the carpet back,' he said crisply. 'And the television. Get this room back to normal.' Picking up the jar of nails, he walked out of the conservatory and back across the living room. As he came through the door, his wife caught at his sleeve.

'Dan—'

He twitched his arm free and pushed past her, without answering. For a second she stood where she was, staring at the wooden square with its border of nails. Then she dropped her head and went to carry out his orders.

Warren scurried after her. 'I'll help,' he said. He wanted her to smile, but she didn't even look at him. Just nodded and kept walking.

They lifted the carpet back into position and unrolled it, making certain that it covered the trapdoor. Then they carried the television from the side of the conservatory and placed it carefully in the centre of the carpet. As they set it down, Warren's father came back.

'And turn that thing off,' he said sharply, waving his hand at the TV.

It was never turned off. There was always a television on in the conservatory, filling it with light and sound. It was so normal that Warren had never even wondered why it was there.

Now, for the first time, he understood that it was because of Hope. The blare from the television had covered the small sounds she made as she moved around under the floor, muttering to herself.

His mother reached for the button—and then stopped. Slowly she turned to face her husband. 'Hope's dead, isn't she? Tell me. I need to know.'

He answered without looking at her, and there was something in his face that made Warren shiver.

'Our only daughter was called Abigail,' he said. 'She died sixteen years ago, when the doctors insisted on taking her into hospital. We had no second chance. There was never any such person as Hope.'

Pushing past his wife, he pressed the button on the front of the television. The sound stopped and the picture disappeared. For the first time in Warren's life, the conservatory was silent and dark.

# 2

It was almost five o'clock when Warren finally went back to bed. Three hours later, the alarm went off as usual and he sat up sharply, shocked out of a deep sleep.

His father was standing at the end of the bed. When Warren groaned and fell back against the pillow, he looked down at his watch with a frown.

'If you don't get out of bed you'll be late for school,' he said.

'School?' Warren couldn't believe he was supposed to treat this like an ordinary day. 'But—I'm really tired. And the bus leaves in half an hour.'

'If you miss the bus, you'll have to take your punishment,' his father said coldly. 'Don't whine.'

Warren slid sullenly out of bed and headed for the bathroom. As he pushed the door open, he somehow expected the room behind to have changed. It felt as though everything ought to be different now. But it wasn't. The bathroom was exactly the same as before. And, when he went downstairs, so were the hall and the kitchen and the living room. Everything looked as though Hope was still down in her room. But she wasn't.

And he was late.

He tried to catch up the time he'd lost, but he kept forgetting things and having to go back. He missed both the early buses and finally sidled into his classroom just as the second lesson was about to begin.

He deliberately chose the moment just before Mr Robinson arrived, when the whole room was in an uproar. He was hoping that no one would notice—but that was pathetic, of course. Steven Platt spotted him before he'd even sat down.

'Hey up! Here's Rabbit! He *finally* finished his breakfast!'

Everyone laughed, and Platt leaned across and patted Warren's stomach. 'Just *couldn't* resist those last sixteen kilos of carrots, could you?' He chewed grotesquely on the empty air, puffing out his cheeks and twitching his nose. 'Watch out your buttons don't burst, little Bunny.'

Warren sat down quickly, before anyone could twang the waistband of his trousers. That was always good for a laugh. For everyone except him.

'Got to sit on his bottom, hasn't he?' jeered Platt. 'To protect his little powder puff.'

Warren stared down at the table, trying to shut his ears. *I have to keep my head down. To guard the secret.* That was almost the first thing he'd ever learnt, even before his first day at school. *Don't draw attention to yourself. Try and stay invisible.* It was his secret weapon. Platt always thought he was so clever—but he didn't know about Hope. He didn't know that Warren was a special boy, with special responsibilities.

Only the secret weapon didn't work any more. When Warren tried to conjure up Hope's face in his mind, all he could see was his father's cold, domineering stare.

*Hope—*

It wasn't going to work. Not ever again. He wasn't special at all. Just ordinary—and pathetic. The shock of it hit him so hard that he closed his eyes.

That was asking for trouble, of course. David called across the classroom. 'Hey, Bunny! You can't nod off here.'

'Oh—I can't help it!' Platt squeaked in his rabbit voice. 'I'm so full of food my tiny bunny-tummy is going to

POP!' He reached over and slapped Warren hard on the stomach. Then he raised his eyebrows comically, grinning round the room.

Everyone laughed, even the girls. Even Karen, who sometimes told Platt to shut up when he was being really cruel. When he pulled that humorous face, Platt was irresistible and he knew it. It was no use protesting. The only thing to do was wait until he got bored. Warren hunched forward, miserably, protecting the soft round curve of his belly.

*Only six more hours to get through. Only five lessons until it's time to go home.*

That was the other chant that got him through the day. But that one didn't work either. Not now. Because when he thought *home,* the only picture that came into his mind was a dead television standing over an empty hole in the ground.

By the time the bus turned into the estate that afternoon, he was numb with misery. Platt had sensed something different about him—some extra weakness—and he hadn't let up all day. Even the bus wasn't a refuge. Warren sat at the front, as near as possible to the driver, but Platt slotted into the seat behind. All the way home, he kept making little bunny-snuffles and pulling at Warren's ears.

'Mmm!' he muttered. '*So* big and soft and furry!'

And the girls giggled at that too.

Warren hunched forward in his seat, hating them all. Hating himself. There were no secret places in his mind any more. He could feel himself giving in. *Becoming* Rabbit.

When the bus reached the estate, he let everyone else get off before he stood up. Then he loitered at the bus stop until they were all heading home. For a nasty moment he thought Platt was going to wait for him, but the girls saved him by trooping off together. The rabbit game was no fun without an audience. After one backward glance, Platt went with the crowd.

As soon as it was safe, Warren dragged himself up the road and round the corner. The close seemed twice as long as usual and the house at the end—his own house—looked dark and grim. The curtains were pulled, but there was no car on the drive and the windows were all unlit.

He wanted to turn back, but there was nowhere else to go. He trailed along the pavement with his shoulders sagging and his bag hanging off one arm. When he reached the house, it took all his energy to find his front door key and slip it into the lock.

He was just about to turn the key when he heard a voice. It was very faint and at first he caught just the intonation, without being able to make out any words. But, even so, there was something about it that made him hesitate. Something that made him turn his key very quietly.

As the door swung open, the words suddenly came clear. The voice was saying the same thing, over and over again.

'Out . . . out . . . out . . .'

He stopped, half in and half out of the house. Listening so hard that he couldn't move. Stunned.

'. . . out . . . out . . .'

It was Hope's voice. He could almost see her frown as she concentrated on making the shapes with her mouth, sounding the last letter separately, to get it right. *Ou-T . . . ou-T . . .*

He stepped into the house, pulling the door shut behind him. The voice stopped instantly, halfway through a word. *Ou—* For a second he couldn't bear to move, in case he'd imagined the whole thing. But he had to know. He went forward and pushed at the living room door.

His mother was in there. On her own. She was kneeling on the floor, with a little tape player in front of her. In her arms she was cradling a cardboard shoe box, with the lid half off, as though she had snatched it up quickly.

'Warren,' she said. She looked awkward and defensive. 'I didn't realize it was so late.'

'Sorry,' Warren mumbled. 'I didn't mean—I just heard—'

He started to back out of the room, but his mother leaned forward urgently, still clutching the shoe box.

'Yes? What did you hear?'

'I thought—' Warren didn't know what he was supposed to say. His mouth was dry. His tongue felt huge. He looked down at the carpet. 'It was Hope,' he muttered. 'Wasn't it?'

He heard a slow, soft sigh as his mother let out her breath. 'We didn't make her up, did we?' she said. 'She's real.' Pulling the lid off the shoe box, she held it out for Warren to see. 'Look! She's *real*.'

The box was full of photographs. Little coloured snaps, slithering over each other in untidy heaps. Warren glanced down nervously at the top one. It showed a baby in a frilly dress, sitting on a blanket. She was smiling and waving her arms as she looked towards the camera. Just like any other baby.

'Go on,' his mother said eagerly, shaking the box. 'Look at them!'

He pulled out another one. It showed a girl of five or six, with a pale, narrow face and braids in her hair. She was kneeling by the entrance to the secret room, gazing down gravely into the darkness. Her head was turned to one side, in a slightly odd way, and she had a distant look that he recognized.

'I didn't know we had any photos of Hope,' he said.

His mother reached out to take the picture back. 'Your father doesn't know,' she said quickly. 'You mustn't tell him. If he finds out, he'll take them away and burn them. And the tape as well.'

'It's OK,' Warren muttered awkwardly.

'I *have* to have them.' There was a defiant edge to his mother's voice. 'I can't just wipe her away. You understand that, don't you?'

Warren didn't understand anything. And he didn't want to answer the question, because he didn't know where that would take him. All he wanted to do was keep his mouth shut and forget what he'd seen. But that wasn't an option. His mother was looking straight at him, waiting for an answer.

'You *do* understand, don't you?' she said. 'You do know that Hope's real?'

Slowly, reluctantly, Warren nodded.

'Then you'll help me to find her?' his mother said quickly.

He hadn't expected that. All he could do was stare, with his mouth open. Did she really mean them to do it on their own?

All his life, he'd done whatever his father said. Sometimes his mother gave him instructions, but he'd known that she was only repeating things that came from his father. Now his father was telling them that Hope had never existed. She was gone, hidden behind some mysterious door that his father had slammed shut. The truth about what had happened was locked away. How could he and his mother find it out by themselves?

'Well?' she said. Still watching his face.

He dropped his head and muttered. 'Might be better if we didn't . . . don't really know what happened . . . it must have been . . .'

*It must have been terrifying*. That was what he wanted to say. If his father couldn't rescue Hope, if he couldn't even talk about what had happened, then it must have been . . . must have been—

Warren's mind cut out, refusing to let him imagine horrors.

Refusing to let him imagine his father being afraid.

'I don't care what it was like,' his mother said fiercely. '*Nothing's* as bad as not knowing. If only we could find out who took her, that would be a start. How did they know she was there? *Who are they?* I didn't even see their faces.'

Warren didn't want to hear what she was saying. He wanted to stay safely outside that locked door, where his father meant him to be. But he'd crossed the line and taken sides, before he realized what he was doing.

'There's a . . . a photo,' he stuttered. 'Of the tall one.'

His mother's mouth fell open. 'Where? *How?*'

'That day the security light came on. Remember?' He could see she did. 'That was him, snooping around. We took a picture before we threw him out.'

His mother scrambled to her feet. 'Where is it? Show me.'

'It's on the computer—'

She was at the desk before he'd finished speaking. As the screen lit up, she grabbed at Warren's sleeve and pulled him into the chair.

'Find it. Quickly.'

This time, it only took him a couple of seconds. She stood over him impatiently while he opened the folder and selected the file. As the tall kidnapper's face came up on the screen, she drew in her breath.

'He looks like a giant. A monster. If he's taken her away to hurt her—'

'I think . . . he's just tall,' Warren said hesitantly. 'He's not much older than me.'

'You mean he's still at school?' His mother's voice was sharp.

'I . . . suppose so.' Warren nodded, thinking about it. 'Yes. He's got to be. And the others as well.'

His mother stabbed a finger at the picture on the screen. 'Print that.'

Warren obeyed, without asking questions. His mother stared at the photo coming off the printer. As soon as it was ready, she darted forward and snatched it up by one edge, flapping it to dry the ink. Then she held it out to Warren.

'There you are,' she said. 'Go and find him.'

*'What?'* Warren looked at her in horror. *'Me?* But I can't—'

'Yes you can.' She took his fingers and closed them round the edge of the paper. 'All you have to do is find the right school and ask someone who he is.'

The idea made Warren feel sick. 'Why can't you do it instead?'

'Because I'm an adult. No teenager's going to answer my questions. But you won't frighten anyone off. They'll tell you, if you do it right.'

Warren looked at her stupidly. He couldn't quite believe that she meant it.

But she did. She grabbed his other hand and took it between hers, holding on tightly. 'Please,' she said. And he could hear how desperate she was. '*Please*. It's the only thing I can think of. And I have to find out what happened to her.'

Warren looked down at the picture. *I can't,* he thought again. But he already knew that he would. He'd spent his whole life doing what he was told.

# 3

For an hour the next morning, he thought it was going to be all right after all. He thought his mother had given up her idea of sending him out as a spy. When he came down to breakfast, she was scurrying round in the usual way, making toast and filling up his father's tea cup as she'd done every other day of his life. He almost expected to see Hope's tray standing ready on the side, with her bowl of porridge and her plastic mug full of milk.

But there was no tray. No Hope. Everything had changed.

As soon as his father walked out of the house, his mother dropped her pretence of being ordinary. She took a sheet of paper out of her pocket and slapped it down on the table in front of Warren.

He stared at a list of times and numbers. 'What's that?'

'Buses,' she said briskly. 'If you catch those, you can visit three schools today. Two when it's break and one at the end of the afternoon. Those are the most likely schools, but if you don't strike lucky today you can do three more tomorrow.'

'You mean—go on my own? In school time?' He couldn't believe that was what she meant.

'How else do you think you're going to find out?' His mother whisked away his cup and plate and took the cloth off the table. 'Go and fetch the street map and I'll give you your fare money.'

'But what if people ask me why I'm not at school?' He was struggling now. Snatching at any excuse.

His mother gave him a scornful, impatient look. 'Tell them you're on your way to the dentist. Tell them *anything*. What does it matter? Hundreds of children skip school every day.'

*But not me. I can't, I can't . . .*

It felt as though the dull, familiar city had turned into a jungle. Behind every window, in every shop doorway, there might be danger lurking. Someone who would grab his collar and haul him off to the police station. *Officer, I found this boy playing truant.*

He wanted to scuttle around, darting from one hiding place to another, but he had enough sense to see that he would be in more danger if he behaved like that. He could only survive by walking boldly, looking straight ahead, as though he had a right to be around.

And there were other survival skills he had to learn. When he reached a school, it was no use just standing at the gate, hoping to recognize one of the kidnappers. There were too many people milling around, and too many places to watch. He was never going to get anywhere without producing the photograph.

But that had its problems too. He began by picking people who looked quiet and safe and asking the question straight out. *Do you know this boy?* That was disastrous. Even the most stupid-looking people edged away suspiciously. If he was going to get any answers, he needed a cover story.

It took him most of the day to invent one that sounded plausible. By then, he was on his third school. One of the big glass and concrete comprehensives that squatted outside the ring road, on the far side of the city. Loitering by the gate, he peered up at the classrooms, piled one on top of another, and told himself that it ought to be simple.

No one would pay him any attention as long as he stood quietly at the gate. He knew that already. All he had to do was take his time and wait for the right person. Someone sympathetic who would take a proper look at the picture.

It *should* have been like that. But he couldn't get rid of the terrifying, tormenting thought that this time it might be the right school after all. And if it was, he might suddenly find himself facing one of the kidnappers.

They knew who he was. If they saw him there, they were bound to guess what he was doing.

He pictured them as massive, nameless figures who would come striding towards him like shapes from a nightmare. They would be relentless and sadistic. That day before the kidnap, when they'd cornered him on the way home, they'd known exactly how to frighten him. They'd played on his worst fears, not spelling anything out clearly. Just hinting at danger, with little pinprick jabs to make him panic. That was how they'd bullied him into turning off the burglar alarm. They'd forced him to help them.

*But it wasn't my fault. I didn't know what they were going to do.*

He didn't know which of them was the worst. The tall one, the short one, or the ginger-haired girl with the sharp fox-face. He hated all three of them.

The idea that they might appear made him much too anxious to ask his question and escape. Instead of waiting for some lumpish, kindly girl who would give him a proper hearing, he spoke to the first person who looked his way. He blurted out his cover story all in one go, without a proper introduction.

'Hi, can you help me I'm looking for someone—picked up my bag instead of his own—on the bus—no name—just a photo—'

Before he was halfway through, he knew he'd made a dreadful mistake. The boy he'd stopped was already smiling down at him with a cruel, amused smile. Like Platt's. Even before Warren had finished explaining what he wanted, the boy was calling over his shoulder.

'Hey, Fipper. Come and take a look at this. What do you reckon?'

And then there were two of them. And other people were looking curiously as they went past.

The boy called Fipper rolled his eyes in a way that was horribly familiar. He glanced at the photo, obviously recognizing the face straight away, but he didn't say who it was. Instead, he turned back to Warren with an elaborate, pantomime frown.

'Looks like the Queen to me,' he said.

The first boy peered at the photo again and snorted scornfully. 'You're crazy. It's Beckham. Old picture, before he changed his hair.'

Fipper craned his head round to study the photo upside down. 'Give it a rest, Ned. You've only got to look at the *nose*. It's *regal,* that nose is.' He was holding on to the end of the paper now. Twisting it round.

'Please.' Warren tried to work it free without tearing it. 'Please can I—'

The instant he heard his own voice, he knew he was just making things worse. He was whining. And to boys like that he might just as well have been saying, *Kick me. Pull my hair*. They knew he was a loser now and in a moment they would start jostling him and stepping on his feet. Seeing how far they could go before he ran away.

Fipper twitched the picture away from him, flapping it out of reach, and Ned laughed scornfully, glancing backwards to see how many other people he and Fipper were amusing.

'Please—' Warren said again, sounding even more hopeless. Knowing that he might just as well abandon the picture and go. No one was going to answer his questions now. It was no use—

And then he was saved. Just when he was about to turn and run, a girl came swooping through the crowd, elbowing Ned out of the way.

'What are you *doing*?' she said. 'Don't you two ever stop?'

She was just the person Warren would have picked, if he'd had the sense to wait. Plump and confident, but slightly awkward, with big, soft eyes. She tweaked the picture away from Fipper and held it out to Warren.

'Here. This is yours, isn't it?'

She obviously expected him to take it and scuttle off, but some instinct told him that this was the best opportunity he was going to get. He took the picture and held it up for her to see.

'I was just asking—'

She leaned forward to take a look and Fipper rolled his eyes at her. 'Oh, come *on*, Shelley! You're not going to *tell* him anything?'

Warren started gabbling, desperate not to miss his chance. 'I only want my bag. He took it on the bus. By mistake. I've got his, and I need my bag back—'

His tongue was falling over itself, going round and round in his mouth, like Hope's when she couldn't get her words out right. *Hasmegg. Nowass. Dohfuss.* He was starting to panic.

The girl's face softened sympathetically and she put a calm, heavy hand on his shoulder. 'It's OK,' she said. 'You don't need to take any notice of Fipper and Ned. Nobody else does. Let's get away from them.' She took his arm and led him off to one side.

'Use your brains!' Fipper called after her. 'You don't

know who he is. Maybe he's working with international terrorists. His parents might be serial killers.'

Shelley looked over her shoulder. 'Don't be ridiculous,' she said scornfully.

Ned was already shrugging and turning away towards the bus stop. 'Give it a rest, Fip. What does it matter what she says? Robbo's big enough to take care of himself.'

Then, miraculously, they'd gone. And Shelley was listening to Warren, drinking in his cover story without questioning a single word. When he held out the photograph, she gave a disconcerting giggle.

'I've never seen him look like *that*! What was he *doing*?'

'I don't know,' Warren said hastily. 'I just found it in his bag. It's the only thing I've got and if I can't find him—'

'It's OK. Don't worry.' Shelley patted his arm. 'I can tell you who he is. His sister's a friend of mine.' She looked round at the people flooding out of school. 'I can't see him, though. He might not come out this way.'

'I only need his name,' Warren mumbled. 'And maybe . . . his address?'

He was afraid that would make her suspicious, but she was too busy being helpful to think of anything else.

'I can't remember the number, but I know the house all right. It's by the Memorial Park—almost opposite the main gates—and it's got a big bay window on the ground floor. With a bush growing up against the wall underneath. If you go there you'll be able to spot it easily.'

'And . . . his name?' Warren prompted. Hardly daring to breathe.

Shelley giggled again. 'Fancy forgetting to tell you that. He's called Robert Doherty.'

For a second, because he was so nervous, Warren thought she said *Robber Doherty*. The shock must have shown in his face, because Shelley gave him a curious look. Then she glanced at her watch.

'Robert's OK. Really. But I'll come with you if you like. I've just about got time.'

'No,' Warren said hastily. 'No, I'm fine. I just need to phone my mum and then I'll go round there. Thank you. Thanks a lot.'

He backed away round the corner, as quickly as he could. He'd almost done it. He'd almost found out where one of the kidnappers lived. But his whole body was shaking with nervous tension. It was all he could do to walk as far as McDonald's.

He ordered fries and a milkshake and sat at the nearest table, eating handfuls of fries and taking the lid off the shake so that he could drink it in big gulps. A couple of girls were watching him and giggling, but he couldn't help that. He needed something to get himself through the last bit of his mission.

By the time he came out of McDonald's, it was almost dark. It took him ten minutes to walk to the Memorial Park and he was out of breath again by the time he reached the gates, but he was determined now. He wasn't going to go home without knowing the house number.

Crossing the road, he walked along the row of houses on the other side. There were only a couple with bay windows and their front gardens were dark and shadowy. He couldn't see which was the one with a bush under the window. Not without going closer.

For two or three moments he dithered, shivering in the cold wind. His feeling of danger was stronger now. This was the kidnappers' lair. It might be the place where they were keeping Hope. He had to check it out properly. But suppose they saw him? He had never felt so vulnerable and afraid.

Then he pushed his hands deep into his pockets—and felt the balaclava his mother always made him take to school in the winter. He'd never worn it. That would have been asking for trouble. Platt would have had a field day if he'd turned up at school with his whole face covered except his eyes.

But now, suddenly, the balaclava was perfect. He pulled it on and headed towards the first house with a bay window.

With his face hidden, he felt almost brave. As he drew level with the house, he glanced around quickly, to check that no one could see him. Then he ducked into the front garden and squatted down behind the low front wall.

Most of the garden was car parking space, with just a narrow flower bed immediately behind the front wall. And, now that he was near, he could see the dark, angular bush growing under the window, close against the house.

He could have left then. But there was a narrow line of light showing between the curtains in the bay. Someone was obviously in that front room.

And it suddenly occurred to him that it might be Hope.

For almost five minutes, he crouched behind the wall, wishing he had enough courage to creep forward to the window. Hope might be in there. She might be in terrible danger. Maybe even being tortured. But he didn't dare go any closer. If she was in there, she wouldn't be alone. The tall kidnapper would be there too. The one called—

Warren was too frightened to sound out the name, even in his head. He set the letters dancing, disguising them quickly. Trying to get them to say something more reassuring. But the words that came back terrified him even more. *Rot by the order . . . The Terror Body.*

The words curdled in his mind. *Run, Rabbit, run, Rabbit, run, run, run.* He was just a coward. A hopeless coward. *I can't . . . I can't . . .*

The voice in his head was still whining when he began to crawl forward through the shadows.

He crept across the garden and when he reached the bay window he pulled himself up, slowly, until his head was just above the level of the windowsill. Leaning forward over the stiff, scratchy branches of the bush, he peered between the curtains. By moving his head around, he could see the whole, lighted room.

And the girl inside.

It wasn't Hope—there was no sign of her—it was another girl. The kidnapper with the fox-red hair.

For a second, Warren was shocked to see how ordinary she looked. He'd remembered a fierce, malevolent face. An evil witch with sharp features and a river of burning hair. But she was just a girl on a sofa, reading a book. Her hair fell round her face as she leaned forward. As he watched, she picked up a pad and scribbled a note. She was doing her homework.

He squashed forward, to get a better view. As he pressed against the bush in front of him, a stray twig hit the window. *Tap.*

And the girl jumped.

Her head jerked up and for a second her eyes were wide and startled. Then she looked down again and went on reading.

Warren felt a small, surprising flicker of satisfaction. Last time he'd seen her, she was towering over him in the street, shaking her gleaming hair and taunting him. But when she heard a strange noise, she jumped, just like anyone else.

He reached out, deliberately this time, and bounced the twig against the glass again. *Tap, tap.*

This time, she didn't jump. It was even better. She glanced up nervously, with a little frown. Putting her book down, she leaned forward, ready to stand up—and then hesitated, uncertainly.

*Tap, tap, tap.*

He wanted a reaction—but he hadn't expected her to move so fast. Before the twig had sprung back from the third tap, she was on her feet and heading for the window. He ducked down quickly, pressing himself into the sharp branches. By the time she dragged the curtains apart, he was too low for the light to catch him.

Crouching there, with his heart thudding, he held his breath and tried not to think what would happen if she left the curtains open and crept away. If she tiptoed to the front door and jumped out at him. What would he do then? There was no getaway car waiting to carry him off. Only a bus stop, five minutes' walk away. If she decided to come out and investigate, he wouldn't stand a chance.

But she didn't. After a few seconds, she drew the curtains together impatiently and he heard her walking away. Straightening up cautiously, he peered between the curtains and saw that she was back on the sofa, reading again.

Warren's heart was still beating furiously, and he was breathless and shaking as he slipped out of the garden. But he felt—triumphant. He'd done much, much more than his mother had asked. He hadn't just discovered Doherty's name and address. He'd actually been to the house, on his own, to check it out.

And he'd *frightened* one of the kidnappers.

There was no doubt about it. He remembered her wide, startled eyes and the way she'd held back from coming to the window. He'd *scared* her.

If only he'd had a car waiting! Then he could have stayed where he was, instead of crouching down. She would have opened the curtains and seen a face in a black balaclava, pressed up against the glass. Would she have screamed?

He felt a wild, intoxicating sense of strength. If the kidnappers could be frightened, then maybe it wasn't crazy to think of finding Hope. Maybe they could even get her back.

Maybe Robber Doherty would turn out to be Rabbit Doherty after all.

# 4

When the bus stopped in the estate, he jumped off eagerly. He would have run all the way home if he could. For the first time in his life, he had important news to tell, news that could change everything. He reached the house and panted up the path—and the door swung open in front of him, before he had time to ring the bell.

His father was waiting for him.

If his father had spoken—if he'd said even a single word—Warren would have had some idea how he was supposed to react. But there was nothing. Just a steady, expressionless stare, and his father's heavy body, blocking the doorway. Waiting.

Did he know how Warren had spent the day? It was impossible to tell. But surely—surely—he would be pleased with the result? Warren blurted it out, stumbling slightly over the words. 'I've found—found the kidnappers. I know what that tall one's called. And where he lives. I can take you—'

And then he saw his father's eyes narrow. And he knew he'd made a mistake.

'I haven't given anything away,' he said, back-tracking fast. 'I was really careful—'

Was that right? Wrong? There was no sign to help him. His father just took a step back, letting Warren sidle past him, into the hall. He didn't speak until the front door was closed.

Then he pointed up the stairs. 'Go to your room,' he

said. In the chilly, controlled voice that was worst of all. 'Wait for me.'

'But I didn't mean—' Warren started babbling, in a panic. 'I thought—'

'Your room,' his father repeated. Not even looking at him.

Warren saw his mother come out of the living room. She stood with a hand over her mouth, following him with her eyes as he trailed slowly up the stairs and into his bedroom. He sat on the edge of the bed, listening for the sound of his father's feet coming up behind him.

Afterwards, his mother came and sat beside the bed, smoothing his hair and patting his hand. When he was little, she'd cried and tried to explain that his father was only looking after them all.

*He just wants you to be careful. We all have to be careful. To protect Hope.*

She didn't cry this time. She just sat there, patting his hand gently. And Warren didn't cry either. He lay on his front, with his head turned to the wall, looking away from her.

When he was small, he'd looked forward to growing up. To being too big for his father to hit. But now he knew that would never happen. It didn't matter what size he was. He was never going to resist. He was defeated before the first blow landed. Flattened by the look of cold disgust in his father's face.

After a long time, his mother stopped patting his hand. She sat back in the chair, looking down at him. 'Did you really find them?' she said quietly.

'It was a mistake,' Warren said dully. 'There weren't any kidnappers. Because there was no one to kidnap.'

There was a small, tense pause. Then his mother said, 'What about Hope?'

'There's no such person as Hope.' The words came out of Warren's mouth on their own, saving him the effort of thinking. 'Just Abigail, who died before I was born. I've always been an only child.'

His mother made a strange little sound in her throat. With a great effort, Warren turned his head and saw that she was crying now. The tears were running down her cheeks and dripping off her jaw. He stared at her for a while without speaking.

Then he said, 'Why do you always give in to him? Why do you let him tell us what to do?'

She shook her head without answering, dragging the back of her hand across her face. 'Please,' she said. 'What did you find out?'

Warren rolled over to face her. 'When I was little,' he said, 'I used to think that he had secret cameras hidden in my room. I thought he could see into my mind. Because you always told him everything.'

His mother looked away. 'He's not a *bad* man,' she muttered. 'He's only trying to look after us all. And I've tried to be strong. But I don't understand what he's doing now. And I can't bear—' She turned back. 'Please, Warren.'

Warren felt so tired that he could hardly put the words together. It seemed like an impossible effort. For a few seconds he just stared at his mother, without focusing. Then he mumbled, 'The tall one's called Doherty. He lives in a house near the park.'

He closed his eyes to shut out the eagerness that flared in his mother's face, but she wouldn't let him stop there. She pulled impatiently at his arm.

'If you know where he is, we have to get hold of him.' She was whispering now, in a low, quick voice. 'We have to find him and *make* him say what they've done with Hope.'

'But suppose it's too horrible,' Warren said. Speaking into the darkness behind his eyelids. Even thinking about it was hard, like carrying a heavy weight up a hill. 'Dad was there. He *knows*. And if he won't tell—if he won't even talk about Hope—it must be something dreadful.'

'You think it's worse than the things I'm imagining?' His mother's voice was still low, but now it was savage. 'I'll go mad if I don't find out. You have to help me, Warren.'

He wanted to say *No*. He wanted to say, *I'm scared. I can't do it.* But he was afraid she would start to hate him if he said no. She'd always taught him to look after Hope, because that was what brothers were meant to do. And he'd found it for himself, in the dancing letter of Hope's name. *Program the son.*

Opening his eyes, he looked at his mother's wet face. 'I saw one of the other kidnappers,' he said abruptly. 'The girl. I tapped on the window and she was afraid. So I thought . . . maybe—'

The words clogged his throat. It had all seemed so clear, so possible, when he was hurrying home from the bus stop, but now it felt as feeble and foolish as everything else he did.

But his mother didn't seem to think it was foolish. She leaned forward intently. 'Maybe what?' she whispered.

Warren swallowed. 'Well, maybe—if we could frighten them a bit more—they might give something away.'

He wasn't expecting his mother to understand. She didn't know what it was like to be so frightened that you would say anything, do anything, to get rid of the threat. He thought she would laugh at him.

But she didn't. She met his eyes steadily. 'How can we do it?' she whispered. 'How can we scare them?'

Warren looked at the door for a moment, listening until he was sure that he could hear his father downstairs, out of earshot. When he was sure it was safe, he told his mother about the idea he'd had on the bus.

He hadn't been planning to do it straight away, that evening. But his mother wouldn't let him wait until the next day. When he suggested that, she shook her head furiously.

'Think how *terrified* Hope must be,' she whispered. 'She won't know what's going on. And we've got to rescue her quickly, before—'

She didn't spell it out, but Warren knew what she meant. *Before the social workers find her. And the police.* If anyone like that got hold of Hope, she would never come home again. If there was even a chance that his plan might work, they couldn't risk waiting. They had to try it *now*.

'But what about Dad?' Warren muttered. 'He'll go berserk if he hears us—'

'He's not going to hear us.' His mother had it worked out already. 'It's my evening for shopping, isn't it? If I tell him I feel too ill to do it, he'll go instead—and we'll have an hour and a half to ourselves.'

Was it really that simple? Warren couldn't believe it was going to work. By the time they went downstairs his mother's face was pale and tense, but he worried that she wouldn't be able to keep up the pretence. Surely his father would see she was acting. Or sense that something odd was going on. Or refuse to go shopping. Or—

But none of those things happened. An hour later, Warren stood at the front window nervously watching his father back the car out of the garage. The engine didn't stop suddenly. His father didn't come storming back into the house, shouting furiously. *Did you really think you could trick me?* The car just turned on to the road and drove off round the corner, and for an instant, the house was totally still and silent.

Then Warren heard his mother's voice behind him. 'Come on. Let's do it.'

He turned and looked at her. She was standing in the doorway, with the tape in her hand.

'You've found the phone number?' she said.

He nodded. He'd checked it five times in the phone book. Taking the cassette from his mother, he slid it into the tape player. When he switched on, it rustled for a moment, and then Hope's thin, clear voice spoke.

'Ou-T . . .'

Warren pressed the pause button and picked up the phone. Quickly, before he had time to think about what he was doing, he dialled the number. His mother held the tape player up to the mouthpiece and they both leaned in close, ready to catch any sounds from the other end.

The phone rang four times, five times, six times. Then the ringing stopped suddenly, and Warren braced himself, ready to speak. *Is Robert there?* But he didn't need to say anything.

'Hello?' It was Doherty himself. Warren would have known that loud, arrogant voice anywhere. He pressed the button and set the tape player going.

'Hello?' Doherty said again. Impatient now. 'I can't hear you.'

The voice that answered him was Hope's, utterly distinctive and unmistakable. 'Out . . . out . . .'

Doherty drew in his breath sharply. 'Hello?' he said once more. But this time he sounded hesitant and uncertain. Warren had to bite his tongue to stop himself yelping with triumph.

'Out!' said Hope again, more insistently this time. Warren could almost see her standing in the secret room with her arms held up.

Very tentatively, Doherty said, *'Hope?'*

Warren pushed the phone at his mother, making her hold it so that he could turn up the volume on the tape. Then he leaned in again, to make sure he didn't miss anything.

'. . . out . . . out . . .'

'Hope?' Doherty was speaking faster now. 'Is that you? Where *are* you?'

Warren recognized that anxious note—and he knew the feelings that went with it. They'd knocked Doherty off balance. Made him unsure about what was happening. *Good!* He turned up the volume again.

*'Out!'*

Doherty drew in his breath—and then a different voice came down the phone. It was fainter, as if the speaker was standing on the other side of the room. 'Rob? What's the matter? Are you all right?'

It was the fox-girl! It had to be!

Doherty didn't answer, but Warren heard her coming across to the phone.

'Hasmegg,' Hope's voice said, conversationally. 'Dohfuss, Wonn. Hasmegg.'

This time the fox-girl's voice was much clearer. 'It's not her, Rob. How could she reach a phone?'

'Ssh!' Doherty said fiercely. 'Listen.'

Then the phone went dead.

'Quick!' Warren's mother said. 'What's the number? Get it again!'

Her finger was already on the button, rewinding the tape. It took a few moments, but as it finished Warren was already redialling. This time, the phone hardly had time to ring before it was answered. Doherty said something very fast. Hardly above a whisper.

It sounded like, *'Law?'*

What did that mean? Did he think they were the police? Warren strained his ears to catch the next word, but when it came, it was the fox-girl speaking.

'It's *not her,* Rob. You know it's not. It must be someone imitating her voice. Ring off.'

'Be quiet, Em!' Doherty snapped.

*Emma,* Warren thought, snatching at the name. *Emma Doherty*. It was a second before he realized that the phone had gone dead again. He put the phone down, feeling drained and disappointed.

'Sorry,' he muttered. 'That wasn't a lot of use, was it?'

'Oh yes, it was.' His mother's eyes were glittering. 'Didn't you hear the boy say, *Hope, where are you?* He was very surprised. And the girl said, *How could she reach a phone?* They weren't expecting to hear her on the phone—because they know where she is. They've got her shut up somewhere.'

Warren's throat was suddenly dry. 'You don't think she's dead, then?'

'No. *No.*' His mother screwed up her fists. 'If she was dead, that boy would have guessed it was a recording. She's alive—and they know where she is. We've got to make them tell us. If only we could get them here and lock them up until they talk!'

She said it wildly, thumping the air with her fists. But as soon as the words were out, she froze. For a second she was very, very still. Then she lifted her head and looked at Warren.

His mind made a huge, terrifying leap. *But we can't—*

'We *have* to,' his mother said fiercely, as though she'd read his mind. 'Otherwise we'll never see Hope again. We have to get them here and make them tell us.'

Warren was trembling, but he couldn't look away. He'd never seen her like that before. The need to find Hope scorched out of her, obliterating everything else. He could feel himself being caught up and swept along by it.

'B-but how can we?' he stuttered. 'We'll never manage—'

'Yes we will,' his mother said. She was calm now. Perfectly, terrifyingly calm. 'We have to watch them. Watch everything they do and everywhere they go—until we know the right one to take, and the right moment to do it. And then I'll hire a van.'

That was when Warren really understood that she was serious. His mind made a picture of her walking into a van-hire office and holding out her licence. She was going to do it. And she thought he was going to help.

'What about Dad?' he muttered.

'We won't tell him,' she said. 'Not until we've found Hope.'

That was the most frightening thing of all. Warren had never even imagined his parents on different sides. Now he was being asked to choose between them and he didn't know how. His whole life had suddenly become impossible.

'But what can *I* do?' he muttered. 'I'm no use—'

'You can help me shadow them,' his mother said quickly. 'And when the right moment comes, you'll have to help. I can't do it on my own.'

Warren didn't say anything. Looking at her, he understood that it was too late to draw back. Somehow, without realizing it, he'd already become part of the plan. He and his mother were going to kidnap one of the kidnappers.

'There were three kidnappers,' said Zak. 'A tall one, a short one, and a witch with ginger hair. They carried off the old man's daughter and took her far away from home.'

Bando leaned forward anxiously from his place beside Lorn. 'Did they kill her?'

All round the circle, people held their breath—and so did Lorn. *Are you going to make that up too, Zak?* she thought bitterly. *Are you going to twist the story some more?*

But Zak shook his head at Bando. 'Oh no, they didn't kill her,' he said. 'Nothing as simple as that. They wanted to keep her alive. So they took her far, far away, into a great dark forest. And there they cramped her and bent her and squashed her and SHRANK her—'

He lifted his hands from the drum-skin, spreading the fingers like claws. Twisting them cruelly to compress the empty air until Lorn could almost see the tiny, soft body of the old man's daughter, shrinking, shrinking, shrinking . . .

'They squeezed her smaller and smaller and smaller,' Zak whispered. 'Until she was no bigger than a bean. Until she was—as small as we are.'

A long, shocked sigh ran round the cavern. Suddenly, the story had come very close to everyone. They all knew what it was to be snatched away from the ordinary, familiar world and plunged into a totally different life. They all knew what it was to find themselves trapped in bodies so small that each day was a fight for survival. Every person there had been snatched away and shrunk—without knowing why or how.

Was Zak's story going to explain all that at last? Was it going to unravel the mystery? That was what they all wanted and their longing drew them deep into the story. Lorn saw their faces grow rapt and intent.

And she knew they were all on the side of the old man and his family—and against the robbers who'd snatched the old man's daughter away.

*It wasn't like that*, she wanted to shout. *You're hearing it wrong.*

*It wasn't like that at all.* But she couldn't say the words. How could she interrupt and break the spell of the story?

Zak waited until the cavern was completely silent again. Then he went on. 'They shrank the poor, stolen girl until she was no bigger than—this.' He held up a hand, with the thumb and forefinger nearly touching. 'Then they squashed her into a hole in the ground and stopped up the hole with thorns. She couldn't escape. She was trapped in the forest, unable to go home to her father. And as for him—'

*As for him—* A huge, dark shape loomed suddenly in Lorn's mind, blotting out the firelight and the familiar, friendly faces. *As for him—* She could hardly breathe, hardly hear Zak's voice as it went steadily on and on.

'The old man's heart was broken,' Zak said. 'The hole in the ground was empty. His daughter was gone.'

For a second, he let the words hang. Then he rattled his fingers sharply against the drum-skin.

'His wife and his son couldn't bear to see him so distraught. They pulled on their battered old boots and their shabby hats, picked up their walking sticks and set out into the world to find the precious girl who'd been stolen away.'

'NO!' said Lorn.

The word was out before she could stop it. She found herself on her feet, yelling across the circle at Zak.

'Why are you telling them lies? That's not how it was! It's not *true*!'

There was a gasp, all round the circle. No one had ever challenged Zak like that before. No one had ever broken a story. Horrified faces looked up at her and Bando tugged her arm, trying to pull her down again.

'Don't be cross, Lorn,' he whispered. 'It's only a story. Stories don't have to be true.'

He sounded bewildered and upset. The others were starting to look angry and Lorn knew they wanted her to sit down and be quiet, but she couldn't stop. Her whole body was rigid with fury.

'You're twisting everything!' she yelled. 'That old man kept his daughter locked up—and you're turning him into a hero.'

'Oh, come *on*!' Perdew joined in, rolling his eyes at the ceiling. 'He kept her locked up because he was trying to protect her. It's not like real life. It's a *story*.'

But it was like real life. Couldn't he see that? That was why Zak's stories held them so that they listened almost without breathing. He knew how to mirror the things they tried to hide. Perdew was the bravest hunter of them all, and the strongest too, apart from Bando. But even he was afraid, like the rest of them. Afraid of the animals that could gulp him down in a second. Afraid of the terrible, deadly cold that would kill anyone who stepped outside the cavern now. When Perdew listened to Zak, surely he knew—

But none of them seemed to know. They were all muttering at Lorn, as though she'd interrupted just to be awkward.

'Why don't you sit down?'

'Wait and see what happens!'

'It's Zak's story. He knows what he's doing!'

They just wanted her to be quiet, so they could find out what happened next. But how could she be quiet? Zak had taken Hope's story—*her* story—and turned it into something false. She had only just got her memories back and now he was trying to take them away again. Twisting them into nonsense.

'That's not how it was,' she said again. Speaking steadily this time. Meeting Zak's eyes across the circle.

Zak didn't attempt to contradict her. He danced his fingers lightly over the drum-skin. 'All right, then,' he said. 'Give us your version, Lorn. What was it like?' He smiled a small, taunting smile.

For a second, she couldn't speak. *What was it like?* She knew now, but there were no words to fit what she knew. The memories were too strong, too vivid. They wouldn't fit into the neat pattern of a story. *I was . . . I felt . . . it was like . . .*

How could she make the others understand?

Zak's clear, blue stare was fixed on her face as he went on with his version of the story again, speaking every word as though it was aimed straight at her. 'The old man's wife and son set out from their house, looking for clues to help them find the lost girl. Their darling. Their treasure. They were determined to get her back from the wicked robbers.'

Lorn couldn't go on standing where she was. All the others were scowling up at her, angry and impatient, because she was in the way. She had to let Zak go on—or tell them her own version.

But where could she start? Zak had already conjured up three evil robbers, three villains who kidnapped defenceless people and imprisoned them in a tiny world. His words were echoing in every heart in the cavern. *Snatched away . . . too small to get home . . .* They all knew how that felt.

That was what Zak's stories did. He told them who they were. They'd all been shocked and helpless when they arrived in the cavern, terrified at finding themselves in a world that had suddenly become unimaginably huge. Patiently, Zak had reshaped it to fit them, so that it made a different kind of sense. He'd given new names to the plants and animals—and to everyone in the cavern as well.

Lorn remembered his blue eyes staring into hers the first time she sat in the circle. *What is your name?* he'd asked, and she'd stared at him blankly, not knowing what to reply. When he said, *Your name is Lorn*, it had felt like a sign of belonging, of leaving her old life behind.

That was how it had been for each of them. Zak had given them a way to survive. *We don't remember. We look forward*. How could she stand against him now and ask them all to look back? She almost gave up and sat down.

And then she remembered Robert.

When they brought him into the cavern, he'd been horribly injured, his leg clawed open by the nightbird. The shock of finding out where he was—and how tiny he'd become—was fresh and raw in his mind. But he'd still had the courage to challenge Zak, refusing to let go of the truth he knew.

*My name is Robert Doherty*, he'd said.

He wouldn't pretend, and he wouldn't forget. From that first moment, he'd been determined to get back to his real home. And his real size.

And he'd done it.

He'd made the long and dangerous journey back to the place where he really belonged and *somehow* he'd managed to reverse the terrible change that had brought him to the cavern. Even Cam and Zak, who'd gone with him, couldn't explain how it had happened, but everyone knew it was true. Robert had rejected Zak's picture of the world—and achieved what they'd all thought was impossible.

*That* was the way to get the others to listen to her story! If she could get them to remember that, they would know that Zak wasn't infallible. Lifting her head, Lorn looked round the circle again. Everyone was watching her now.

'The old man had it wrong,' she said firmly. 'He thought he had his daughter under the ground for ever, with no way out, but the robbers knew better—because one of them was Robert Doherty.'

She felt the shock as she spoke his name. They thought she was the first one to break the rules of storytelling by cutting through the neat line between *real* and *imagined*. They didn't realize that Zak had already done it.

Sitting down slowly, with everyone's eyes fixed on her face, she plaited her fingers together in her lap. In a steady voice, she launched into the story. As she wanted to tell it.

'You all know what Robert's like. When he decides that something needs to happen, he won't give up until he's done it. From the moment he found out about the old man's daughter, in her miserable prison, he was determined to rescue her. With two brave friends, he planned a daring rescue, risking his life to snatch her away to a new life. And he almost succeeded. At the risk of their lives, he and his friends broke into the old man's house and carried her off, running through the night with the old man chasing them. But, just when they thought they'd escaped, when they thought the girl was free at last—that's when they lost her . . .'

# THE TERROR BODY

# 5

Robert was alone in the front room when he first picked up the phone.

'Hello?' he said.

There was no answer. Only a strange rustle.

'Hello?' he said again. 'I can't hear you.' He was about to ring off when the voice came at last, out of the blue.

*'Out . . . out . . .'*

His brain froze.

It was Hope's voice. That was exactly how she'd sounded when he and Tom had lifted her out of that horrible, dank hole under the Armstrongs' conservatory.

He didn't know how he replied. He couldn't think about anything except the sounds coming down the line. Was it possible? Could Hope really be there? Talking to him?

*'. . . out . . . out . . .'*

When Emma came in, he hardly noticed. But she must have seen something strange in his expression, because she crossed the room and stood beside him, listening. Then—so quickly that it took him by surprise—she pulled the phone out of his hand and rang off.

Robert reached out angrily, to snatch it back, but she held it behind her body and shook her head. Her face was white and tense.

'It wasn't really her,' she said. 'It can't have been, Rob. It must have been some kind of recording.'

'But it was her voice—' Robert protested.

'How can it have been?' said Emma. 'The past doesn't

change. You *know* what happened to Hope. We rescued her and took her to the wood—and she shrank away into the cavern. There's nothing left of her now, above the ground. She's smaller than my little finger. With no way back.'

Robert looked away. Emma was right, of course—but he didn't want her to be. He desperately wanted the voice at the other end of the line to be Hope's. Because Hope was *Lorn*. The friend who'd saved his life by taking him into the cavern. What he wanted, more than anything else in the world, was to see her again. To speak to her.

'It was a recording,' Emma said. 'And you'd better stop fantasizing and think about that properly. Don't you realize what it means?'

For a second, Robert didn't understand. He just stared blankly at her, wondering why she looked so grim.

Emma walked back to the door and closed it quietly, to make sure they couldn't be overheard. Then she spelt it out. 'If there's a recording, then there has to be someone playing it. And you know who that's got to be. There's only one person who's likely to have a recording of Hope's voice.'

She was right, of course. Only Hope's family had known she was there, under the floor. If he had been listening to a recording, one of them must have made it. *And no prizes for guessing which one,* Robert thought. That family was dominated by a single, terrifying person.

'So you think Mr Armstrong's tracked us down?' he said slowly. 'You think he knows where we live?' It was horribly easy to picture that heavy slab face leaning in close to the phone. The thick, cruel finger waiting ready over the PLAY button, poised to send the fragile thread of sound moving towards them.

*. . . out . . . out . . .*

'He knows where we live—and he wants us to know that he's watching us.' Emma shuddered. 'He's trying to scare us. We were idiots to think he'd just go away and leave us alone. If he'd kept Hope hidden under the floor for years, he was never going to give up overnight, was he?'

'But he knows he can't get her back,' Robert said. 'He saw her shrink. We were all holding on to her and she just disappeared.'

'You think he understood what was happening?' Emma shook her head. 'There's no way he could have worked it out. *I* wouldn't have had a clue what was going on if you hadn't told me about the cavern already.'

Robert didn't look convinced. Emma pulled an impatient, exasperated face at him.

'Don't you see?' she said. 'He knows that Hope disappeared, but he thinks *we did it*. So he probably thinks we know how to get her back.'

'If only,' Robert nodded ruefully. 'If we could only find out—'

He didn't finish, because the phone started ringing again. Before he could stop himself, he snatched it out of Emma's hand. In spite of everything they'd said, he couldn't quite believe there was no point. If there was even a chance—

'*Lorn?*' he said desperately. Emma made a quick, impatient sound and he flapped his other hand at her, straining to hear. 'Be quiet, Em.'

But he knew he was being stupid. This time he could hear the flutter of the tape and it was obvious that the sounds were simply being repeated, exactly the same as before. After a few seconds, he rang off and put the phone slowly back into its cradle. Emma was right. It was Mr Armstrong at the other end of the phone.

They were being watched. He might be outside the house at that very moment, waiting for them to come out. Wherever they went, they'd never be sure that they were alone.

'What are we going to do?' Emma said.

Robert sighed, gloomily. 'We can't do anything, can we?'

'But we must,' Emma said. 'We've *got* to get our bikes back. Suppose he sees us doing that.'

They'd ditched their bikes in the dark, when they were running away with Hope. They'd climbed over fences, to get from one back garden to another, and it was impossible to carry Hope and cope with the bikes as well. All three bikes—theirs and Tom's—were still hidden in one of the gardens.

At the time, it hadn't seemed important—not compared with Hope's safety. But Tom's mother was already asking awkward questions. They needed their bikes back.

'We'll just have to be careful,' Emma said at last. 'Mr Armstrong's got to take a break sometime. And he won't expect us to be out so late, will he?'

Robert pulled a face. 'I hope not. I really don't fancy meeting him in the dark.'

They lay in bed, fully dressed, waiting to hear the soft, snoring sounds that meant their parents were asleep. As soon as it was safe, Robert ducked under the covers and phoned Tom.

'Hi, Tosh,' he whispered. 'Ready to go?'

'Thought you'd never ring,' Tom whispered back. 'My mum's been asleep for hours. See you down by the park in ten minutes?'

'No problem. But be careful. We think Mr Armstrong's watching our house.'

Robert heard Tom's quick gasp, but he didn't stop to explain. They had a long way to walk and it was time they got started. Ringing off, he dropped his phone into his pocket and slid out of bed, pulling on his trainers.

Emma was already out on the landing, waiting for him. She didn't risk speaking, just beckoned impatiently and led the way downstairs. As they crept out of the house, Robert looked up and down the road, feeling exposed and vulnerable.

Was Mr Armstrong hiding somewhere close? There was no sign of him, but that didn't mean anything. Every bush and every shadowy corner was a possible hiding place. His eyes darted left and right as they crossed the road.

As they went round the corner, Robert looked down the side of the park and saw Tom away at the far end, by the wood. But he wasn't watching for them. He was facing the other way.

'He's *talking* to someone,' Emma hissed. 'Who on earth—?'

Robert's heart thudded. The figure beyond Tom was half-hidden in the trees, but he could see that it was a man. And surely there was only one man who would stop and talk to Tom so late at night. Only one, terrifying person . . .

'Mr Armstrong's got him!' he gasped. 'Come on.'

He and Emma broke into a run, racing down the side of the park towards Tom. But as they drew closer, the dark figure in the trees began to look shorter than Robert was expecting. Less threatening. Maybe it wasn't Mr Armstrong. But if it wasn't—who could it possibly be at that time of night?

They were only a dozen steps away when the dark figure walked out of the trees, stepped round Tom, and came down the pavement towards them. As he reached them, he lifted his head and looked Robert straight in the face.

For a split second, Robert found himself staring into a shadowy face that he knew—and didn't know. Even in the orange light from the street lamps, he was aware that the man's sharp eyes were impossibly blue and bright. They made everything else seem far off and insignificant. Somewhere, off to his left, he could hear Emma muttering something, but that was in another world, another life. There was no room in his brain just then for anything except the face in front of him.

*What do you want? Why are you here?* It was the man he'd seen on the plane, at the start of all this strangeness. Their eyes had met as they walked past each other. *And after that—I was small and alone. Down on the dark ground.*

He wanted to say it, but he couldn't get the words out. Couldn't move at all. He could only stare.

Then the man turned his head, breaking contact. He stepped off the pavement and went past the two of them. By the time Robert had gathered his wits enough to look round, he'd already disappeared.

Now—when it was too late—the questions came flooding into Robert's head. He wanted to run after the man and make him answer them. But he couldn't. Emma was tugging frantically at his sleeve.

'Rob. Rob—look at Tom! What's the matter with him?'

Reluctantly, Robert turned back. Tom was standing very still, gazing at the empty pavement where the man had been standing.

'He's not all right,' Emma said. 'Come on!'

She and Robert covered the last few steps at a run and Emma caught hold of Tom's shoulder and pulled him round to face her.

'Tom! Wake up. You can't go on standing there like a zombie.'

The word hit Robert like a blow in the chest. *Zombie* was the word Emma and Tom had used to describe him—when he wasn't really there. The Robert they could see had just been an empty shell, because the *real* Robert had been down in the cavern, with Lorn and the others.

That couldn't have happened to Tom. It *couldn't.* Robert took hold of his arm and shook him fiercely.

'Don't do that,' Emma said.

But Robert couldn't help it. He had to get some reaction. 'Tosh! Snap out of it!'

Very slowly, Tom blinked and began to move, knocking Robert's hands away.

'Cut it out!' he muttered shakily. 'What's your problem, Robbo?'

'I thought there was something wrong,' Robert said. 'I thought—'

*I thought that man had changed you. I thought he'd sent you down to the dark ground.*

'There's no time to hang around thinking,' Tom said. His voice was strange, as if he was struggling to speak clearly. 'If we don't get going, it'll be morning before we've fetched the bikes. Come on.'

Without waiting for the others to answer, he turned away and began to walk briskly up the road, towards the city centre.

'What was all that about?' Emma said.

'Did you see . . . that man?' Robert said tentatively. He was already beginning to wonder if the whole thing had happened inside his own head. 'He was—did you *see* him?'

'Of course I saw him.' Emma scowled. 'Couldn't miss him, could I? Not with you standing there, goggling at him like a codfish and blocking his way.'

'I've . . . seen him before.' Robert was still trying to make sense of it all. 'I saw him on the plane. Remember?'

'On the *plane*?' Emma looked baffled.

'I told you. When I went off to the washroom, I passed a man coming the other way. It was *him.* As I went past, he looked straight into my eyes, the way he was looking at Tom just now. And a couple of seconds later—pow! Everything exploded and disappeared. When I woke up, I was small and lost and alone.'

Emma gave him a long, cautious stare. 'So?'

Robert was sure she knew what he meant. But she was obviously going to make him spell it out. 'Well . . . now he's looked at Tom,' he muttered. 'So is Tom—?'

'Tom's nothing like you were,' Emma said firmly. 'When you came back from that washroom, you were polite and laid back and—*empty*. Tom's not like that at all. *Look* at him.' She pointed down the road. Tom was striding away energetically. 'We need to stop worrying about him and concentrate on catching him. Come on.'

She broke into a run and Robert jogged to keep up with her. But he was still worrying. Was Tom *really* all right? Or was the Tom they could see now just an empty zombie? Was the real Tom somewhere in the wood with Lorn and the others, down on the dangerous dark ground?

# 6

They'd left the bikes right over on the other side of the city, in the estate where the Armstrongs lived. It took them over an hour to walk there, ducking into the shadows from time to time to avoid anyone who might cause them trouble.

All the time they were walking, Robert was trying to work out a way of asking Tom about the man from the plane. But every question he invented sounded sillier than the one before. *Hey, Tosh, are you just a zombie? Is the real Thomas Hastings down in the cavern with Lorn?* They were all pointless. If the Tom they could see really was a zombie, he wouldn't know anything about it.

Robert did once get as far as saying, 'You know that man—?' But Tom changed the subject immediately, with a sharpness that discouraged any more questions. There was something he didn't want to talk about. Robert could tell that. But there was no real chance to discover any more. What they were doing was hard enough on its own.

And Emma kept hassling them. The nearer they came to the estate, the more she worried about how they were going to find the right place.

'I just don't *remember,*' she muttered. 'We were going so fast, and there were so many gardens. We could spend all night looking.'

'It's OK,' Tom said. 'I'm pretty sure I know where we need to be.'

Emma didn't look convinced but, when they finally reached the estate, Tom turned confidently off the main road. He began to work his way through the network of little streets as though he knew exactly where he was going.

'We go right here,' he murmured, 'and then right again—and the road curves round to the left. The house we want is about halfway along. With a red door.'

Robert didn't remember, but he recognized it as soon as he saw it. An immaculate semi with identical net curtains at every window and a neat, paved path leading up to the front door. There was no light showing at any of the windows, and no one around in the road. With luck, they could sneak in and out of the side gate without being noticed at all.

Even so, it was hard to take the first steps. They hovered on the pavement for a moment, looking nervously at each other.

Last time, it had been simple. Once they'd rescued Hope, they'd been so desperate to escape that they were ready to do anything. It had been easy to open any gates that blocked their way, easy to slip into strange gardens and clamber over rickety fences. But it was different now. As they looked at the house, all the dangers they'd ignored before jumped into their minds. *What if someone calls the police? What if there's a dog in the garden—or an angry man with a gun?*

Emma bit her lip. 'We should have come in the daytime. Just knocked on the door and explained what we wanted.'

'We've discussed all that,' Robert said patiently. He didn't want to go through the arguments again. 'It's too late now, anyway. We're here. And we'd better get on with it before anyone spots us. Come on.'

Stepping on to the grass, he walked quickly to the side gate and tried the latch. It lifted easily. He opened the gate without a sound, beckoning to the other two as he crept through.

Beyond the gateway, the garden was very dark, but he could just make out the shape of the shed at the far end. That was where the bikes were, hidden between the shed and the back fence.

Emma came up behind him, not realizing that he was still standing there. When she bumped into him, she gave a small, startled squeak.

'Sssh!' Robert muttered under his breath.

'It was your fault,' Emma said indignantly. 'You were in the way. If you'd just kept going—'

'*Sssh!*' That was Tom, following behind her. 'Get into the garden quickly, before someone comes. And be *quiet*.'

Robert couldn't believe they were being so loud. He'd learnt about being quiet in the cavern, when he was small. If he'd gone outside and made the kind of noise they were making, some greedy predator would have come along and eaten him. Tom and Emma wouldn't have survived for five minutes the way they were behaving now.

He pulled them into the garden and shut the door, lowering the latch carefully. Then he turned and began to pad down the garden, keeping to the grass and feeling the way with his feet. The others followed, as silently as they could.

They were halfway to the shed when a window opened behind them.

'What are you doing?' said a child's shrill voice. 'Go away, or I'll call the police.'

A light came on suddenly, catching all three of them out in the open. There was a girl at one of the upstairs windows and she was pointing a powerful torch straight at them. They stopped dead, turning to face her.

'It's all right,' Robert said gently. 'We're not doing anything wrong. We've just come to fetch something that belongs to us.'

That didn't make any impression on the girl. 'I'll call the police *now,*' she said, 'if you don't get out of here. I've got the phone in my hand. Look.' She turned the torch towards herself and they saw her for the first time. She was only about eight. A thin, lanky girl with hanging hair and nervous eyes. Her left hand was gripping a phone and they could see it shaking as the hand trembled.

'You really don't need the police.' Emma was trying to sound gentle too. 'We're not doing anything bad. Why don't you go and fetch your mum or your dad? Then we can explain.'

The torch whipped back towards the garden, dazzling them all, and the girl gabbled a sentence that sounded as if she'd learnt it by heart.

'It'snotconvenientformymothertospeaktoyoujustnow.'

As she said it, they heard another sound from behind her. It sounded like a much younger child, whining as if he'd just been woken up. The torch wavered again as the girl called back into the house in a sharp voice.

'Get back in bed, Callum. Everything's all right. I'll come in a minute.'

Tom shifted uneasily beside Robert. 'Isn't there anyone else there?' he muttered under his breath.

'Doesn't sound like it,' Robert muttered back.

Emma raised her voice and spoke to the girl again. 'We'll only be here for a minute. It's just that some stupid kids have dumped our bikes behind your shed, and we need to get them back.'

The girl hesitated for a second. 'There's no bikes in our garden,' she said warily.

'Yes there are. Look. We'll show you.' Emma began to walk in that direction, very slowly, so that the girl could follow her with the torch.

Robert nudged Tom. 'Get going, Tosh. What are you waiting for?'

Tom was staring back at the house. 'How could anyone leave her like that?' he whispered fiercely. 'She's terrified.'

Robert shrugged. 'She seems pretty brave to me. And maybe she loves being in charge and bossing her little brother around. We don't know what she's thinking.'

'I *do* know,' Tom muttered. 'I can feel—' He broke off suddenly and began to follow Emma, making for the shed.

Last time they'd been there, it had been much too dark to see what the garden was like. Now, as the torch lit the way ahead of them, Robert saw that the garden was as perfect as the house. The edges of the lawn were cut into crisp curves and the beds round the sides were full of tidy shrubs standing in a layer of bark chippings.

It didn't look like a garden where children ever played.

The bikes were very well hidden. Tom had jammed them right in behind the shed, so that they were invisible from the house. Emma was leaning into the space and pulling at the nearest bike, but she couldn't move it.

'Hang on,' Robert said. He squatted down and took out the little torch he'd brought with him.

Peering into the gap, he saw that Tom had locked all three bikes together. The loop of one of the locks had caught on a nail and there was no hope of getting them out without unhooking it. He wriggled the bikes, attempting to work them free, but there wasn't enough space to manoeuvre properly. They would have to undo the lock.

The girl from the house was still watching them. They could see the beam of her torch flickering up and down as she tried to work out what they were doing.

'We won't be long,' Robert called over his shoulder. Then he lowered his voice. 'Can you reach in there, Tosh? It's too narrow for me.'

There was no answer.

Looking over his shoulder, Robert saw that Tom wasn't listening to him. He was staring back at the house, looking grim and miserable.

Emma had noticed that too. She gave Tom's shoulder a brisk shake. 'Stop daydreaming!' she said roughly. 'We've got to get on with this. Unless you *want* that girl to panic and call the police.'

'Be quiet,' Tom muttered. 'You'll scare her even more if you start shouting. Why can't we just take the bikes and go?'

'They're stuck,' Robert said. Even he was starting to get exasperated.

'Let me see.' Tom squinted into the space between the shed and the fence. When he saw the lock, he nodded. 'I'll have to get in there and undo it.'

'The nails'll rip your jacket to pieces,' Emma said.

'Not if I take it off.' Tom unzipped it and pushed it into her hands. Then he looked again and took off his sweat-shirt too. 'Might as well be as thin as possible. Hold the light steady, Robbo.'

Emma stepped back, out of the way, to let Robert stand at the corner of the shed. Lifting his torch high, Robert shone it down on to the tangled bikes and Tom breathed in and wriggled towards the lock. When he was near enough, he stretched down to reach it with both hands, leaning away from Robert.

As he bent, his T-shirt caught on a different nail. The cloth was pulled up, leaving the whole of his side exposed as he bent into the torchlight.

Robert was shocked into speech. 'What's *that*?' he whispered softly.

There was a dull red bruise under Tom's ribs, running all the way across his side. It had a raw, new look, as though it had just happened.

'What's what?' Tom whispered back, glancing round.

When he saw where Robert was looking, he dragged his shirt down hastily, tearing the material. 'Oh. That. It's nothing.'

'Nothing?' Robert was horrified. 'You must be joking. How on earth—?'

'Don't fuss,' Tom muttered. He looked quickly at Emma, who was standing just out of earshot. 'Let's just get the bikes out of here as fast as we can. That girl's very frightened already. If it looks as though we're hanging around, she'll get even more suspicious—and we could land up in big trouble.'

That certainly made sense. Robert put his questions on hold and waited to take the first bike as Tom worked it loose. A few seconds later he had all three of them and Tom was backing out into the garden.

'Let's go,' Emma said cheerfully. She took her own bike and began to push it up the garden, waving at the window where the torch was still shining.

The girl didn't give any signal in reply. But as they reached the gate she turned off the torch and they had a brief glimpse of her standing in the window. She had a small child on each side of her now. They were both whining and tugging at her clothes and she kept thrusting their hands away irritably.

'It's not *right*,' Tom said, as he pushed the gate open.

'Perhaps their mum's ill,' said Robert. 'Or maybe she's just a heavy sleeper. It's probably no big deal.'

'Yes it is,' Tom said stubbornly. 'She's always leaving them alone. Can't you *tell*? Someone ought to do something.'

Why did he think he knew? And why was he getting so agitated about it? 'Isn't there enough to worry about already?' Robert said. 'At least those three have a roof over their heads.'

'And plenty of food, I expect,' said Emma. 'Not like some people.'

Tom scowled at them both. 'Don't start going on about the cavern again. Haven't you ever thought there might be worse things than nightbirds and hedge-tigers? Wasn't Hope's life worse than that, before we rescued her?'

'Of course it was,' Robert said. 'In a way. But—'

How could he explain what it was like to live in constant physical danger? Tom knew that *nightbirds* and *hedge-tigers* were owls and weasels—but he couldn't understand how different they were when they loomed over you with outstretched claws or sharp and savage teeth. *If you could only see, just for a minute . . .*

But Tom wasn't interested. Without waiting for Robert to finish, he jumped on to his bike and pedalled off.

Emma pulled a face. 'Well, at least you can't say he's a zombie,' she said wryly. 'He's certainly got a mind of his own.' She set off after Tom and Robert pedalled along slowly behind her. Still wondering.

It wasn't like Tom to be short-tempered and impatient. Something strange had happened to him. He certainly wasn't blank and empty, but he wasn't like himself either. He'd never been so vague and erratic before. What had changed him?

And had it got anything to do with Hope—with Lorn—and the people down in the cavern?

Robert's head was bursting with questions. He didn't know any of the answers, but he knew that he had to talk to Tom. As soon as possible. *I'll do it first thing in the morning,* he said to himself as he cycled off down the road.

But overnight the temperature dropped, without warning. And that put everything else out of his head.

As soon as he woke up, he knew that something had changed. A narrow strip of sky showed pale and clear between the curtains and when he pulled them apart he saw the dark leaves of the front hedge crisp with frost. Under the street lamps, the grass verges beyond glimmered icy-orange. Last year, he'd seen the same thing and thought, *How beautiful.*

Now, he thought of death.

Last year, he hadn't known what it was like to live in a cavern under the ground, with no kind of heating except a brazier that burned little scraps of wood. Last year, he'd thought that the life he lived was the only kind of life that there was. He'd been very unhappy, but he hadn't been in danger of dying.

Now, as he looked at the frost, he could almost feel the cold air filtering down into the cavern where Lorn and the others slept. The brazier couldn't give out any more heat. There were already two people stoking it constantly, day and night, and it was burning flat out. How could they all survive if it got any colder?

Zak had spelt out the answer, ruthlessly. *Their body mass isn't big enough to retain the heat . . . Lorn will die first. She's very small . . .*

Frantically Robert started dressing. He had no real plan. All he knew was that he had to do *something*. Pushing his feet into his trainers, he went out on to the landing—and bumped into Emma as she emerged from the bathroom.

She saw him heading for the stairs and pulled a face. 'What are you doing? Aren't you going to wash?'

He couldn't believe she was being so trivial. 'Haven't you looked outside? It's *frosty*.'

'So?' Emma said. 'That doesn't mean—' And then she got it, and her eyes widened. 'Oh, of *course*. What are you going to do?'

'I'm going to the park,' Robert said gruffly. 'I don't know what use I can be, but I can't just sit around here.'

'But suppose Mr Armstrong's watching already?'

'I'll just have to be careful. If you come too, one of us can keep a lookout.'

'OK.' Emma nodded quickly. 'Give me a couple of seconds.'

While she was dressing, Robert went quickly downstairs and found a few currants and a piece of bread to take to the cavern. It was frustrating to see all the tins heaped up in the cupboard. There was lots of food in the house, but none of it was any use to Lorn and the others. He could only give them a few tiny fragments at a time. Feeling miserable and useless, he wrapped the bread and currants in his handkerchief and slipped them into his pocket.

Emma came running down the stairs, calling over her shoulder. 'Rob and I are just going out for a walk. We'll come back and have some breakfast before we go to school.' They went out quickly, before their mother had a chance to reply.

The park hadn't opened yet and the big memorial gates opposite their house were tightly shut, but that was just a formality. There was a fence most of the way down the side of the park, but, once they'd walked past that and reached the wood at the far end, there was nothing to stop them heading straight into trees.

The wood was still dark, its narrow, twisting paths shaded by tangles of brambles and gaunt, leafless branches. They hurried along one of the paths, towards the hedge that separated the wood from the playing fields.

When they reached the hedge, Robert led the way along the little ditch just inside it. Even in the dim light, he knew exactly where to cross the ditch, but he took his time, stepping very slowly and placing his foot down carefully on the other side. While he was still glancing round, to make sure that no one was watching them,

Emma dropped on to her knees and peered into the shadows under the hedge.

'Look,' she whispered. 'It's sheltered. There's no frost here.'

Robert knelt down beside her. He ran his hands lightly across the hedge bank until he found the tiny tunnel entrance. Emma was right. The ground was very cold, but not frozen. Step by step, he walked his fingers up the bank to the little patch of warmer earth, close under the bushes.

'The fire's still going,' he murmured. He took out his handkerchief and unrolled it. Finding a small, straight twig, he began pushing the bread and currants into the small, dark tunnel entrance.

'A bit more insulation might help.' Emma leaned forward and scooped up a handful of dry leaves from under the hedge.

'Careful!' Robert said sharply. The picture in his mind was clear and violent. *Thick fingers digging. Heavy. Hard. Nails crashing into soft flesh and crushing tiny bones . . .*

'I know, I know,' Emma said. 'But we've got to do something, haven't we? We can't worry about every little danger.'

She knew she was wrong, though. Robert could tell from the way her movements changed. She arranged the leaves carefully down the slope, not scattering them at random but placing them, one by one. As she reached up for more, she slid her fingers gently into the brittle heaps.

When there was a thick layer of leaves all down the slope, she sat back on her heels, looking satisfied. 'That has to make a difference.'

Robert shrugged. He was snapping twigs into neat, short lengths and stacking them next to the entrance tunnel, so that they were ready for the woodpile. He hoped that would make a difference too. But how could they tell? How did they know what it would take to keep the cavern warm enough?

Emma stood up and started to move up and down the hedge bank, hunting for more wood. 'If we break up some wood at home, we won't need to hang around here so long,' she said over her shoulder.

As she spoke, Robert thought he heard something else in the wood behind them. A faint noise, like feet stepping along the soft earth path. He put up a hand, to tell Emma to be quiet.

'What's the matter?' she whispered.

He waved his hand impatiently and listened again, but there was nothing now except the rumble of traffic on the road outside. He covered the wood stack with leaves and stood up. His feet were numb and the knees of his trousers were damp.

'Let's go,' he muttered. 'You're right about the wood. I'll put it in my bag.'

Slowly he stepped across the ditch. Then he turned and looked back at the entrance to the cavern. *I was in there with them,* he thought. *I was there.* But it was already becoming more and more distant. Less real.

Emma came past him, pulling at his arm. 'We're going to be late,' she said. 'Get a move on, Rob. Or do you *want* to stand there until you freeze to death?'

Robert stared after her as she went back along the ditch. How could she say something like that, so casually? Did she think it was all a game?

# 7

Even with Emma chivvying him, he was still late for school. She grabbed a piece of toast and went off straight away, but he needed to wash and change his clothes. The school bell was already ringing when he finally turned in at the gates, and by the time he made it to the classroom, registration was over.

Mrs Pearson looked at him sharply over the top of her glasses. 'Late?' she said, with a question in her voice. Robert wasn't one of those people who made a habit of missing registration.

'I'm sorry,' he mumbled, not offering any excuse.

Mrs Pearson frowned and looked back in the register. 'You were late on Tuesday too. What's the matter, Robert? Have you started oversleeping?' She raised her eyebrows and someone tittered at the back of the class.

'Sorry,' Robert muttered again, ducking into his seat next to Tom. As Mrs Pearson moved to mark him late, Tom leaned sideways to ask him something. But Mrs Pearson's head snapped up before he could get the words out.

'There's no time for chattering. You all need to listen hard. Even you, Thomas Hastings. There are dozens of notices today.'

Tom lurched back into his seat as she started firing information at them. He began scribbling on a piece of paper, as if he was taking notes, but a second or two later the paper came slithering across the table.

Robert reached out for it but, before he could take a

look at it, Mrs Pearson was glaring at him again. Just waiting to catch him reading it.

'I hope you're remembering all this information,' she said sharply. 'Where have I told you to be in period four, Robert Doherty?'

She was in the worst kind of mood, just looking for an excuse to hand out punishments, but she wasn't going to catch him like that. Robert returned her look with wide, innocent eyes.

'We have to go to the hall for a talk,' he said.

She nodded, grudgingly. 'And what will you need?'

He'd missed that bit while he was reaching out for Tom's note, but it didn't sound too hard to guess. 'Pens and paper,' he said, as confidently as he could.

'Pens and *link notebooks*,' Mrs Pearson said, pursing her lips.

It wasn't enough of a mistake to lose him his break, but he suspected that he couldn't afford another one. It was another two or three minutes before he risked looking at Tom's note, and when he did, it didn't make any sense.

WHAT KEPT YOU? it said. DID YOU MEET HIM AGAIN?

Did you meet who? He didn't know what Tom meant—but it wasn't sensible to ask him at that moment. If they upset Mrs Pearson again, they'd be in real trouble. So he crumpled up Tom's note and pushed it into his pocket.

By the time Mrs Pearson reached the end of the notices, he'd forgotten all about it.

All day, at school, he thought about freezing to death. About blood growing solid and sharp ice crystals piercing the lungs. It was the kind of day when everyone made a rush for the seats at the back, near the radiator. People kept their jackets on in the classroom and skulked in the cloakrooms at break time, trying to avoid being sent outside.

Robert couldn't concentrate on anything except the cold. He wanted to invent a way of making a second brazier and getting it into the cavern without enlarging the tunnel. But his mind couldn't make that work. It kept bringing him back to the same depressing conclusion. The only thing that would really help the people in the cavern was to get them out of there, and back to normal. He'd done it for himself and there had to be a way of doing it for them too.

But what *was* it?

By the end of the day, he was feeling stupid and frustrated. He'd completely forgotten that he was supposed to stay behind for a basketball practice and he was already heading out of the gate when Tom came running after him.

'Hey, Robbo! What are you doing? Dazzer'll go nuclear if you miss this practice too. Have you forgotten there's a match next week?'

Robert stopped and turned round, frowning. Yes, he had forgotten. And even now he'd been reminded, it all seemed impossibly trivial. He could hardly believe that basketball had once been the centre of his universe. He'd missed the last two practices without even noticing.

'I haven't got my kit,' he muttered.

'It's in your locker,' Tom said. 'Been there for weeks.'

Robert looked back at the school. 'Don't you think it's a bit of a waste of time? With all we've got to do?'

Tom shook his head. 'You'd be dumb to miss it. Unless you *want* Dazzer asking lots of awkward questions.'

There was no arguing with that. Mr Dawson wasn't a man who gave up on things. Reluctantly, Robert started back towards the gym.

Tom was absolutely right about his kit. It was there in the locker, still clean, because he'd forgotten the last practice too. He pulled it out and followed Tom into the gym.

'You're late!' Mr Dawson yelled. 'Get yourselves changed and get out here! And remember you're not the only post player in the squad, Doherty. Don't think you can swan in and take your place for granted.'

That was an empty threat, and everyone knew it. Robert was the best player in the school. Not just because he was tall, but because he was fast and intelligent and knew the game inside out. If he was available, he'd get picked. No competition.

By the time he'd changed, Tom was already out in the gym, dribbling along the back line. As soon as he saw Robert he fed him the ball.

Robert shot out a hand to trap it, without really thinking. He and Tom had been passing balls to each other since they were five and it was completely automatic, like breathing. Tom never got it wrong.

But he did this time.

The ball went sailing past and cannoned off the changing room door with an embarrassing thud. Bret Leavenholme scooped it up, looking smug, and lobbed it back to Robert. Insultingly slowly.

'You need to play a bit of patball, Robbo. You're losing your touch.'

'That's what happens when you start skipping practices,' Mr Dawson said sourly. 'Get your stretching done, Doherty. And then I want you and Hastings passing up and down the court for five minutes.'

Robert pulled a face and went into his warm-up stretch routine. Basketball might not be the most important thing in the world, but he was determined not to give Dazzer another excuse to bawl him out. From now on, he was going to get everything a hundred per cent right.

It was much harder than he thought it would be.

As soon as he and Tom started passing, he knew there was something badly wrong. Tom's first mistake hadn't been just a stray fumble. All his passes were like that. Just slightly skew. And it was the same when he sent the ball back. Tom was reaching for it in the wrong place. If Robert hadn't fed it to him carefully he would have missed three passes out of four.

'What's up?' Robert hissed, the second time they turned at the end of the court. 'Why are you fooling around?'

'I'm not fooling,' Tom muttered. 'It's just—'

He didn't get to finish the sentence. Mr Dawson spotted them talking and bellowed across the gym. 'OK, ladies! If you're good enough to stop for tea and a chat we'll have you dribbling now. And shooting from the dribble. Ten each. *Go!*'

Tom groaned and started down the court, but it was a disaster from the beginning. He missed every shot.

He wasn't a natural, like Robert, but he was a moderately competent player—and he didn't usually miss *like that.* Steadying himself too long and frowning up at the basket, then pitching the ball over his head at completely the wrong angle.

Mr Dawson thought he was doing it on purpose, of course. By the end of the practice, he was so angry that he had Tom running laps round the court while the others played one short. And Tom ran round perfectly happily, as though he would rather have been doing that than actually playing.

'What's the matter with you?' Robert muttered again as they went off to the changing rooms. 'I could play better with my eyes shut. What were you *doing*?'

Tom hesitated. For a second, Robert thought he was going to say something. Then Peter Wimborne came up behind and jeered at him.

'What did you do, Hastings? Disconnect your brain before you started? You were serious rubbish.' And he dug Tom in the ribs, in an amiable way.

Hitting the precise place where Robert had seen the bruise.

Tom drew in his breath sharply—and then tried to disguise it by slipping into his Dazzer imitation. 'That's no way to behave in the changing room! Where's your team spirit, boy? This side's never going to top the league until you learn to support each other *on and off the court*!'

Wimborne laughed and disappeared into the toilet. Tom sat down on the bench and quickly pulled on his sweatshirt, over his basketball kit.

'There *is* something wrong, isn't there?' Robert said.

Tom hesitated. 'This isn't the place—' He ducked sideways, peering back into the gym. 'They'll all be in here in a couple of seconds.'

Robert nodded. 'Come back to our house and have some soup then. Before you take Helga out.'

'If you like,' Tom said. He shrugged and started to undo his shoes.

They were out of the changing room while the others were still hunting for their socks and they cycled away from the bike sheds down an empty drive. Most people had gone home an hour earlier and the street was almost deserted, but there were the usual loiterers around the corner shop.

As Tom and Robert cycled away from school, one of them peeled off from the crowd. 'Hey, Robbo!' he shouted. 'Someone's looking for you.'

It was a boy from Emma's year. What was his name? Phipps? Phipson? Robert couldn't remember exactly, but he recognized him all right. A real joker.

'Don't stop,' Tom muttered. 'It'll be some kind of nonsense. We'll get stuck for hours if we start talking to Fipper.'

Robert had no intention of stopping. He cycled on, pretending not to hear. All he wanted was to go home as fast as he could, so that he could ask Tom some serious questions.

But he didn't get to ask anything. When they came round the corner by the park gates, there was a bus just leaving the stop outside his house. As it drew away, Emma came charging out of the front garden, on to the pavement. She stared left and then right, turning her head wildly from one side to the other as if she was searching for something. Robert had never seen her like that before.

She looked hysterical.

'He was right by the window,' Emma said. She was still shaking so hard that her coffee slopped out of the mug and on to the kitchen table. 'I opened the curtains and he was *there*. Staring straight at me.'

Robert and Tom had taken her into the house and made her sit down. She could speak coherently now, but she couldn't stop talking about the intruder.

'He was crouching down, and his face was so close it was like . . . like—' She moved her hands and the coffee slopped again.

'Who was it?' Robert said. 'Did you recognize him?'

'I couldn't really see his face. He was wearing some kind of mask. Like a balaclava. But his eyes looked horrible. And I was so *feeble*.'

'It wasn't feeble to chase after him,' Tom said, very quietly. 'Not when you were frightened.'

That hadn't struck Robert before. He put a hand on Emma's shoulder. 'Pretty brave of you,' he said.

'Pretty *stupid*,' Emma said. She was starting to sound more like herself. 'Suppose he'd had a knife?'

'Did he look violent?' Tom murmured.

'How would I know?' Emma shrugged. 'I just saw him crouching at the window—only his head—and then I was running. By the time I came out of the front door he'd disappeared.' She leaned back in her chair and drank down half her coffee in a single gulp. 'That's better. Chuck the cloth over here, Rob, and I'll clean up this mess on the table.'

She started wiping energetically. *Not much wrong with her,* Robert thought. For once he was glad to see her organizing things.

She balled up the cloth and tossed it into the sink. 'At least I got across to the park before it happened. I've stacked up a load of wood for them.'

'Is that where he saw you?' Robert said. 'Did he follow you back?'

Emma thought it over. 'I don't think so. I checked very carefully before I went into the wood. There was no one around at all. And I checked again when I got to the cavern, just to be on the safe side.'

'It's probably just some random snooper,' Tom said mildly. 'Nothing aimed specifically at you. Forget about it, Em.'

Emma nodded. 'That's what I want to do. I'm sick of all this drama. I'd just like things to be *normal* again.'

Tom looked hard at her and Robert thought he was going to say something else, but he didn't. After a second, he stood up, pushing his chair away from the table. 'I'm off then. Before Helga goes completely berserk and thinks I've abandoned her. See you tomorrow.'

He waved a hand and let himself out of the kitchen door. As he closed it behind him, Emma looked up at Robert.

'D'you think he's right?' she said. 'Was it just some random intruder?'

Robert hesitated. 'I don't know. It seems a bit of a coincidence, having so many weird things happening at the same time. I wondered if it was—'

'One of the Armstrongs?' Emma said quickly.

'Ye-es. Or maybe—' Robert glanced down. 'What about the man we saw yesterday?'

'For goodness' sake!' Emma stood up impatiently. 'Why do you keep banging on about him? Don't complicate things. There's enough to worry about, without that.'

She walked out of the kitchen, leaving Robert staring miserably at the table. He wanted to talk to her, to tell her about Tom's bruise, and the odd way he'd been behaving. But she obviously wasn't going to listen. And Tom had gone off too, without answering any questions. No one was interested in talking about the strange man.

But Robert was sure he was important.

That night, he had a slow, detailed nightmare, full of dark images. He was in the wood, unable to move or speak, but seeing everything around him with agonizing clarity.

He saw Mr Armstrong standing beside the ditch, looking across at the low hedge bank and the tiny cavern entrance. Everything was utterly, unnaturally, silent. There were no car sounds from the road. No leaves rustling as a fox padded through the undergrowth. The wood was motionless, holding its breath around the dark, menacing figure beside the ditch.

And then the figure moved. One instant it was on the far side of the ditch. The next it was kneeling in front of the hedge bank with its huge, brutal hands going out like grabs towards the earth. It pushed the soil aside so fast that a great pit opened up in seconds. And then—and then—

Robert saw Lorn's tiny, defenceless face gazing up in horror as the ground opened over her head and the cold air flooded in. He saw the dark figure reach down into the earth and scoop her up.

For a split second, she was there in the palm of the great left hand. Lorn. Hope. The friend he would have given anything to rescue.

Then the giant fingers closed around her living body, not clenching tight and squeezing her to death, but trapping her for ever. With its hands cupped, the massive, ugly figure strode away into the trees.

Robert woke suddenly, sweating and appalled. For the first time, he understood that being small put Lorn into a new kind of danger. If her father got hold of her now, he would be able to hide her in his pocket. Or keep her in a matchbox. Or shut her into a tin. No one would ever be able to rescue her again.

For five or ten minutes, he couldn't do anything except lie still, paralysed with fear. But gradually he became aware of sounds coming through the wall. It was before four o'clock in the morning, but someone was moving round in Emma's room.

Why was she awake? Had she had a nightmare too? He listened for another couple of moments and then he slid out of bed and went to find out.

# 8

He tapped on Emma's door and she opened it cautiously. When she saw who it was, she stepped back quickly to let him in. Her room was dark and the curtains were pulled wide open.

'What are you doing?' Robert whispered.

She put a finger to her lips and shut the door behind him. 'It's them,' she muttered, nodding at the window. 'They're outside. Go and take a look. But keep out of sight.'

Ducking down, Robert crept across to the window and knelt down to one side of it, peering out at the orange darkness of the street. Emma slipped into place on the other side, frowning as she stared down. For a few seconds, there was nothing to see. Then Emma tapped Robert's arm and pointed.

Someone was coming along the pavement. A person in a long coat, with the hood pulled up. The dark figure stopped opposite them and looked up, scanning the front of their house.

Robert's heart twisted and he caught his breath. That was how Lorn moved. That was how she lifted her head.

'It's too small for Mr Armstrong,' Emma whispered.

Did she really not see who it was? Robert could hardly believe it. There was only one person he knew who moved like Lorn. Who looked exactly as Lorn would look in forty years' time—if she managed to live that long.

'It's *Mrs* Armstrong,' he whispered back. 'And if she's here, he can't be far off. They're not going to let go, Em.'

'Then we'll just have to be cleverer than they are,' Emma said stoutly.

She sounded as though it was a game. Something they could 'win' if they tried hard enough. Robert didn't know how to explain what it was like to be caught up in something that might not end.

It was like the moment in the nightbird's tree when he'd realized, for the first time, that he was trapped in a body the size of a bean. That he could be stuck with being small for the rest of his life. What worried him most, then and now, was the idea that he might just . . . give up.

If protecting Lorn became too dangerous, too much of a burden, would he shrug his shoulders in the end and give up on the whole thing? *Because I'm never going to see her again* . . . He couldn't bear the thought of that.

'We've got to get rid of them!' he said fiercely.

Emma pulled a face, warning him not to raise his voice, but she was too late. They heard a door open and feet came towards them across the landing. There was a soft tap on the door.

'Emmie?' It was their mother.

Emma went across to open the door. 'Sorry, Mum. Didn't mean to wake you up.'

'You're in the dark,' Mrs Doherty said.

No direct question, of course. She never asked questions aloud, even when the air was thick with them. Robert went across and turned on the light.

'It's my fault,' he said quickly. 'I had a nightmare and I came in to see Em. But I'm fine now. I'll go back to bed in a minute.'

'So will I,' Emma said. 'We were just having a bit of a chat.'

'You ought to close the curtains,' Mrs Doherty said faintly. 'The room will get cold. And if you're not all right, Robbie—'

'It's OK,' Robert said. 'Honestly. It was just a stupid dream.'

Emma grinned brightly. 'We're absolutely fine, Mum. You can go back to bed.' She stood in the doorway smiling and waiting for her mother to leave.

It felt disturbingly like bullying. Robert turned away towards the window. As Emma closed the door and flicked the switch, his eyes adjusted and he saw the hooded figure outside, staring up at him.

He felt a brief flicker of pity. Then he remembered Hope scuttling backwards in her hole under the floor and every drop of sympathy drained away. That woman down there had helped to keep her a prisoner. Whatever Mr Armstrong had done—whatever had gone on in that black room—his wife had been part of it.

Abruptly he went across and closed the curtains. 'I'm going back to bed. There's nothing we can do about *her*.'

He went out and back into his own bedroom, padding across the floor in the dark, without bothering to switch on the light. As he reached the bed, he trod on the trousers he'd taken off the night before.

Something crackled slightly between his toes. Not cloth, but paper. For a second he couldn't think what it was. He bent down and picked up the trousers, feeling in the pockets. As soon as his fingers touched the crumpled note, he remembered. He pulled it out and turned on his lamp to read it again.

SO WHAT KEPT YOU? DID YOU MEET HIM AGAIN?

He still didn't understand it. Did Tom think he'd met Mr Armstrong on the way to school? That was what the note seemed to mean. But why jump to that conclusion? It didn't make sense. Robert fell asleep with the question going round and round in his head.

It was only when he woke up in the morning that he realized the note had nothing to do with Mr Armstrong.

Tom was asking him about the man from the aeroplane.

Once he'd understood, he knew that he and Tom had to talk, straight away. In private. It was no good waiting until they were at school, with hundreds of people milling around. He had to catch Tom on his own, while he was out walking Helga.

Robert was up and dressed by seven. He slipped out without telling anyone where he was going and went off to Tom's house. When Tom came out with Helga, Robert was waiting for him.

Tom looked surprised—and oddly wary. 'What's this about? Has something happened?'

'We need to talk,' Robert said. 'But not here. Where are you going?'

'Along the canal.' Tom gave him another odd look, but he didn't ask any questions. He just set off down the road, leaving Robert to follow.

They reached the bridge and walked down on to the towpath. Helga was fizzing with excitement when Tom undid her lead, clearly delighted at having two people to play with instead of one. As soon as she was free, she raced ahead, stopping every couple of seconds to look back and wag her tail.

Tom started along the path, not saying anything. Just waiting for Robert to begin.

'You know that man you were talking to on Wednesday night?' Robert said carefully. 'By the park—when you were waiting for us to go and fetch the bikes?'

There was a tiny pause. Then Tom said, 'What about him?'

It was like trying to squeeze a hard, dry lemon. *Why don't you talk to me?* Robert wanted to shout. *We're supposed to be friends. You're supposed to trust me.* But he knew that wouldn't work. If he wanted Tom to trust him, he had to explain.

'I know you think he's important,' he said. 'Because you wrote that note, asking if I'd met him again. I haven't, but I think he's important too. Because—'

Tom was listening now. Watching him with cautious, glittering eyes. 'Because what?'

'He was the man I met on the plane,' Robert said steadily. 'And when he stared at *me*, I landed up in the cavern. So I wondered . . .'

Tom stopped dead, staring at him. And then he began to laugh out loud.

'What's so hilarious?' Robert said.

'You think I've become a zombie? Without any feelings?' Tom shook his head as though he couldn't believe it. 'You think I've changed the way you did?' He was still laughing, but there was an odd, uncomfortable edge to it now.

'It wasn't funny when it happened,' Robert said stiffly.

'I know. I'm sorry.' Tom gave him a rueful smile. 'I'm only laughing because—well, you couldn't be more wrong. There's no Tiny Tom out there in the park, hiding under a heap of leaves. I'm all here. So you can stop worrying.' He looked up the path. 'Hey, Helga!'

Snatching up a stick, he threw it for her, obviously meaning to end the discussion. But the stick flew sideways, erratically, over the canal. It dropped into the water with a splash and Helga jumped in eagerly, paddling towards it.

Tom made a small, irritated sound under his breath. Helga was too small to jump back up on to the bank by herself. When she came swimming back, he had to bend down and haul her out. By the time she landed on the towpath, they were both wet and Tom's hands were covered in mud.

Robert looked at him. 'You didn't mean to throw the stick there, did you?' he said quietly. 'What's the matter with you?'

The moment the words were out, he knew that was the question he should have asked in the first place. Tom was suddenly very quiet.

That didn't matter. Robert knew he would get an answer if he waited. They turned and walked silently back along the towpath and up the steps on to the road. Tom didn't speak until they had almost reached his house.

Then he said, 'I can't see properly. It was like that at the practice, too. I get . . . distractions.' He frowned miserably.

Robert had no idea what he was talking about. 'What sort of distractions?'

Tom shrugged. 'Well—remember that boy we passed on the way here?'

Robert vaguely remembered seeing some kid in a hoodie coming the other way. 'What's he got to do with anything?'

'There's something black inside his head. I don't know what it is, but I can still *see* it, like a filthy cloud. And I can feel it too.' He pressed a hand to his side, just under the ribs.

Something slid into place in Robert's mind. 'That girl,' he said slowly. 'When we were fetching the bikes back. Were you seeing weird things then as well?'

Tom pulled a face. 'When I first heard her voice, I could hardly breathe. That was the first time it gave me a bruise.' His voice was completely matter-of-fact, as though he was talking about something ordinary, like measles.

'You ought to go and see a doctor,' Robert said uneasily.

'A *doctor*?' Tom looked at him as if he'd gone mad. 'What use would that be? I'm not ill.'

'So what's all this stuff about getting bruises and seeing things that aren't there? Are you trying to tell me that's normal?'

'Why not?' Tom said irritably. 'Have I got to be ill just because I don't see the same way as you do? The things I see are *real.*' He stopped for a second, as though he was making a decision. Then, very deliberately, he added, 'And Magee says it's going to get worse.'

Tom watched Robert, waiting for him to understand.

When he did, it knocked the breath out of him, so that he could hardly speak. 'You mean the man on the plane, don't you? The one you were talking to on Wednesday night. *He's* Magee. And he's mixed up with this too!'

'Maybe,' Tom said warily. He looked down at Helga and she whined, pushing her nose into his hand, and he patted her head without looking down.

'Why didn't you *tell* me?' Robert said angrily. 'He's right in the middle of everything. So we've got to find him and make him explain. Then we might even have a chance of saving Lorn and the others—before it gets too cold.'

They'd reached Tom's house now. He opened the front gate, and let Helga into the garden. Then he paused, blocking the way.

'Magee's not—like you think,' he said. 'You can't just ask him questions and get answers. He'll only say what he wants to say.'

Robert scowled. 'So what did he say to *you*? Or aren't you going to tell me that either?'

Tom ignored the jibe. He was very pale now, quite unlike his normal, cheerful self. 'I couldn't tell you before. It was too . . . too—' He stopped and spread his hands, hunting for the right word. 'When he stared at me, it was like—like having him inside my mind. And when we met outside the park, he said, *You can see like me, can't you? And you want to do something*. He knew exactly how I was feeling.'

'Didn't you *ask* him anything?' Robert said impatiently.

'Of course I did.' Tom grinned ruefully. 'I said, *I don't like seeing into people's heads. How can I make it stop?* And he just laughed and said, *It'll get worse before you find that out. You need to know how to help them*.'

'He's got you taped, hasn't he?' Robert said. Tom was a sucker for trying to help people. 'But it's all nonsense, Tosh. What could you possibly do to help that girl where we hid the bikes?'

'I asked that too,' Tom muttered. 'But he wouldn't tell me. He laughed and said, *When you're ready, you'll know*. And then he went.'

'And you let him go? Without any way of finding him again?'

'Oh, I know where to find him,' Tom said mildly. 'He gave me this.' He put a hand in his pocket and pulled out a little white card.

MAGEE, it said, 17A STEPNEY PARADE

Robert wanted to go there straight away, but Tom persuaded him that they ought to wait until after school.

'If we keep skipping school, people are going to start asking awkward questions,' he said. 'A few hours won't make any difference, and if we go this afternoon, Emma might come too. It'll be better with three of us.'

Grudgingly, Robert agreed. 'Let's tell her at break. She might have some good ideas about what we need to ask.'

That was what they both expected. But they were completely wrong. When they told Emma, she didn't waste time thinking up ideas. She hit the roof.

'Are you *insane*? You don't know a thing about this Magee man. I can't believe you're planning to go off to this address he's given you. It's as stupid as going to see someone you've met on the internet.'

'There'll be two of us,' Tom said. 'Three, with you. And Robert's taller than he is. Come with us, Em.'

'No,' Emma said. 'No, no, *no*! Things are crazy enough without that. I'm not getting mixed up with anything else. I told you. I just want a bit of *normal life*. If you're determined to go, you can go on your own.'

'There's nothing to be frightened of.' Robert couldn't think why she was being so awkward. 'What could possibly happen?'

'Suppose he *attacks* you?' Emma said.

It was all Robert could do not to laugh in her face. 'He's only a man—shorter than me. Why should I be afraid of *him*, when I survived being grabbed in the night-bird's claws?'

'That was different,' Emma said. 'I mean, I'm sure it was terrifying, but if Magee does something it'll be—' She stopped.

'Real?' Robert said spikily.

Emma went red. 'That's not what I meant.'

'Yes it is.' Robert's voice was cold. 'You think Lorn and the others are less important because they're small. You think they can't feel things the way we do.' He turned away quickly, picturing his friend Nate in the mouth of the hedge-tiger. That death was more horribly *real* than anything Emma had ever seen. *And I did it. I persuaded him to come on the journey.* The breath in his throat almost choked him.

'It's OK,' Tom said quietly, from behind him. 'Don't worry about what Emma says. We can go without her.'

Robert had an uncomfortable sense that Tom knew exactly how he was feeling. He pushed the thought away and squared his shoulders.

'Of course we can,' he said. 'And we must. We have to go.'

He was absolutely convinced that Magee understood what was going on. And no one else did—except possibly Zak, who seemed to have all kinds of mysterious knowledge. But there was no hope at all of talking to Zak. Not ever again. They had to find Magee.

Secretly, Robert was still hoping that Emma would give in and go with them. But when they met her at the school gates, at the end of the afternoon, she clearly hadn't changed her mind. She scooted up on her bike looking cross and prickly.

'Well?' she said. 'Have you given up your stupid plans?'

'What do you think?' Robert said stiffly.

Emma shrugged. 'All I can say is, don't go inside the flat if you know what's good for you.'

Tom was watching her face. 'Won't you change your mind?' he murmured.

'I told you. I'm going to have a *normal* weekend.' Emma tossed her head. 'Shelley's having a party, and I'm going to stop over at her house.'

'*Shelley?*' Robert couldn't believe what he was hearing. 'I thought she was an airhead.'

Emma shrugged. 'So? At least I can spend a few hours without thinking and worrying and having the world turned upside down. I just need a *rest* from it all.'

Robert was too annoyed to answer. He watched in silence as Emma cycled away out of the gates.

'I'm going home to change,' she called back over her shoulder. 'See you tomorrow night.'

It was already beginning to get dark. Robert wondered, for an instant, how Emma would cope if Mr Armstrong came lurking round the house again. Then he hardened his heart. What did that matter, compared with the risks that Lorn was running every day? Emma might be scared, but she'd survive.

He looked away, nodding at Tom. 'Let's go and see Magee,' he said.

Lorn was still telling the story—*her* way—and she was trying everything she knew to hold the others' attention. But she could see their eyes wandering. The power wasn't there and, any minute now, someone was going to interrupt.

It was Annet who cracked first. She stood up suddenly, brushing the dust off her hands. 'I'm bored with this. The robbers are just wandering around, moaning about losing the girl. Why don't they find out why she shrank? And why don't they do something to get her back?'

*How can I tell you that when I don't know the answers myself,* Lorn thought. But she couldn't say that out loud.

The others all looked as though they agreed with Annet. 'It's time something happened,' said Dess. 'When are we going to get to the real stuff?'

Lorn didn't know how to reply. 'What's *the real stuff*?'

Dess stared at her. 'When the robbers and the old man fight, of course. Isn't that what the whole thing's about? I want to know who gets the girl in the end?'

'Why does she have to belong to someone?' Cam said belligerently. 'She ought to be free, like the robber girl. That would be a better ending.'

'She's certainly not free at the moment,' said Tina. 'She's squashed into that hole in the ground. The first thing she has to do is get out of there.'

'Her dad's going to pull her out, isn't he?' Shang said.

Now everyone was talking at once.

'—but she'll still be small—'

'—maybe he can force the robbers to make her big again—'

'—but in Lorn's story the robbers are the heroes—'

They crowded together, making suggestions and arguing, and Lorn found herself squeezed out on to the edge of the group. Only Zak was still looking at her now.

She looked helplessly at him. 'What's going on?'

Zak grinned. 'You've let them take over the story. They're squeezing it like a berry, and the juice is trickling off in all directions.'

'So have I got to leave them to work out an ending?'

'They'll never do that.' Zak's grin broadened. 'When they're tired of guessing, they'll come back to us and ask, *What happened?*'

'How can we know what happens?' Lorn said wildly. 'It's not over yet.'

'We're not writing history,' said Zak. 'Stories don't have to be true—they just need to be *right*.'

Lorn frowned. 'So how do I make this story right?'

'There has to be a battle,' Zak said gently. 'The robbers have to meet the old man.'

'But they can't!' Lorn felt herself begin to panic. 'You don't know what he's like. They couldn't possibly—'

He was suddenly there in her mind, not a *poor old man*, but real and terrifying. Frantically she tried to shut the memory away. If she let herself think about him, he would swamp her.

Zak was watching her face. 'It's no good,' he said quietly. 'You'll never be able to end the story unless you let him into it.'

It was easy to say that, but how *could* she talk about him? How could she ever make the others understand? He was like . . . like—

All her words failed. He was *there*, huge and dark, beyond description. His eyes saw her, his huge hands could reach out and grab her wherever she was. When she tried to picture him in her head, she was swamped by a wave of fear that obliterated everything else.

'I can't—' she said. And then her clenched fist started hitting the side of her face, punishing her into silence.

Zak caught hold of her fist in both hands, pulling it away from her cheek. 'That's why your story doesn't work,' he said quietly. 'You want the robbers to be heroes, but how can they be heroic unless they defeat the monster?'

Lorn couldn't speak. She stared at Zak, willing him to stop.

But he didn't. 'What's the monster's name?' he murmured. 'Tell me, Lorn. What's he called?'

She couldn't say the word. If she tried to talk about him, he would destroy her.

The others were turning round now, tired of arguing. Some of them were already sitting down again. As they settled back into the circle, Bando came across to Lorn and tugged at her arm.

'What really happens, Lorn?' His voice was plaintive. 'Tell us the end of the story.'

*I warned you*, said Zak's eyes. But Lorn still couldn't speak.

Zak gave a faint nod and stepped into the centre of the circle, pulling her with him. 'There are two stories,' he said, in his light, clear voice. 'I'll tell you the end of mine today. But you'll have to wait until tomorrow for Lorn to finish hers.'

There was an instant buzz of excited voices and Lorn could see that everyone liked the idea. 'But I *can't*,' she muttered to Zak. 'You know I can't.'

Zak loosened his fingers, one by one, setting hers free. 'Not in words. But I think you can finish your story a different way. With your hands.'

The others had all stopped talking now. They were watching Zak and Lorn, trying to understand what was going on.

Lorn didn't understand it herself—but Zak's words teased at her mind. Spreading her hands in the air, she flexed her fingers, feeling their power. Imagining a dark, solid mass between them, gradually taking shape.

'What can I use?' she said slowly. 'Where can I make it?'

Zak shrugged. 'There's only one place with enough room, where you can be private. But it's going to be cold down there. You'll need to take some furs. And a blade.'

He waved a hand at Bando and Annet. Without any questions, they went to the corner of the cavern and picked out a sharp, light blade and a couple of bat-fur blankets. Lorn took the blade in her hand and slung the furs over her shoulder. Then she walked out of the circle and down the cavern, towards the brazier.

The others stood aside to let her go. She wanted them to ask about what she was going to do—and about whether she needed food and water with her. But no one said a word. They all watched her, but there were no sympathetic smiles. They looked annoyed and impatient, not understanding why she'd had to disrupt the story. Not understanding *anything*.

She felt like an outcast as she went past the brazier and down the ramp into the storeroom under the cavern. No one spoke until she was halfway across the storeroom. Then the voices started up overhead. She knew they must be talking about her, but the earth muffled their words, so that she couldn't work out what they were saying.

Down in the storeroom there was no light at all, but she moved just as easily without it. That was how she'd grown up. Shut away under the floor, in the dark, with nothing but what she could hear and smell and feel. When she couldn't see, her brain had learnt how to make pictures out of what her other senses told her. She could navigate by the soft, padding sounds of her feet and the swirl of the air she disturbed.

Without hesitation, she made her way to the wall at the far end of the storeroom. Beyond that were the huge dark tunnels where her story could take shape. Kneeling down, she unblocked the entrance to the secret passage that ran through the wall. Pushing the furs and the blade ahead of her, she wriggled into it.

When she came out at the other end, the air was cold and damp. She stood up and wrapped the furs tightly around her shoulders, breathing in the musty, animal scent of the tunnels. The roof arched high above her and the wide space curved away in both directions, inviting her to begin. She began to move forward, impatiently.

She found the right place very soon, a narrow side tunnel where the roof had collapsed. As soon as she saw it, she realized that the great mound of loose soil gave her the start she needed.

She began work immediately, not visualizing the result in her head, but digging straight into the earth with her fingers and the blade. But the thing she had to make was too big for her imagination. Too frightening to think about. And if she couldn't think about it, how could she get the others to see what she saw?

*But I've got to. I have to find a way.*

It was impossible to build anything big enough without stones and water to bind the earth. She hunted back through the tunnels for stones, prising them out of the side walls and lugging them back to the place where she was working. But there was no source of water down there, and nothing to carry it in.

It would have to come from the storeroom.

She knew there was a good supply there. It was stored in big snail shells, just on the other side of the wall. Wriggling back through the narrow passage, she scooped out what she needed, dipping with one of the smaller shells that Annet used.

She needed a lot of water. Dozens of times she walked through the tunnels, carrying the full shell back to the place where she was building—*HIM*.

Even to herself she couldn't name the shape she was making. It was beyond naming. Each time she came back with the water, she sensed it ahead of her, a vast dark mass that absorbed the noises she made and blocked the flow of air along the tunnel. Its sour, fresh smell was like the scent of an alien creature and she had to force herself to take the final steps round the corner to confront it.

By the beginning of the second day, she was too weak to go on without food. She'd sipped at the water she fetched, but that was all she'd had, and she was hungry and exhausted. Twice she stumbled when she was carrying water, spilling half of it over her feet. Once her mental picture of the space around her blurred confusingly. She was clambering up the huge mound of earth, to add more to the top, and she fell sideways, tumbling head-first to the ground.

All she wanted to do was keep working until *HE* was finished. Her mind was completely focused on what she was doing—but her body wouldn't let her go on. She had to have a rest, and something to eat.

And that meant going back up into the cavern. She could take water from the storeroom, but taking food was utterly forbidden. All of them would drink mouthfuls of dew if they were outside on their own, but no one (not even Dess, not even *Ab*) would eat anything.

Every seed, every berry had to be brought back and shared. It was the only way they could survive. Once she'd taken a thorn-berry to Robert, before he found the cavern. She'd taken the risk because she was desperate to keep him from starving, but she'd known what the penalty was. If anyone had found out, she would have been thrown out of the cavern for ever.

She hated the idea of breaking her concentration. She hated the idea of facing the others before she had something to show them. But there was no way out. Without food she couldn't go on working.

Slowly she walked back along the tunnels, to the wall that closed off the storeroom. As she crouched down to crawl through the secret passage, she heard something at the other end. The sound of someone breathing.

'Hello?' she called. 'Who's there?'

The reply came quickly. 'Lorn! Where are you? Are you all right?'

It was Bando, of course. She ought to have known he would be worrying about her. 'I'm fine,' she called back soothingly. 'Wait a moment, and I'll be right beside you.'

She wriggled through the tunnel. He was crouching at the other end, feeling for her in the darkness.

'I was going to come and find you,' he muttered. 'Only I didn't know where you were. But you need to eat. I've got some food for you.'

'That's wonderful,' Lorn said.

She was grinning broadly, even though he couldn't see, from sheer relief that the others hadn't forgotten her. They weren't angry after all. They understood that she had to be on her own—and they'd sent her the food she needed.

It was bundled up in a piece of bat leather, tied with a clumsy knot. Bando pushed the bundle hastily into her hands. 'Here you are,' he mumbled. 'You can take it back into the tunnel with you. I'll bring some more tomorrow.'

'Thank you,' Lorn said. 'Oh, thank you, Bando. Tell the others—'

But he was already backing away, muttering at her over his shoulder. 'I've got to get back now. I'm supposed to be helping Annet with the wood.' He stumbled against a heap of grain and almost lost his footing, but he didn't stop. 'I'll see you tomorrow, Lorn.'

'OK,' Lorn said. 'I'll be here.'

She waited long enough to be sure that he'd reached the ramp safely. Then she sat down on the ground, where she was, and untied the bundle he'd given her. If she hadn't been so tired, she would have taken the food back into the tunnels, but she couldn't face doing anything else until she'd eaten. As soon as she smelt the fruit, as soon as she laid her hands on the first grain, she realized how hungry she was.

Sitting with her back against the wall, she began to eat as fast as she could, chewing the dry food greedily. She was still eating when she fell asleep, slumping forward over the grain in her lap.

She didn't hear the footsteps coming down the ramp. She didn't see the red glow of the torch moving across the storeroom.

# MY OTHER DAME

# 9

Afterwards, Emma couldn't believe she'd been such a *fool*. Why hadn't she used her brains? Why hadn't she *guessed*?

It was the boys' fault.

She was worried and distracted, because they were going off to this weird Magee man's flat. And she was angry, too, about having to go to Shelley's party. She'd only accepted as a way of saying no to Robert, because she wanted him to understand that he was being obsessive. But he hadn't understood—and now she was stuck with the party.

She was furious with Robert for his stubbornness. And miserable too, because she had an uncomfortable suspicion that she was behaving like a selfish coward.

It was all boiling in her head as she cycled out of school and she began the journey on autopilot, mechanically following the usual route home. Pedalling hard, she swung round the corner and then turned sharp left into the pedestrian alley. When she saw that the alley was empty, she didn't get off her bike. She just put one foot to the ground, and scooted quickly between the high brick walls.

There was a blue van parked across the opening at the far end. As she came out beside it, she was startled by a sudden noise from inside. Bare knuckles knocking against metal.

'Hello?' said a woman's voice. It had some kind of odd accent. Slightly foreign. 'Is zere someone there?'

Emma stopped uncertainly.

'Hello?' said the voice again, slightly louder. The woman sounded tentative and embarrassed. 'Please can you 'elp me?'

Emma took a step nearer. 'What's wrong?'

'Oh, sank *goodness*!' There was a light, apologetic laugh from inside the van. 'Zis 'orrible 'andle is broken and I'm stuck in ze van. Please—could you give ze doors a pull?'

It seemed straightforward enough. Emma relaxed. (How could she have been so stupid? So *gullible*?) 'No problem,' she said cheerfully. 'Hang on.' She leaned her bike against the alley wall and then reached for the handle on the right-hand door of the van.

After that, everything happened very fast. As she opened the right-hand door, the left-hand one flew open as well. Inside the van was a woman in a stocking mask. She grabbed at Emma's wrists and pulled her forward. At the same moment, someone charged from behind, knocking Emma completely off-balance and seizing her legs.

*This can't be happening. It CAN'T.*

As she started to fall, she opened her mouth to scream. But before she could make a sound, the left-hand door swung back accidentally and hit the side of her head. The inside of the van blurred in front of her eyes and then she lost consciousness, sliding down into the dark.

When she came round, she was shocked and shivering and desperately thirsty. And her head was pounding as though it was ready to split in half. She was lying on her side, with her clothes clinging damply to her skin, and her whole body felt aching and peculiar.

Where was she?

She opened her eyes, still half-dazed. There was nothing to see except darkness and the ground underneath her smelt of mould and decay. When she tried to open her mouth, her jaw wouldn't move. Her whole face seemed to be paralysed.

Wild thoughts raced through her mind. Was she near the cavern? Had she been changed, like Robert? Closing her eyes, she sniffed hard, trying to catch the scent of wood smoke, but all she could smell was wet, stinking earth.

Then she tried to sit up—and she knew this had nothing to do with the cavern.

She couldn't move. Her body was trussed up with long, sticky strips that felt like parcel tape. There was a piece right across her face and it pulled at her cheeks when she struggled to open her mouth.

More tape spiralled up her legs, binding them tightly together, and her arms were fixed behind her back with the wrists crossed. Underneath the tape, she could feel the slow beat of blood in her veins.

*Don't panic. THINK.*

She lifted her head slightly and felt something tug at her hair. She'd plaited it into the twelve-strand braid that Robert had taught her—the braid he'd learnt from Lorn. Someone had used that braid to tie her down, knotting a cord round it and pegging it into the ground.

And that wasn't the only cord that fixed her there. She wriggled, experimentally, and felt resistance in every direction. The people who'd tied her up hadn't left her any chance of escaping. She was completely immobilized.

But why had they done it? Who *were* they?

She fought back a surge of useless, feeble panic. There was no point in getting hysterical. What she needed to do was think coherently. She might not be able to move or see, but she still had the rest of her senses.

Slowly, she worked out as much as she could about the place where she was lying. The surface underneath her was smooth and pliable, and slightly noisy, like polythene. The ground underneath was hard and cold, but not as hard as concrete. It felt slightly uneven, as though the polythene had been laid over bare earth.

It was very quiet where she was, but there was a radio playing somewhere nearby. And, with her head pressed to the ground, she could hear a constant hum like the sound of distant traffic.

She lay still and concentrated, trying to work out how she'd got there.

She remembered coming out of school, distracted by worrying about Tom and Robert. She remembered scooting down the alley and seeing something blue. And then her memory cut out. Every time she tried to get beyond that glimpse of blue, she hit a blank. There was no link between *then* and *now*, between *there* and *here*.

She longed to tell herself that it wasn't real, that she was dreaming. But she knew that wasn't true. Ever since she'd seen Robert come back from being small, she'd known that *real* was a much bigger word than most people realized. And the cords and the sticky tape were certainly real.

And so were the people who had tied her up and left her in the dark.

All she could do was lie and wait for them. Every time a board creaked above her, every time a draught of cold air slid across her face, she peered into the darkness, thinking they must be coming. But nothing happened. She simply lay there, getting thirstier and stiffer every minute.

When the noise came at last, it was so sudden and shocking that it gave her a jolt. It sounded like a television, turned up to full volume, blaring directly overhead.

Then there was a sequence of small scraping sounds.

Metal moving over wood. Emma tried to work out what it was, struggling to add up all the clues, and make some kind of deduction about where she was, but her brain was slow and stupid. It wouldn't make any sense of the sounds.

And then she was blinded by a sudden rush of light.

For a second she was totally dazzled and her eyes closed automatically. She forced them open and found herself staring at a hole in the darkness. There was a square opening above her head, giving her a view of grey sky, seen through glass. It looked like a huge window crossed by a single diagonal strut.

*I ought to recognize that—*

But before she could grab at the memory, a head appeared in the opening. It was hardly more than a silhouette, but its ungainly, short neck was angled towards her and she knew instantly who it was. Suddenly, everything slid into place.

She was trapped in the secret room, under the Armstrongs' conservatory floor. The room where they'd kept Hope hidden all her life. The diagonal strut was part of the conservatory roof, and below it was Warren Armstrong, staring down at her.

She hardly had time to think it before she was blinded again. A torch shone into her face, and there was an awkward scrabble as Warren let himself down through the trapdoor. She closed her eyes quickly, listening as he blundered towards her across the polythene.

As he crouched down beside her, she held her breath, determined not to react. She could feel him peering at her, panting slightly from the effort of climbing down into the hole, but she resisted the urge to look at him. She concentrated on staying totally still.

After a second or two, Warren began muttering to himself. Odd, incomprehensible words that were barely audible.

'Tread my home . . . Mary the demo . . . my other dame . . .'

Emma had to hold her body tense to keep herself from shuddering. He was mad. Completely mad.

Then one of his pudgy hands prodded at her cheek—and she couldn't bear it any longer. Her eyes opened, involuntarily, and for a split second she saw him staring down at her with a look of desperate anxiety.

And then he realized that she was looking back at him, and the anxiety was replaced by an overwhelming flood of relief.

*He thought I was dead.*

That was staggeringly obvious. Emma didn't know whether he'd been part of the kidnap, but he was clearly worried about the result. She wondered, suddenly, whether she could turn him into an ally.

Jerking her head upwards, she grunted as loudly as she could to let him know that she wanted to be free. The noise she made was pathetically small—she could hardly hear it herself above the sound of the television—but even that made Warren uneasy. He jammed his hand over her mouth, crinkling the tape so that it pinched her skin.

'Be quiet!' he hissed urgently. He tapped her cheek with his hot, sweaty fingers and leaned forward, putting his mouth next to her ear. 'We'll let you go soon. When you've told us where to find Hope.'

That was what they wanted, of course. They wanted the one thing she couldn't tell them. The thing she *mustn't* tell them. She frowned and made an attempt to shake her head.

Warren leaned even closer. 'You've got to tell us,' he whispered. 'Or you'll have to stay here for ever.'

He nipped Emma's cheek painfully, between his fingernails. Feeling his power, and her helplessness. *In a minute,* Emma thought, *he's going to start enjoying it.*

She had a sudden, shameful memory of feeling like that herself. When she and the boys were working out how to save Hope, they'd cornered Warren in the street. *You don't want us poking round in the conservatory,* she'd cooed. *We'll have to look for your sister.* When his mouth trembled, she'd had an exhilarating sense of control. *He'd have done anything he was told,* she'd said to Tom afterwards.

Now she was the helpless one, and he was doing his best to frighten her. Emma felt the stirrings of a different kind of panic, deep and dark. For the first time, she understood that she might get hurt.

She took a long, slow breath, determined to stay calm. Wrenching her head round, she looked Warren straight in the face. Raising her eyebrows, she opened her eyes wide and shrugged her shoulders, miming as hard as she could.

*I can't help you. I don't know anything.*

Warren's mouth tightened and he leaned forward so that their noses were almost touching. 'You *do* know where she is,' he hissed. 'We heard you on the phone. You've got her locked up and you have to tell us where. Because she's *ours*.'

Emma shook her head fiercely, trying to get away from the feel of his breath and the glare of his eyes. But there was no way of escaping. *This is how he felt,* said a little voice in her head. *You had him trapped exactly like this and you made him do something he'd been told not to do.*

She forced herself not to listen. What they'd done was different. It was all about rescuing Hope. What Warren wanted was to get her back into this horrible prison. Emma clamped her mouth shut, determined not to give in.

When they took the gag away, she wasn't going to tell them anything. She was going to resist everything they tried—and escape if she could.

Warren saw the stubborn look in her eyes. He frowned and sat back on his heels. 'She *is* ours,' he said. 'Look.'

He started to fumble in his pocket, pulling out pieces of paper and dropping them impatiently as he hunted for something. When he found it, he held it up and shone the torch at it, so that Emma could see.

It was a photograph of a pretty little baby girl, with her hair tied up in a wispy bunch on top of her head. She was grinning happily and waving her arms at the camera.

It took Emma a full minute to realize that she was looking at a picture of Hope.

'You see?' Warren said emphatically. 'She was here all the time. From the beginning. If she has to live anywhere else, she'll die.'

Helplessly, Emma stared at the photograph. How could anyone be *so wrong*? Didn't he understand what his parents had done to Hope? She'd started out as the baby in the photograph—animated and happy and *normal*—and ended up as a stunted, miserable captive, so afraid of making too much noise that she hit out at her own face.

If Emma had been able to speak, she would have argued and shouted and *made* Warren understand. But all she could do now was pull faces and grunt. And what use was that?

For a second longer, Warren waved the photograph in front of her eyes. Then he glanced suddenly over his shoulder. As he scrambled to his feet, Emma realized what he'd heard.

Footsteps were coming quickly across the floor above their heads. Someone else was approaching the opening. *Mr Armstrong!* she thought, before she could stop herself.

And she felt a jolt of fear that went through her whole body.

# 10

But it wasn't Mr Armstrong. It was a woman. A small, slight woman, with a long tail of hair that hung down into the opening as she leaned forward.

Emma had forgotten all about Mrs Armstrong. She'd dismissed her as a passive, frightened person totally dominated by her husband. But now, as she recognized her, one more piece of the puzzle slid into place and she began to understand her mistake. She remembered the woman in the van.

*It was her. She was the one who trapped me.*

Mrs Armstrong peered down for a second and then swung herself expertly through the trapdoor. Crouching under the low roof, she came quickly down the secret room, watching Emma as she came.

For an instant, the two of them stared at each other. Emma heard Warren start breathing faster and she thought, *He's nervous. He doesn't know what she's going to do*. She tried to hold her eyes steady, but her own breathing quickened too.

When Mrs Armstrong reached them, she knelt down on the polythene, still not shifting her eyes from Emma's. 'I want to know where my daughter is,' she said.

Emma tried to shake her head vigorously, but the cord attached to her plait was too tight. All she could do was grunt behind the tape, getting as close as she could to the words she needed to say, *We haven't got her. It's not like that.* But even while she was making the sounds, she knew they were incomprehensible.

'I gave up my life to keep Hope safe,' Mrs Armstrong said softly. 'For years I haven't had any friends, or a job, or a holiday. Just her. I'm not going to let anyone take her away from me.'

In the dim light, she looked painfully like Hope, with the same narrow mouth, the same sharp jaw and finely arched eyebrows. It was terrifyingly easy to imagine Hope herself kneeling just like that in the middle of the polythene. Except that she wouldn't have had anyone with her. She would have been down there on her own.

*You chose to give up your life!* Emma wanted to shout. *But Hope didn't have any choice. You stole hers from her*. The words beat inside her head, clamouring to be spoken.

Mrs Armstrong lifted a hand. For the first time, Emma saw that she was holding a small plastic bottle. She brought it round into the torchlight and tilted it slightly so that Emma could see the water inside.

'If you promise to keep quiet, I'll take off the tape and give you some of this,' she said.

Emma's eyes locked on to the water bottle and she swallowed dryly behind the brown tape.

'Well?' The raised hand gave the bottle a tempting little shake.

Emma knew what she had to do. She took a quick breath and nodded, as well as she could. Mrs Armstrong leaned forward and ripped the tape off her mouth in a single, quick movement. It felt like having the skin ripped away, but Emma didn't let the pain put her off. She opened her mouth and looked up at the square opening, yelling as loudly as she could.

'HELP! I'M A PRISONER UNDER THE FLOOR! GET ME OUT!'

But even while she was shouting, she could hear that it was no use. The earth around soaked up her voice, and any small sounds which reached the outside were hidden by the noise of the television. When she looked back at Mrs Armstrong, she could see that it had all been planned. She'd been meant to shout, so that she would understand how pointless it was.

When she stopped, Mrs Armstrong leaned forward and slapped her face. Just hard enough to hurt. 'Liar,' she said evenly.

'Why should I tell you the truth?' Emma croaked, hoarse from the shouting. 'I don't owe you anything. You *kidnapped* me.'

Mrs Armstrong shrugged. 'Please yourself. But if you don't co-operate, you'll never get out of here.'

'Yes I will,' Emma said fiercely. 'Robert and Tom will guess where I am and they'll call the police.'

'Not yet,' Mrs Armstrong said. She sat back on her heels and smiled a small, tight smile. 'They think you're staying at your friend's house. Remember?'

Emma felt the cold of the earth seep into her bones. She could hear her own voice, calling out to the boys. *I'm going to stop over at her house . . . See you tomorrow night.* Where had Mrs Armstrong been hiding? How had she overheard that?

'No one's going to come looking for you,' Mrs Armstrong murmured. 'Not for a long, long time. We've got plenty of time to persuade you to tell us what we want to know.'

It would have been less frightening if she'd sounded angry. But her voice was low and even, without any emotion. She unscrewed the top of the water bottle and tilted it again, letting a drop of water fall on to Emma's hand.

Emma swallowed and tried to ignore it. (How long could a person survive without anything to drink?)

'A couple of words will do for now,' Mrs Armstrong said mildly, letting another drop fall. 'Just give us a hint and you can have some water.'

Emma licked her lips. 'Ask your husband what happened to Hope,' she muttered. 'He was there.'

Mrs Armstrong didn't reply to that. But her mouth tensed and she started to pour the water straight out on to the ground, in a slow, continuous stream, right in front of Emma's face. When the bottle was empty, she dropped it and pulled a roll of brown tape out of her pocket.

'No!' Emma began to move her head furiously, trying to avoid the tape. 'You don't need to do that again. No one can hear me anyway.'

It was all useless. Mrs Armstrong pulled off a length of tape. Then she caught Emma's bottom jaw firmly with one hand, jamming it shut and digging her fingers in under the chin. With her other hand she plastered the tape across Emma's mouth, running it from ear to ear to make a tight, efficient gag.

'I *know* you've got Hope,' she said. 'Do you think I'm a fool?' Leaning forward, she snatched at Emma's plait, tugging it free and bringing the end round to flap in her face. 'Did you think I wouldn't recognize one of her braids? She did this, didn't she?'

She plastered another loop of tape around Emma's jaw and then took a pair of pointed scissors out of her pocket. Before she cut the tape, she held them for a second in front of Emma's eyes.

'Next time I take off the tape, you *will* tell me,' she said coldly. 'You'll tell me everything.' Then she started to snip.

She began with the parcel tape, cutting the roll free and letting it fall to the ground. But she didn't stop there. Pushing Emma's head sideways, she bent closer, working the scissors quickly over her head. *Snip, snip, snip.*

Emma heard Warren draw in his breath sharply, but it took her a moment to realize what Mrs Armstrong was doing. As soon as she did, she began to wriggle and grunt in protest, but that was useless. She was rolled firmly on to her face.

'Hold her down, Warren,' Mrs Armstrong said crisply.

He threw his weight across Emma's back and she was pushed down on to the wet polythene. All she could see was the spilt water around her head and the scraps of paper that Warren had pulled out when he was hunting for Hope's picture.

She strained at the parcel tape, trying to open her mouth enough to let some of the water leak in, but it was impossible. The water lapped tormentingly at the tape and the words on the paper mocked her, dancing in front of her eyes. They were disconnected and incomprehensible, like the weird things Warren had muttered at her when he thought she was dead. Surreal nonsense, scribbled in capital letters.

*DRY ME AT HOME . . . MY OTHER DAME . . . HAMMERED TOY . . . MARY THE DEMO . . .*

They were totally mad—like everything else in that horrible, nightmare house. The phrases danced tauntingly in her head, in time to the snipping of the scissors and the slither of dirty water over the polythene.

*TREAD MY HOME . . . MAD EM THEORY . . . MEMORY DEATH . . .*

At last the scissors made their final snip and Mrs Armstrong stood up, tugging at Emma's arm to roll her on to her back again. The long red braid was dangling from her other hand.

'This is just the beginning,' she said. Her voice was still cold, but this time there was an edge to it. Emma could hear that she was near breaking point. 'It will be worse next time—and every time after that. I won't give up until I get Hope back here.'

She nodded at Warren and he scuttled back to the trapdoor, taking the torch with him. When he had heaved himself out, she picked up the empty bottle and the roll of tape and followed, taking Emma's braid with her. Emma had a last glimpse of her familiar red hair gleaming in the winter sunshine and then it was gone. The trapdoor thumped down, the carpet slithered over it, and there was a soft thud as the television was lifted back into its place.

Emma was alone, in the dark, lying in a pool of cold water. Her clothes were already soaked. Now, when she tried to move, the water slurped across the polythene, washing against the bare skin of her neck.

She hadn't had short hair since she was five.

Her hair had always been the first thing people noticed. *Who's Emma Doherty? Oh, you know. She's that girl with the wonderful red hair.* Now, when she turned her head, all she felt was the prickle of stubble and the chilly movement of the water.

She didn't feel like Emma Doherty any more. Emma Doherty was a bright, capable girl who sorted out everyone else's problems. *She* was a different girl—thirsty and bald and terrified.

She let her face fall down on to the wet polythene and cried, without being able to wipe the tears from her face or the snot from her nose. She'd lost herself. She was no one.

The water lapped against her cheeks, and Warren's crazy pieces of paper brushed her forehead. It was too dark to read them now, but the meaningless phrases had lodged in her mind, mocking her with their nonsense.

*MAD EM THEORY . . . TREAD MY HOME . . . HAMMERED TOY . . . MY OTHER DAME . . . MEMORY DEATH . . .*

*Hammer. Death. Mad.* They were nonsense, but they seemed to threaten darkness and violence, stirring up the terrors at the bottom of her mind. She wanted to be positive and plan an escape. *I'm Emma Doherty, and I don't let anything beat me.* But how could she be Emma when the things that made her special—the briskness, the upbeat efficiency, even the hair—had all been stripped away? What was left?

*Mary the Demo.*

The nonsense words resounded in her head, making a raw new picture.

Mary the Demo had short, spiky hair, thick with earthy dust from the torn black polythene. Mary was afraid of the little, rustling noises that came through the darkness. She couldn't keep herself cheerful. She was afraid of hunger and thirst and cold. Afraid of being trapped—

*I'm NOT like that. That's NOT me.*

But the picture grew, sucking the strength out of her. Mary was different from Emma. Emma had never thought of wondering how Robert had felt when he was up in the nightbird's tree with his leg slashed open. When he saw the familiar, terrible view below him and knew that he was shrunken and trapped. But Mary thought about it now. She began to imagine the agony and the panic and the terror—

*No! I'm NOT going to give in!*

Emma screwed up her eyes and pushed the thoughts away, wishing that Robert was there. For the first time in her life, she needed him. He could have told her how to survive.

# 11

'You smell,' Warren said.

He was there when Emma woke, squatting beside her again. She couldn't believe that he'd come without waking her, but he was there, shining the torch full into her eyes. His face was so close that she could have spat on to the end of his nose if her mouth wasn't parcelled shut.

'You smell,' he said again. 'You need a wash.'

She was completely at his mercy. For an instant her mind raced, imagining horrors. As long as he left the tape in place, he could do anything that came into his weird little head. Anything at all . . .

Then her common sense kicked in. *Don't be so melodramatic. He's not a Dracula-psycho. He's just a pathetic fat boy who's trying to scare you. Stop giving in and THINK.*

Warren ran a finger lightly up and down one side of her head, rubbing at the stubble. Was he gloating? Or was he sorry to see her hair cut off? There was no way to tell. Emma realized how little she knew about him.

There might even be a way of getting him on to her side, if only she could find out some more. But how could she do that? She had no way of asking questions, and no way of watching him, except in this strange underground setting. What could she do to catch him off guard?

As an experiment, she tried pulling faces. She tilted her head to one side and attempted to smile behind the sticky tape—struggling not to wince as it dragged at her skin.

The hand that was rubbing her bristly hair stopped

dead, just above her left ear. Warren leaned closer, peering at her. She let him look for a second—and then winked.

Like lightning, Warren pulled his hand away. He sat back on his heels and the torch wavered sideways so that Emma saw his face for the first time. He looked nervous and uncertain.

That wasn't what she'd meant to achieve, but at least she'd had some kind of effect. What could she try next?

There wasn't a great deal of choice. She tilted her head the other way, raising one eyebrow, as if she were asking a question. But Warren just kept very still, frowning warily.

If Emma could, she would have shaken him. *What do you think I'm going to do? Eat you? For goodness' sake, REACT!* How could he be so frightened of someone who was completely wrapped up in parcel tape?

Maybe it would be better if she tried to make him laugh. She thought for a second and then stuck her tongue into her left cheek, bulging it out while she opened her eyes wide and looked to the right. She counted up to three and reversed the movement. And then did it again.

It was hard work and it made her eyes feel strange, but she kept it up for several seconds. Then she stopped and grinned again. The most uncomplicated, friendly grin she could manage under the circumstances.

'Why are you doing that?' Warren muttered shakily. 'Stop it.'

She shrugged and raised her eyebrows again. Then, still smiling, she started wiggling her ears.

For a moment, Warren obviously had no idea what she was doing. He kept looking nervously at her eyes and nose and mouth, waiting for the next movement. It was only when she rolled her head—first one way and then the other—that he saw her ears going up and down.

A slow, unexpected smile spread across his face. Propping the torch on the ground, he moved back slightly so that Emma could see his whole head. Then he began wiggling his own ears.

He was way beyond Emma, in a class of his own. He could move his ears together, but he could move each ear separately too. And he could do it at different speeds, setting up a rhythm. *Left, right, left RIGHT, RIGHT, left, right, left, RIGHT, RIGHT*. Before she knew what she was doing, Emma found herself putting words to the rhythm.

*We are the champions, we are the champions . . .*

She began to laugh, snorting helplessly through her nose because she couldn't open her mouth. It messed up her face, but she couldn't help herself. Warren looked irresistibly funny, frowning with solemn concentration as he wiggled out the song. She rocked her head from side to side, hiccuping with laughter.

Warren stopped at last, looking pink and gratified. If he'd been standing on stage, he would have taken a bow. Emma gazed up at him, still grinning, and he studied her face for a second.

Then he muttered, 'When Hope was here, I sometimes used to—she didn't mind—can I—?'

What did he want to do? All the laughter drained out of Emma. She remembered Hope's wasted body and her mumbling voice.

'It's all right,' Warren muttered. 'I'm not going to hurt you. I just—look, it's all right.'

He took a handkerchief out of his pocket and blew Emma's nose, very gently. Then he began wiping the tape underneath it and the skin all round the tape. As he worked, he muttered in a low, soothing voice.

'It's OK. I won't be a minute. You'll look much nicer when it's done. Just keep still . . .'

Emma knew, without being told, that he was talking to her the way he'd talked to Hope. It was like peering through a window into the past. She hated the touch of his fingers, but she lay still and let him clean her face. Even when he licked the handkerchief without thinking, with his own tongue, and then rubbed it on her chin. She let him do it.

Until the handkerchief reached her right cheekbone. And it *hurt*.

Taken by surprise, she gave a loud grunt. Immediately Warren dropped the handkerchief and flapped his hands at her, signalling that she had to stay silent.

'I'm sorry,' he gabbled. 'Sorry, sorry, sorry. Didn't mean to hurt you. We didn't know how hard we needed to hit. And then the van door—sorry. We just had to be sure we knocked you out.'

Suddenly, everything they'd just been doing seemed ridiculous. Emma cringed at the memory of herself pulling faces and trying to win him over. How could she ever have thought he might be on her side? The Armstrongs were all maniacs, completely cut off from reality. And they were never going to let her go. Never, never, never.

'No,' Warren said desperately, flapping his hands again. 'Don't cry. You'll be home soon. The moment we get Hope back.'

*You'll never get her back. And nor will we. Not even Robert—though he wants that more than anything in the world. Hope's lost for ever. And now I'm lost too.*

She was gagged and trussed—and if she died down here, in this horrible, stinking hole, no one would ever know where her body was. Robert and Tom would try to find her, but the Armstrongs would be expecting that. They were bound to have some plan to keep her hidden.

Warren was patting her arm frantically, to try and keep her quiet. Babbling stupid reassurances into her ear. 'Mum will give you a drink soon. I know she will. And something to eat as well. You're going to be all right. All you have to do is be sensible—'

And then he froze.

A second later, Emma heard the noise he'd picked up. A car, crunching over gravel, close to the house.

Warren's panic went into overdrive. 'Sssh!' he hissed. 'I've got to go. I'll come back and talk to you soon, but just be *quiet* for now—or Dad will find you.'

He scuttled towards the trapdoor and scrabbled up into the conservatory. As the car's engine stopped, Emma heard the noises she was coming to recognize. The scrape of the metal catches that fastened the trapdoor in place. The carpet sliding over it. The television being put back.

The television landed on the mat just as the front door opened. It was turned off now, and there was nothing to mask the sounds drifting down to Emma. She heard feet coming into the hall. The soft sound of Mrs Armstrong speaking and then another, deeper voice.

Mr Armstrong.

What had Warren meant? *Be quiet for now—or Dad will find you*. Didn't he know already that she was there? Surely he was the person who'd come up behind and hit her on the head?

Surely Warren and his mother couldn't really have done it all on their own?

Could they?

It was a startling idea—but it had to be important. If they'd done it without telling Mr Armstrong, that meant there was a split in the family. And she might be able to take advantage of that. She needed to think how she could play them off against each other. Forcing herself to ignore the pain that thudded in her head, she concentrated as hard as she could, trying to gather together everything she knew about the three of them.

If there was a chance for her to help herself, she had to be ready when it came.

# 12

After Warren ran away, Emma was on her own for a long time. At first, she tensed at every noise overhead, every voice and footfall. But gradually she came to understand that none of them were aimed at her. No one came.

She began to wriggle as much as she could, shifting her body to avoid getting numb. There wasn't much scope for movement but she worked out a sequence of exercises, flexing her muscles and arching her back and rolling her hips from side to side.

The exercise made her slightly warmer, but it made her feel even more hungry and thirsty. Her headache was almost unbearable now. She didn't know whether it was caused by thirst or whether it had something to do with the blow to her head. What had they used to hit her from behind? And what had Warren meant about the van door?

Her memory of the kidnap was still very vague—and that was worrying too. She thought they must have snatched her as she came out of the alley. But what had happened to her bike? Was it still there, propped against the wall? Why couldn't she remember? Warren's weird words danced in her head: *Memory death. Mad Em theory. Hammered toy*. Perhaps the blow had given her concussion. Or even some more permanent kind of brain damage. How would she *know*?

She worried about how they were treating her now, as well. Why weren't they feeding her? Maybe they meant to starve her until she was so desperate that she would say anything. She told herself that she would never do that, that she would keep on resisting them until Robert and Tom came to rescue her.

But when she dozed off, she babbled in her dreams. *Hope's very small now. If you dig up the hedge bank you'll find her.* She woke in a panic, clamping her lips together to keep the words back. Forgetting that she was gagged and couldn't talk in her sleep.

The next time the trapdoor opened, it was dark outside. The blinds were closed in the conservatory and the light that came through the trapdoor had a yellow, electric glare.

Mrs Armstrong lifted the lid away from the opening and came down fast. As soon as her feet hit the polythene, she turned round and reach up for something that Warren was handing down to her. A loaded tray. She took it quickly and scurried towards Emma. Warren was crouching up above, shining a torch so that she could see.

Emma's eyes locked on to the tray, focusing on the important details. The plastic mug. The banana. The thick slice of bread. Behind her sticky gag, she swallowed drily, wondering what she would have to do to get them.

Whether she would have to refuse.

But there was obviously no time for negotiations. Mrs Armstrong put the tray down and knelt beside her. 'I've brought you some food and water,' she said hurriedly. 'But there's not much time—and I'll take it away if you make a noise.'

Emma nodded, to show that she accepted the conditions, and Mrs Armstrong pulled off the tape over her mouth.

'If you want me to hurry,' Emma croaked, 'you'll have to let me sit up. Otherwise I'll choke.'

Mrs Armstrong sighed impatiently, but she didn't argue. Reaching over Emma's head, she untied some of the cords that held her down. Then she put an arm behind her shoulders and heaved her up into a sitting position.

Emma felt dizzy, because she'd been lying so long. And, because of the way her legs were taped, she couldn't keep herself upright. As soon as Mrs Armstrong let go of her and turned round for the tray, she thumped backwards on to the ground.

'For goodness' sake!' Mrs Armstrong said. She called up through the trapdoor. 'Warren! You'll have to come down and hold her, or she won't be able to swallow anything.'

Warren leaned over the edge of the opening. 'But if I come down, there won't be anyone to watch—'

'That doesn't matter.' Mrs Armstrong was starting to get hassled. 'She's got to eat, and I can't manage by myself.'

'All right,' Warren said. But he didn't sound very happy about it. He jumped down clumsily, staggering as he hit the ground.

'*Hurry*,' Mrs Armstrong snapped. 'Or he'll be back before we've done anything.'

Warren dropped the torch and scuttled towards them. Mrs Armstrong pointed irritably and he wriggled behind Emma and heaved her up again, propping her in place with his body. The whole thing was very quick, as though he knew what to do without thinking. Because he'd done it a hundred times before.

The instant Emma was upright, Mrs Armstrong held the mug to her lips—and for a moment, nothing mattered except the water. Emma ducked her head forward and drank, so fast that she almost retched.

All the time she was drinking, Mrs Armstrong was hissing in her ear, in an angry whisper. 'We can't keep you hidden like this for much longer. If you don't tell us what we need to know soon, my husband will find you. And you'll wish you hadn't been so stupid.'

Leaning back against Warren, Emma felt him grow tenser as his mother talked. Was he afraid of his father? She remembered how Hope had cowered and hit her own face when she thought she'd made too much noise. This was the room where she'd learnt to do that. Had Warren learnt to be afraid here too?

The last few drops dribbled out of the mug. Emma twisted her head away, to show that she'd finished, and Mrs Armstrong's free hand shot out for the banana. Dropping the cup, she pulled back the skin and aimed the banana at Emma's mouth.

'All you've got to do is say a few words,' she muttered. 'Just enough to tell us where to find Hope.' She was pushing the banana between Emma's teeth with practised efficiency. Not enough to choke her, but enough to keep her quiet. 'As soon as we know that, you can go home.'

Emma felt Warren shift uneasily. 'You'll have to promise not to talk,' he said. 'Otherwise—'

He stopped, and there was an uncomfortable stillness. Gulping at a mouthful of banana, Emma suddenly understood that they hadn't really planned what was going to happen after they kidnapped her. They didn't know how to get the information they wanted—and, if she did give them the information, they had no idea how to stop her going straight to the police as soon as they let her go.

They weren't terrifying criminal masterminds. They weren't expert kidnappers. They were a couple of ordinary people, bumbling around. They'd probably only managed to snatch her in the first place because she'd knocked herself out by accident, on the van door.

And that was much more frightening than being in the hands of experts. Because they might suddenly panic—and what would happen then?

She swallowed the banana in her mouth, very fast. 'It's all right,' she said quickly. 'You don't need—'

But she obviously wasn't meant to be discussing anything. Mrs Armstrong pushed the banana at her again and it squelched into her mouth, catching on her teeth and smearing itself over her top lip. Emma had to bite off the next piece to keep herself from choking.

Before she could eat it, Warren jumped up, letting go of her so that she went sprawling backwards. 'It's Dad!' he said. And he sounded scared now. 'Listen!'

Emma heard the car now, coming up on to the gravel much faster than last time. Mrs Armstrong dropped the banana and hissed at Warren.

'Out! As fast as you can!'

They made straight for the hatch. Warren went up first, with Mrs Armstrong pushing at his legs to speed him up. As she pushed, she snapped over her shoulder at Emma.

'Keep *absolutely silent*. If you don't he'll find out you're here—and then you'll be sorry.'

Then she hauled herself out of the hole, abandoning everything that she and Warren had brought down. In the torchlight, Emma could see the half-eaten banana and the lovely, thick slice of bread, just too far away for her to reach. She stared at them as the hatch cover went on and the carpet slapped down, quickly followed by the television.

It was all done just in time. A split second later, Emma heard a man's voice, away at the front of the house.

She couldn't make out what he was saying, and she had no idea whether it was really Mr Armstrong or not. But it wasn't one of her bumbling, panicky kidnappers. It was another person—and there was no gag over her mouth, and no television blaring overhead.

She didn't waste time trying to decide what was the most sensible thing to do. She just seized the opportunity she'd been given. Gulping down the piece of banana in her mouth, she started to yell.

'Help! Help! Come and get me out of here!'

The earth still absorbed most of the noise she made. But this time there was a real chance of being heard. And she wasn't in any mood to give up. If she didn't do something, she'd soon find herself gagged once more. She'd be shut up on her own in the cold darkness again, and she couldn't bear the idea of that.

'They're keeping me a prisoner!' she bellowed. 'Help!'

She fumbled around with her crossed hands until she found the empty plastic mug. Grabbing it tightly, she began to bang it up and down on the metal tray.

'Help! Get me out! HELP!'

She could tell the exact moment when the man up above realized where the noise was coming from. His voice sharpened suddenly and his feet came running towards the hatch.

'I'm down here!' she shouted, hearing the television slide sideways.

(*What have I done?* whimpered Mary the Demo inside her head. But she hardly heard it. The Emma part of her mind was too busy saying, *Good!*)

The hatch cover came off with a thump. She stopped shouting and held her breath.

'Who's down there?' Mr Armstrong's voice said sharply. 'Come here!'

He was over the opening now, leaning down into the hole and angling his head to try and see up to the end of the secret room.

'Come here,' he said again, beginning to sound impatient. 'Come where I can see you.'

Emma had forgotten how big he was. Lit by the torchlight from below, his heavy, jowled cheeks were grotesquely shadowed. His hands loomed huge as they gripped the wooden frame of the hatch. She took a quick, nervous breath.

He heard it. For a second, there was an odd silence. And then, in quite a different voice, he said, 'Hope? Is that you?'

It was the smell of smoke that roused Lorn. She opened her eyes before she was properly awake and saw a dazzle of red light in front of her. For an instant, in the dark, she thought she was still Hope, staring up at the black, accusing figure behind the light.

Then her nose caught the other scent, behind the wood smoke, and her mind clicked into gear.

'Perdew!' she said.

He was standing over her with the glowing wood burning low in his hand, staring at the half-eaten grain in her lap. At the woody ends of the dried berries she'd eaten, and the shelled nuts lying on the square of leather.

'What have you done?' he said. He looked disgusted.

For a moment, she didn't know what he meant. She looked up at him, bewildered, not realizing what he was seeing.

'You've been *eating*.' His voice was furious now. 'How could you, Lorn? How *could* you?'

'I was hungry,' she said. 'I needed food—'

And then she understood. Not from what he said, but from the expression on his face. He thought she'd taken the food herself.

*It wasn't me. It was Bando*. The words were almost out when she knew that she couldn't say them. She remembered Bando's low, mumbling voice and his clumsy haste as he backed away towards the ramp. He must have been terrified. What had it cost him to break the rules like that?

Perdew was already edging away, towards the bottom of the ramp. Still watching her, he yelled up into the cavern. 'Come into the storeroom! Quickly!'

That was all it took to set feet running overhead and bring the others racing down the ramp. Cam was in the lead, with a new, bright torch in her hand. When she saw Lorn she stopped in amazement. Looking horrified and scornful.

The others crowded down behind her. Lorn heard them gasp as they saw her sitting there. And then there was a terrible, angry silence. If they'd spoken, she might have tried to invent some kind of explanation, but she dared not speak into that anger.

Zak came down the ramp last, with Bando beside him. Lorn crouched where she was, staring up at the two of them. Bando looked puzzled and confused, but it was impossible to tell how Zak was going to react. His face was calm as the others parted to let him through and the first words he spoke were for someone else.

'Perdew,' he said. Not looking round but staring steadily at Lorn. 'Perdew, your fingers are burning. Throw the wood away.'

Perdew glanced down impatiently, as though he hadn't felt the fire. Then he tossed the wood into a corner, throwing it hard so that it burst apart, loosing a shower of sparks.

Zak let the sparks die in the air. Then he said, 'There has always been a punishment for stealing food.'

Bando caught his breath, but Lorn could see that he still hadn't understood. He was waiting for Zak to turn on him. When he found out he was wrong, he wouldn't stay silent, she knew. He would take the blame for what he'd done.

But he'd never cope with the punishment.

'We can only live because we share everything,' Zak said gravely. 'That is the bond that holds us together. You've broken that bond, Lorn, and you can no longer be part of this community. You are not welcome to share our warmth and food and stories.'

That was the moment when Bando realized what was happening. He let out a great roar. 'No! It wasn't her! She didn't do it!'

'Be quiet, Bando.' Zak spoke without looking at him.

'But you don't understand!' Bando shouted. 'Lorn hasn't done anything wrong. I took the food *for* her! It was me!'

Zak didn't speak. He just looked questioningly at Lorn, his shadowed face grim in the flickering light of the torch.

Lorn made her decision. 'Thank you, dear Bando,' she said. Looking down so that she wouldn't have to see his face. 'Thank you for trying to protect me. But I have to take my own punishment.'

'No!' Bando roared again. 'You didn't–'

Zak turned, with a look so terrible that even Bando was silenced. 'Enough!' Then he turned back to Lorn and motioned with his hand. 'Stand up.'

Lorn's legs were stiff and numb from the cramped position in which she'd fallen asleep. She scrambled up and held herself steady with one hand on the wall.

Zak waited until she was still. Then he said, 'Who are you?'

'I'm Lorn,' she said uncertainly.

Zak shook his head. 'Who are you?' he said again. 'What is your name?'

Then she understood that he was taking away the name he'd given her when she first came to the cavern. The name that made her belong and kept her safe.

*You can't do that, Zak. I AM Lorn now. You can't–*

'My name is Hope,' she heard herself say. And as she said it, she felt her identity dissolving. The quick cleverness that had let her run everything when Zak and Cam were away on the journey. The power of telling stories that had come when she needed it. The friendships, the sense of purpose. Even the words fell away. When she spoke again, her tongue scooped awkwardly round her mouth. 'I'm Hope Armstrong.'

Zak stepped sideways and waved towards the ramp. 'Hope Armstrong, you must leave this place,' he said. His voice was entirely dead, without any expression. 'You may take with you as much food and water as you can carry. That discharges all our debts to you for the work you did when you were one of us. From now on, we owe you nothing. You will live on your own. Outside.'

'No,' Lorn whispered under her breath. She knew what the punishment had to be, but hearing it spoken was almost unbearable.

'NO!' Bando shouted, a hundred times louder. 'No! It's not fair!' Stepping up to Lorn, he put an arm round her shoulders, turning to stand beside her, with his face to the others. 'Don't you know what happens if you send people outside when it's cold? They *die*. I have to carry them away from the cavern and throw them into the ravine. And then the steel birds and the plated creatures and the snakes—' His voice broke and he shook his head again.

'She can't stay here,' Zak said.

Bando glared back defiantly. 'If you send her outside, I'm going with her!'

Dear precious, simple Bando. It was all Lorn could do not to cry. He didn't understand how important he was to everyone else, how much they depended on his strength. He had no idea of bargaining or blackmail. What he said had come straight from his heart and he meant it. If she went outside he was going too.

But the others couldn't afford to lose him.

'There must be justice,' Zak said softly. 'That's what gives us the strength to keep the rules when things get hard.'

Bando's arm tightened around Lorn. She could tell that he didn't really understand what Zak was talking about.

But she did. Gently, tenderly, she loosened the arm from her shoulders and stepped sideways, turning to look at Bando. 'I'm not Lorn any more,' she said. 'My name's Hope Armstrong. That's what you have to call me. Say it, Bando.'

He hesitated, but she kept looking at him until he obeyed, shaping his mouth carefully to the unfamiliar words. 'Hope Armstrong.' He said them staring straight into her face and she felt the name cling to her.

*No, no, that's not what I want. I can't bear—*

'You can let Hope Armstrong go, can't you?' she said calmly.

Bando nodded, looking bewildered. Still not understanding, but registering a difference. In the air around them, Lorn felt a faint movement of relief from all the others.

It gave her the courage to ask for what she wanted. They owed her something extra now. Turning towards them, she stared at the rows of angry, unrelenting faces.

'I am Hope,' she said, 'and you've turned me out of the cavern. I accept that. Only . . . please don't shut me out of the tunnels too. I'm trying to find out how to finish my story.

I'll never know how it ends if you make me go outside, above the ground. Let me stay in the tunnels instead. You can block up the hole through the wall, to keep me out of the storeroom.'

'You won't have any chance of surviving there,' Perdew said gruffly. 'Not once you've run out of food.'

'You think I could survive outside in the cold? On my own?' Lorn gave him a long, straight look. 'There's no chance, is there? But if I can stay in the tunnels, at least I'll understand my life before I die. What do you say?'

No one answered, but she sensed something—some faint slackening of tension—that made her feel they were listening. One by one, the others turned to look at Zak, waiting for him to make the decision.

But he wouldn't do it. He stepped across to stand beside Lorn, so that he and Bando were flanking her, one on each side. From there, he stared back at the expectant faces, challenging them.

'What's your answer? Do you agree to what Hope has asked?'

They shifted uneasily for a moment. Then Perdew muttered, 'Yes. Yes, she can stay down here.'

As though he'd given them permission, the others joined in, muttering their agreement in grudging, embarrassed voices. *If Cam dies in the cold, Perdew will be the new leader*, Lorn thought. In a strange, detached way, because it couldn't matter to her any more.

Now that they'd decided, the atmosphere was suddenly easier. Annet came forward, reaching up on tiptoe to untie a half-empty net from the ceiling.

'Let me help you collect the food you need,' she said. 'Let me help you, Hope.'

She opened the net and held it wide. But it wasn't Lorn—it wasn't Hope—who filled it full. All the others began to move towards her, picking up grains and nuts and seeds. They pushed food into the net until it bulged so much that Annet struggled to tie the top. Cam snatched up a couple of bat-furs and bundled them together.

'You'll need these too,' she said gruffly. 'And a shell of water as well. Don't worry about getting them through the passage. We'll take them for you.'

Lorn stood back while Cam and Perdew took the supplies through the wall together. When they came back, she took a long breath and stepped up to the little gap in the stones.

Everyone was watching her. Cam and Zak. Bando. Annet and Dess and Perdew and Tina and—all of them. They were the only group of people who had ever looked after her and needed her and listened to her. She didn't know what to say to them.

'Go now,' Zak said. Not harshly. He came forward and put both his hands on her shoulders. 'Go now, Hope Armstrong, out of this group for ever, to live on your own. May you find food and water and shelter whenever you need them.'

Lorn bent her head, acknowledging what he'd said. Then she went down on her knees and began to crawl through the wall.

As she came out into the darkness beyond, she could already hear the others shifting stones behind her. Dragging them across the storeroom and jamming them firmly into place so that she wouldn't be able to move them from the other side.

Standing up, she hoisted the net on to her shoulder and tucked the blankets under one arm. Picking up the shell of water in her other hand, she began to walk off down the tunnel, on her own.

# TOSH SINGS AT HAM

# 13

*Magee. 17a Stepney Parade.*

By himself, Tom would never have gone there. Not for any of Emma's sensible, careful reasons, but because he was afraid.

When they'd met beside the park on Wednesday night, Magee had hardly said a word. He'd just held out the little white card and . . . stared. But his stare had gone through everything, right into the inside of Tom's head. *No,* Tom had thought, when he looked down at the card. *No, I'm not coming to see you. I'm not as stupid as that.*

And yet . . . something powerful was pulling him there. If Robert was right—if Magee really was the man from the plane—then maybe he had some link with the headaches too. And the bruises. And the blurred, erratic vision. If he understood those, then wasn't it stupid *not* to go and see him?

Left to himself, Tom might have hesitated for ages, torn between his fear and his need to know. But Robert tipped the balance. When he said they were going to see Magee, Tom didn't argue. He simply got on his bike and pedalled.

Stepney Parade was a row of shabby little shops, out on the east side of the city. They cycled towards it down a long, straight road lined with cheap terraced houses. As they approached the parade, Tom could see a bizarre red haze, glowing warm against the dingy shop fronts.

At first he thought it was some kind of optical illusion

and he blinked once or twice, to try and clear his eyes. The red mist shimmered and shifted, like wisps of fog in the wind, but it didn't disappear.

Gradually, as they cycled closer, the thickness at the centre of the haze resolved itself into individual figures. There was a group of teenagers hanging around outside the shops, laughing and chatting together. When Robert and Tom pulled up beside the kerb, they stopped talking and drew together, suspiciously.

Robert looked wary, but Tom could see it was all right. He grinned at the boy in the middle of the crowd. 'We're looking for someone who lives down here. Are there flats over the shops?'

The boy nodded and jerked his head towards an archway halfway down the row. He was cautious, but not unfriendly, and it was a perfectly good answer. Tom replied with a grin and a nod, thinking that was an end of it.

But there was another boy on the edge of the group, outside the red warmth that surrounded the others. A boy with a grey, nervous face and a smile that was too eager.

'I'll show you,' he said loudly. 'Follow me.'

'It's OK.' Tom smiled and shook his head. 'We're fine.'

But the boy wasn't going to be put off. He attached himself to them, with another ingratiating smile, trotting along beside Robert. Tom dropped back into third place, listening to their conversation but not joining in.

'Nice bike,' the boy said. Reaching out as if he wanted to touch it, but not quite connecting.

'It's not bad.' Robert wasn't really paying attention. He was trying to find the street numbers on the shops ahead of them. 'It's a bit small now.'

'Must be difficult,' the boy said, 'being so tall.' And then—hastily—'But it's fantastic for sport. You ought to play basketball.'

'I do play basketball.'

Robert didn't say it unkindly, but the boy's face went red and he started to apologize. As though it mattered.

And it did matter to him. Because everything mattered too much. Nothing was ever easy and natural. Tom could feel that unhappy awkwardness jabbing into him, settling under his ribs into a sharp, familiar pain. *Not again,* he thought. *Why now? This is all trivial stuff.*

But it wasn't trivial to the boy. He wanted to make friends, to be useful and important to them. Tom could feel him wanting it so much that he got everything wrong.

He was asking questions now, still trying to foist his help on them. 'Which flat are you looking for? It's probably someone I know.'

'Don't worry,' Robert muttered. 'We can cope.'

'But I could just—'

'We're fine, thanks. We can sort ourselves out.'

Robert was starting to sound impatient and Tom felt the boy shrink inside. He knew they didn't really need him, but he was desperate to stay with them. He'd made a big deal out of offering to help, and all the others had heard him. Being sent away now would make him look stupid.

The pressure was so strong that Tom could hardly breathe. *Don't be such a bleeding heart,* he told himself crossly. *You can't take everyone's troubles on board. It doesn't MATTER.* But it did matter to the boy. It mattered ridiculously.

When they reached the archway, Robert stopped dead. 'That's great,' he said firmly. 'Thanks for bringing us to the right place. We'll look after ourselves now.'

It was absolutely clear that he and Tom weren't going to move until the boy took himself off. Things were complicated enough, without a stranger tagging along. But the boy was still hovering.

Tom gave him a friendly smile, trying to catch his eye. 'Bye. Thanks for your help.'

The boy wouldn't look at him. He shrugged and shuffled his feet. 'It's all right,' he muttered. He hesitated for a second longer and then drifted back towards the group he'd just left.

'At last!' Robert pulled a face. 'I thought we were never going to shake him off. What a pain.'

'Yes,' Tom said faintly.

Robert looked quickly at him. 'What's up with you?'

'Nothing. Headache.' That wasn't quite the right word for it, but Tom couldn't think of anything better. He pushed his bike under the archway and leaned it against the wall. 'Let's go.'

The archway led into the alley behind the shops. Tom and Robert walked along the alley, looking at all the doors that opened on to it and checking the numbers. At the far end was a plain green door with plastic letters screwed on to it. *17A & 17B*. Robert knocked on the door with his knuckles and they waited for several minutes. No one came.

'He's out,' Tom said, feeling relieved. And cheated.

'Maybe.' Robert frowned and tried the handle.

The door swung open when he pushed it, showing a flight of stairs rising in front of them. The treads were bare and the paint on the walls was peeling.

'I bet the real front door's upstairs,' Robert said. 'Come on.' He dived inside.

Tom followed him up. Before he reached the turn in the stairs, he could hear Robert ringing the bell at the top, but when he came out on the landing nothing happened. Robert was already ringing again.

There were two doors leading off the little landing. 17A was the one on the left, a neat blue door, with a little curtained window beside it. There was no light showing from inside. They could hear the bell echoing in the empty rooms.

'He's not there.' Robert's voice was rough with disappointment. He rang the bell for a third time, even though they both knew it was pointless.

A door knob rattled suddenly, and an old man's voice came sharply from behind them.

'What do you want?'

The door of the other flat was open just wide enough to let him peer out at them. Tom saw his anxious eyes above the security chain—and for a second he glimpsed himself and Robert as they looked from there. *Boys on the landing. Teenagers. Louts.* The old man was afraid of them—and ashamed of himself for being afraid.

'We're . . . er . . . we're looking for Mr Magee,' Tom said apologetically.

'*Mister* Magee?' The old man gave a sudden, wheezy laugh. 'He's gone up in the world. I've never heard him called that before.'

'But he does live here?' Robert said quickly.

The old man nodded. 'Oh, he lives here, all right. But you won't find him now. You'd best come back in the morning.'

'But—' Robert began impatiently.

Tom kicked his ankle. Couldn't he *see* they were scaring the old man? 'Thank you very much,' he said politely. 'We'll do that. Come on, Robbo.'

Robert resisted for a second and then gave in. But he wasn't pleased. 'Why did you do that?' he muttered, as they went down the stairs. 'We could have asked him some questions about Magee.'

'What for?' said Tom. 'We can ask him ourselves tomorrow. No point in hassling the old man. There's enough—'

*Enough pain in the world without making more*. The words were almost out before he realized how weird they would sound.

'Enough what?' Robert said sharply.

'Enough time to wait until tomorrow morning,' Tom improvised.

'There's *no* time to spare.' Robert's voice was even fiercer now. 'We've got to find a way of saving Lorn and the others. Before it gets too cold.'

And it was colder every day. Tom knew that even better than Robert. Now, when he took Helga out before school, the wind was icy round his ankles, and the other dogs and their owners hurried past without stopping to chat. Winter was almost there.

'We'll come back tomorrow,' he said. 'OK?'

Robert gave a grudging nod as they went outside. 'Have to be, won't it?'

They cycled back quickly, without talking. Tom would have liked to go straight home, but Robert obviously assumed that they were going back to his house together. When they reached it, he cycled straight into the front garden, without pausing to say goodbye.

Tom turned in after him, to explain that he was going on. By the time he was close enough to speak, Robert had already opened the side gate. He was frowning at Emma's bike, which was just on the other side, propped against the wall.

'What's the matter?' Tom said. 'Something wrong?'

'Not really. It's just—' Robert shook his head.

'Just what?'

'Well—why has Em left her bike there? It's in everyone's way.'

Tom shrugged. 'Maybe she was in a hurry.'

'But she hasn't padlocked it, either. That's really peculiar. She's always nagging at me about padlocking mine.'

'Well, now you've got a chance to nag her,' Tom said. 'That'll make a change.'

'Not till she gets back from Shelley's,' Robert said. He

wheeled both bikes towards the shed. 'And we'll probably be at Magee's by then.'

'What time do you want to go?' Tom said. Thinking, *Ten? Half past ten?*

'We ought to be there before nine,' Robert said briskly. 'We don't want him going out before we get there. Leave your phone on and I'll call you at half past seven, to make sure you're awake.'

'Great,' Tom said sarcastically. It was no use arguing. There wouldn't be any peace until Robert had caught up with Magee. 'I'd better go and take Helga out for a proper run now, then. She's not going to get much in the morning.'

'Please yourself.' Robert locked his bike to Emma's and shut the shed door. 'I think I'll go in and ring Em, so she knows what's going on. She might decide to come with us tomorrow morning—instead of slopping round Shelley's house in her dressing gown all day.'

*You think so?* Tom had a feeling that Emma wanted to stay a long way away from Magee. And he could understand that. As he pedalled home, there was only one thought running through his head.

*He'll be there tomorrow . . .*

# 14

When Robert phoned in the morning, he was in a very bad temper. 'At least *you*'ve got your phone turned on,' he muttered, when Tom answered it.

'Only because I knew you'd ring early.' Tom was whispering, trying not to wake his mother. 'What's bugging you?'

'I can't get Emma. Her phone's been off all the time.'

Tom laughed. 'Must have been a really great party.'

'But how can she cut out like that? And forget about what's going on?'

'Give her a break, Robbo. She's only having twenty-four hours off. It's been pretty intense for the last few days. Don't *you* wish you could switch off?'

'No I don't,' Robert said. 'But you sound as if you do. Are you going to run out on me as well?'

Tom sighed. 'Of course not.'

'Good. I'll see you round here in half an hour, then.' Robert rang off, before Tom could protest.

Being there in half an hour meant getting up instantly. Tom tried to do it without disturbing his mother, but she appeared in the kitchen doorway while he was swigging down a quick glass of milk.

'This is a surprise,' she said sleepily. 'You're not usually so eager to get to Tesco.'

Tom stared at her. 'Tesco?'

'You *promised,*' his mother said reproachfully. 'Because I need to get all the really heavy stuff today.'

Of course. He had. Dad had always taken her in the car, and she hated going on her own. She couldn't really manage all the bags on the bus. *Don't worry,* Tom had said the Saturday before. *I'll come with you next week.* He couldn't go back on that now. And the shopping wouldn't take more than a couple of hours.

He gave his mother a cheerful smile. 'Don't panic. I remember. But can we go soon? I said I'd do something with Robert afterwards.'

'No problem.' His mother grinned back. 'I'll be ready in twenty minutes.'

She rattled back upstairs, and Tom took out his phone and dialled Robert's number, reluctantly. His head was already starting to ache and he wasn't looking forward to the conversation. Robert was going to be furious with him.

He was.

'What are you talking about?' he said. 'Can't you go shopping this afternoon?'

'No,' Tom said. 'Sorry.'

'Why not?'

*Because I promised. Because Mum always goes shopping on Saturday mornings. Because.* 'It'll only take a couple of hours,' Tom said soothingly. 'I can be back before eleven.'

*'Eleven!'* Robert said. 'That's much too late. Magee might be out again by then and I'm not risking that. If you won't come with me now, I'm going on my own.'

Tom knew that wasn't a good idea, but he wasn't going to let himself be blackmailed. And his headache was getting worse. Soon it wouldn't be safe for him to cycle anyway.

'I've got a terrible migraine,' he muttered, fudging a half-truth. 'If I go shopping with Mum, I'll be able to get some painkillers. Then I can join you afterwards—if you still need me.'

'You've never had migraines before,' Robert said sharply. 'Is it something to do with Magee?'

*Don't start on that,* Tom thought. He could hear his mother coming down the stairs. 'Adolescence often triggers the onset of migraine,' he said. In the best Great Scientist voice he could manage.

'Other people make do with acne.' Robert still sounded annoyed, but he was calming down now.

Tom decided to end the conversation while he was winning. 'I'll phone you as soon as we've got the shopping home. If you need me then, I can be round at Magee's in fifteen minutes. OK?'

'Have to be, won't it?' Robert said grudgingly. 'Just be as quick as you can.'

He rang off, just as Tom's mother came into the kitchen.

But it was Robert who made the next call, long before eleven. Tom and his mother were only halfway round the supermarket when Tom's phone rang, between the pasta and the bread.

Tom took it out of his pocket. 'Hi, Robbo.'

'Can't he leave you alone for a second?' his mother muttered irritably.

Tom put a hand over the phone and grinned at her. 'No one can do without me. I'm indispensable.'

He dodged the amiable cuff his mother aimed at him and ducked away down the aisle.

'Tosh?' Robert said in his ear. 'Are you there?'

'What's up?' said Tom. 'I thought I was going to phone *you*.'

'You don't understand,' Robert said. He was almost whispering. 'I had to phone you. Because of Magee.'

Inside Tom's head everything suddenly went very still. 'What about Magee?'

'He won't talk to me. He just says, "It's the other one I want." You've got to come, Tosh.'

Tom took a long breath. 'He wants to talk to *me*?'

That made sense, of course. He was the one who'd been given the little white card. From the moment their eyes first connected, he'd known that he had business to settle with Magee.

'You've got to come *now*,' Robert was saying. 'Straight away.'

Tom could hear the urgency in his voice. But he could see his mother too. She was watching him anxiously, waiting for him to finish his call. He couldn't just take off and leave her to carry the shopping home.

'Look, Robbo,' he said, 'I won't be long. I've just got to help Mum—'

'I don't *believe* it!' Robert said furiously. 'We've finally found Magee—and all you can think about is *shopping*?'

Tom closed his eyes and took a long breath, trying to stay calm and reasonable. He was still trying to work out how to reply when he heard a completely unexpected sound from the other end of the phone.

Someone was laughing.

'Who's that?' he said sharply.

The voice that replied wasn't Robert's. It was another voice. He knew instantly who it was. Who it had to be.

'Hello, boy,' said Magee. 'How are the bruises coming along?'

How did he know about those? Even Robert didn't really know.

'What do you mean?' Tom said, very fast and low. 'What bruises?'

Magee laughed again. A wry, hoarse laugh. 'They'll get worse before they get better. Believe me.'

'What do you mean?' Tom said again.

But it was too late. Magee had gone. It was Robert who answered the question.

'I don't know what *any* of this stuff is about,' he said, in a low, secret voice. 'But you've got to get over here, Tosh, as fast as you can. When I heard Magee speak, I was—he sounds just like Zak. We've *got* to persuade him to talk.'

Tom glanced quickly at his mother. She was standing further down the aisle, in exactly the same place as before. Staring at exactly the same loaf of bread.

He did a quick calculation. 'I can be there in an hour and a half.' It would take that long to get the shopping home. 'Tell Magee I'm coming.'

'An hour and a half?' Robert said. 'What use is that? I need you here now.'

Tom heard Magee's voice in the background, muttering something. And then Robert spoke down the phone again.

'OK, Tosh, Magee's going to stay around until you come. I'm going off for a walk and I'll probably have some coffee and give Emma a ring. Just call me as soon as you get here. And make sure it's not more than an hour and a half.'

'Don't worry. I'll be there.' Tom rang off and went back down the aisle to his mother. She was still staring at the bread. 'Let's have them both,' he said, putting his head over her shoulder. 'The bloomer for breakfast and the multigrain for tea.'

She turned round with such a wide grin that he knew she'd been afraid he was going to abandon her. 'Boys!' she said. 'You're all the same. Hollow legs and no sense of economy.'

By the time Tom reached Stepney Parade, Robert was back there, hovering outside number seventeen.

He'd obviously been thinking while he had his cup of coffee. 'What's all this with you and Magee?' he said as he opened the door.

'I wish I knew,' Tom said. 'Maybe we'll find out now.'

'But what did he mean about the bruises?'

'Nothing,' Tom said quickly. 'That's not important.'

'Oh, come *on*.' Robert pulled him inside and shut the door behind them. 'If we're going to talk to him, I have to know what's going on. Tell me about the bruises.'

He was obviously not going to be put off. Reluctantly, Tom loosened his jumper and T-shirt and lifted them up, to show the bare skin of his chest.

Robert gasped.

It was a much stronger reaction than Tom was expecting. He knew there were a lot of bruises, and they were very sore, but they'd appeared one at a time and he'd grown used to them. It was only now, looking at Robert's face, that he realized how shocking they were. His whole chest was patched with dull red shading into purple.

'Is that all of them?' Robert said faintly.

Tom shrugged and stripped off the T-shirt and jumper altogether, so that Robert could see the bruises running up his left side. They went all the way from his hip to his armpit. His right shoulder was bruised too. And he could feel a tender patch in the middle of his back.

'Who did it?' Robert said faintly. 'Was it Magee?'

Tom shook his head.

'Not your mother—?'

Tom laughed out loud, even though his ribs were sore. 'Come on, Robbo. You *know* my mum. Do you really think she'd hit anyone?'

'So why are you keeping it a secret?' Robert said. 'If someone's beating you up, you've got to tell the police—'

'It's not like that,' Tom said slowly. 'No one's thumped me. The bruises just . . . come. When I see someone like that boy we met here yesterday, it just *hurts* me. And afterwards there's a new bruise.'

Robert stared at him. 'You mean they just come? On their own?'

Tom looked down at his feet. 'I think so. There doesn't seem to be any other reason.'

He could see Robert didn't want to believe him. If he hadn't been standing there shivering, with his bruises actually showing, Robert would have brushed the whole thing away as 'imagination'. But there was nothing imaginary about those savage red blotches.

'There's the headaches too,' Tom said. 'And my eyes go blurred and I see strange colours. I can't help it.'

Robert was still staring at the bruises. 'You really got those like that? Just from looking at people?'

'It's more like . . . feeling,' Tom said, awkwardly. 'As if I can see inside their heads.'

For a moment, Robert just looked at him, bewildered and speechless. Then he waved a hand at the clothes Tom was holding. 'Put those on again and let's get upstairs. We've got to talk to Magee.'

# 15

Tom hadn't realized how frightened he was until Robert lifted his hand to knock on the door. Then he found he was trembling.

Before he met Magee, his life had been simple. When he looked at people, he'd seen what everyone else saw—ordinary faces that didn't give much away. Now everything had changed. Wherever he went, he was battered by feelings and fears and pain, and he didn't like it. He wanted his old life back.

But that wasn't what they'd come for. They'd come to try and rescue the people in the cavern.

Robert gave him a quick glance. 'You OK, Tosh?'

Tom shrugged. 'Let's get it over with.'

Robert knocked and immediately they heard someone moving inside. A second later, Magee opened the door.

He was smaller than Tom remembered. And older. A thin, wiry man, with greying hair and fine, tired wrinkles at the corners of his eyes. But there was nothing tired about the eyes themselves. They were bright blue, as clear and cool as still water. And they went straight to Tom's face.

'You're here,' he said. 'Good.'

Tom hunted for the right words to answer him, but Robert interrupted before he found them, bursting in eagerly.

'You said you'd talk if Tom came. You said you'd *explain*. Are you going to tell us—?'

Magee was still staring at Tom and his eyes were very sharp now. Probing. 'What do you want to know?' he said, without looking round.

'I want to know how I landed up in the cavern,' Robert said. 'And I want to know about all the others too. What made us shrink? And *why*?'

Magee glanced sideways at him. 'You call that *shrinking*? That was when you started to *grow*. Beforehand—when I passed you on the plane—your body may have been big, but you were shrivelling inside.'

'*What?*' Robert gaped at him.

Tom understood a bit better, but he thought Magee was exaggerating. 'Surely it wasn't that bad? I mean—he wasn't in a prison, like Hope.'

Magee gave a small, wry smile. 'No? You've never lived with a rival who's always better than you are. You haven't got a sister, have you? Or a brother?'

Tom shook his head, not understanding, and Magee's smile twisted bitterly. 'Believe me, it's just another kind of trap. If you met Robert *now*—as he was then—you'd be able to feel it choking him. It nearly knocked me over when I passed him on the plane.'

It sounded wildly exaggerated. Melodramatic. 'Just because Emma kept putting him down?' Tom said, unconvinced.

'Oh, she wasn't the only one.' Magee's eyes swivelled suddenly, fixing on Robert's face. 'Was she?'

Robert went bright red. 'I just didn't know what I could do,' he muttered. 'That's all. I thought—'

'You thought you were pathetic and incompetent,' Magee said evenly. 'And you didn't find out you were wrong until you were put in a place where you had to survive. Where only real things mattered. That's what saved you.'

'But—I could have died,' Robert said.

'And would that have been so bad?' said Magee. 'Everyone dies in the end. Isn't it better to have some real life before that happens—even if has to be short?'

'That's nonsense!' Robert said angrily.

But it made a horrible kind of sense to Tom. He knew what Magee meant. But he couldn't agree with him. He couldn't let himself.

'Robert *escaped,*' he said hotly. 'He did this real life thing of yours and then he came back. That's what we want to do for the others. How can we get them out of the cavern?'

'You haven't even told us how they got in,' Robert said. 'You promised to explain—and you haven't explained anything.'

Magee spread his hands, rejecting the accusation. 'I can only explain what you're ready to understand. I've told you I rescued them—for their own good. What more do you want me to say?'

'You know what we want,' Robert said furiously. 'We want to know *how.*'

He was shouting now and his voice must have carried further than he meant it to. A chain rattled behind them and when Tom looked round he saw the old man peering out of 17B. Magee raised a hand and waved, telling him not to worry.

'It's time you went,' he said. 'I can't tell you any more until you've found out for yourself.'

'That's not fair,' Tom said. 'It doesn't make sense.'

'Oh yes it does,' said Magee. 'You'll discover the game for yourself when you really need it. Just as I did. When I couldn't take any more.'

'What game?' Robert said wildly. 'None of this is a *game.*'

Magee was looking at Tom. 'You'll find it out for yourself,' he murmured. 'When the pressure's strong enough.

All you have to do then is visualize the place—and the power will come.'

Tom scrabbled to grasp what he meant. 'What place? What are you talking about?'

But it was too late. Magee took a step back and shut the door in their faces.

Robert knocked on the door angrily, with his fist, but there was no answer. It was obvious that Magee wasn't going to come back.

'What do we do now?' he said. 'We can't just leave it like that.'

Tom felt the same. Magee's final words were swirling around sickeningly in his head. He knew they were important, but he couldn't make any sense of them.

'Let's go and find Emma,' he said. 'Maybe she'll understand better than we do. She's good at sorting things out.'

Robert scowled. 'That's great—if we can ever get in touch with her again.'

There was a sudden stillness inside Tom's head. 'What do you mean?'

Robert pulled a face. 'Well, she's had her phone off for twenty-four hours now. She just doesn't *care* what happens to us.'

Could he really be talking about Emma? 'I thought you were going to phone her last night,' Tom said slowly.

'Couldn't get through, could I?' Robert was still complaining. 'It must have been a really wild party. Either that, or she's still annoyed with us. But she needn't expect—' He finally noticed Tom's expression. 'What's the matter? Why are you staring at me like that?'

'Think what Emma's like,' said Tom. '*Why* was Emma annoyed with us? Why did she go to Shelley's party in the first place?'

'She did it to get at us. Because she didn't think we ought to go looking for Magee.'

'And that was because she was *worried,'* Tom said. 'So why has she waited twenty-four hours to find out what happened? You know what she's like. Wouldn't you have expected her to keep calling us? Every couple of hours?'

Robert hesitated. 'Maybe her phone's dead.'

'Oh, come on. Won't every single girl at that party have a phone?' Tom shook his head fiercely. 'There's something wrong, Robbo. We've got to go round to Shelley's and see what's happening.'

Robert looked horrified. 'But it's a girlie weekend. They're probably all in their underwear, waxing each other's legs.'

'So?' Tom was heading for the stairs. 'I'm not afraid of a bit of wax, even if you are.' He knew already, in his bones, that Emma's silence had nothing to do with wax. But, for the first time in his life, he really wanted to be wrong. He wanted to turn up on Shelley's doorstep and find Emma inside, making fun of him. *Couldn't you manage without me for twenty-four hours?*

But it wasn't Emma who opened the door. Disconcertingly, it was Fipper.

Robert stared at him. 'I thought this was a girls' party.'

'How could they have a party without me?' Fipper said smugly. 'Anyway, aren't Shelley's friends a bit old for you?'

Robert didn't smile. 'I want to see my sister.'

'Wo-*ho*!' Fipper backed away, shaking his head in mock horror. 'Don't let Shelley hear you mention that name. Emma's not Miss Popularity in this house.'

'We only want to talk to her,' Tom said. 'Can't you ask Shelley—'

'Ask me what?' Shelley materialized from nowhere. When she recognized Robert, she raised her eyebrows. 'What are you doing here? Has she sent you to apologize?'

'Apologize?' Robert said cautiously.

'Or does she think it's all right to dump people without an excuse?' Shelley scowled. 'She was all over me yesterday. *Of course I'll bring a gateau. Do you want some cheese too?* I even paid for her cinema ticket last night, because I was so sure she was coming. And then she didn't turn up.'

'*What?*' Robert said.

That was nearly a disaster. Just in time, Tom realized what would happen if Fipper got the idea that Emma hadn't been home last night. She would never live it down. He kicked Robert's ankle, to keep him quiet, and said, 'Didn't she even send you a message?'

Shelley looked hurt. 'I must have phoned her ten times last night. But she had her phone turned off. She was deliberately avoiding me.'

Fipper leered over her shoulder. 'Maybe she didn't want to be disturbed.'

'Very funny,' Robert said. He'd spotted the danger now. 'I thought she'd come round already, but she won't be long. She'll explain then. She doesn't want you to think—'

'Too late for that,' Fipper said gleefully. 'We've all been *thinking* already. Haven't we, Shells?'

Shelley dug him in the ribs with her elbow. 'Don't be mean. Just because we let you barge in here, it doesn't mean you can be rude.' She pushed him back into the house and gave Robert a pale smile. 'As long as Emma's OK,' she said. And then, 'She *is* OK, isn't she?'

'Yes. Oh yes, she's fine,' Robert said. He was backing away quickly now. 'It's just—well, she'll tell you herself. When she sees you. Bye, Shelley. Bye, Fipper.' He waved a hand and jumped on to his bike as though he hadn't a worry in the world.

Tom let him cycle ahead until they were out of sight of Shelley's house. Then he overtook him and stopped by the kerb.

Robert pulled in behind him. 'There's bound to be some simple explanation,' he said, before Tom could speak. 'She'll have gone somewhere else instead. She's sure to be fine—'

'She's *not* fine,' Tom interrupted, to make him stop. 'She's disappeared, Robbo. What are we going to do?'

For a moment, Robert stared uncomfortably at him. Then he said, 'It's Mr Armstrong, isn't it? He's taken her.'

Tom nodded miserably. 'That's what it looks like. Do you think we should tell the police?'

'What do we say? *Officer, my sister's disappeared and I think I know who's taken her. No, I haven't got any evidence except that we kidnapped his daughter a few days ago.*' Robert shook his head. 'It'll take hours. And she's been there long enough already.'

That was right. Of course. If Mr Armstrong had really kidnapped Emma, he wasn't just going to ask her polite questions. He'd be determined to find out where Hope was. If Emma wouldn't tell—

'Let's go and get her,' Tom said grimly. 'As fast as we can.'

# 16

Twice before, Robert and Tom had clambered along the motorway embankment to reach the back of the Armstrongs' house. The first time, the journey had taken them over an hour. They'd crawled carefully through the bushes, moving silently and making sure that they stayed hidden.

This time, they covered the ground in under twenty minutes.

Robert moved like a wild creature. Not noisily, but fast, unerringly following the route they had used before. He was so quick that Tom struggled to keep him in sight. He panted along behind, ripping his clothes on brambles and grazing his sore, bruised flesh on branches and loose stones.

Robert didn't slow down until he was level with the Armstrongs' high evergreen hedge. Scuttling the last few feet, Tom found him squatting at the top of the embankment, looking into their garden. Although it was only early afternoon, all the blinds were pulled in the conservatory.

Tom's ribs ached as he gasped for breath. 'What now?' he said, as soon as he could speak. His head was spinning and the bushes were beginning to blur around him. He wanted a few minutes to calm down and make some kind of plan.

But there was no time for that. Before Robert could answer his question, there was a noise from inside the conservatory. A loud, hoarse shout that rang through the glass. They couldn't make out the words, but the voice was unmistakable.

'It's Emma!' Robert hissed.

They both moved instantly, instinctively, sliding straight down the embankment through brambles and bushes and mud. Even before they reached the bottom of the slope, the television came on in the conservatory, drowning out any other sounds. But they didn't need to hear any more. Emma was in the house beyond the hedge, and they had to get her out.

Without hesitating, they pulled themselves up into the hedge and dropped over the fence beyond, into the Armstrongs' garden. Crouching under the thick evergreens, they studied the back of the house, wondering how to get inside.

'Do you think the kitchen door's unlocked?' Robert murmured.

There was no way of knowing, but it was worth a try. They sidled round the garden, keeping close to the hedge to avoid setting off the security light. They would have been clearly visible from the conservatory if the blinds had been open. But the blinds were closed, and the noisy television was their ally. It masked the padding of their feet over the grass and the faint click as Robert tried the handle on the kitchen door.

The handle went down, and the door opened in front of them.

For a second, they hesitated, looking at each other. They had no real idea of what was ahead. They didn't even know the exact layout of the house. But, somewhere beyond the kitchen, they could hear a voice that had to be Mr Armstrong's. It sounded as if he was in the conservatory—and if he was talking to Emma, they needed to be there. Robert pushed the door further open and they slipped inside, closing it softly behind them.

Tom's heart was pounding hard. The tiles on the kitchen walls rippled sickeningly in front of his eyes and the air was thick in his lungs, as if he were breathing soup. Everything around him felt dark and oppressive.

Robert had already crossed the kitchen. He was standing in the doorway, peering into the hall. Glancing over his shoulder, he beckoned impatiently. *Come on.*

Together they crept out into the hall and over to the sitting room door. Leaning round the doorpost, they looked past the coffee table and the armchairs, and into the conservatory. Robert tensed, clenching his fists, but at first Tom didn't know what he was seeing. He was blinded by a dirty, swirling haze that smeared itself across his field of vision.

*I can't,* he thought. *I can't.* And then, *I MUST*. Screwing up his eyes, he forced himself to concentrate, peering ahead. Slowly the mist cleared, and he saw the inside of the conservatory, with the television on one side and the carpet rolled up.

The hole in the floor was invisible from where he was standing, but he could see Mr Armstrong kneeling on the edge of it, calling down into the darkness. His voice carried clearly over the sound of the television.

'Hope! Come here when I call you!' He sounded angry and impatient. *'Out!'*

Mrs Armstrong was standing just behind him, her hand held out towards him. Not quite connecting. She was speaking too, but her voice was too soft for Tom to hear. And behind her was Warren.

Warren's plump, pathetic face skewered Tom's mind. For a second, the whole scene blurred again. Because it was unbearable to think about Warren. Unbearable to see him living in a world that didn't make sense, however he tried to rearrange the pieces.

*I don't want to be sorry for Warren. I can't cope with that.*

Tom swung away from the door, standing with his back against the wall and his eyes closed. In the darkness behind his eyelids, he heard Mr Armstrong speak again.

'Out!' And then—impatiently—'It's no good sulking. If you won't come when you're called, I'll come down and get you!'

'No!' said Mrs Armstrong, loud and clear now. 'No, Daniel! You don't understand—'

Tom felt Robert nudge him hard in the ribs. He opened his eyes again and Robert mouthed frantic words. *What are you doing? We've got to get in there!* And he was right, of course. They'd come to rescue Emma. They couldn't stand around doing nothing while Mr Armstrong went down into the black room.

They should have had a plan, of course. But it was too late for that now, and Tom couldn't think straight. His head was throbbing savagely and the world outside seemed unreal and insubstantial. What was happening in this house was worse than anything he had felt before. It was battering at him, demanding . . . demanding—

But he didn't know *what*. What could he possibly do?

Mr Armstrong was letting himself down into the hole now, manoeuvring his shoulders awkwardly through the narrow opening. Robert was on tiptoe, poised to move. As soon as Mr Armstrong was out of sight, he nodded to Tom, beckoning him forward. The two of them stepped into the sitting room.

And Warren turned and saw them.

His eyes were wide with fear. For a second, Tom thought he was afraid of them. That he was going to shout a warning and give them away. But that was wrong. Warren stared steadily at them for a moment and then—quite deliberately—stepped away from the hole in the floor.

Tom wondered what he was thinking, but Robert's response was much more direct. He tugged at Tom's sleeve and then raced forward, crossing the sitting room in three or four strides.

Mrs Armstrong saw him, out of the corner of her eye, and she turned to shout at him. But before she could make a sound, Robert had grabbed her and dragged her backwards, with an arm looped round her neck. His other hand went over her mouth and above the hand her eyes were shocked and terrified.

The pressure in Tom's head beat harder and more insistently. He could see Robert frowning at him, gesturing with his head to tell him to get hold of Warren and keep him quiet. But there was no need for that. Warren was rigid and silent. Tom could feel the cold, paralysing weight of his thoughts. How could he do anything if his world was completely senseless?

Mrs Armstrong was scrabbling at Robert's arms, trying to free herself. But she wasn't thinking either. She was moving, moving, moving—because if she stopped she would despair and fall to pieces. Tom could feel that too.

Everything was focused on that dark hole in the ground and the man who had just gone down into it. He was the key and the cause of it all. From underneath their feet, his voice sounded again.

'Hope!'

Without knowing why, or what difference it could make, Tom went towards that voice, led by some instinct to the very centre of the terrible pressure he felt.

He walked across the conservatory and jumped down into the hole.

As soon as his feet hit the black polythene, the noise from the television faded into the background. There was a torch lying on the polythene and, by its light, he could see a dark bulky shape ahead of him. Its outline was indistinct, because he saw it through a dense, ugly fog, which hung round it like foul smoke. But he knew who it was.

The figure swung round sharply. Tom heard a quick intake of breath. 'You're not taking her away again,' Mr Armstrong said. 'Now I've got another chance, I won't let her go. She's *mine*.'

His voice was like a wall of ice, blocking out any possibility of a reply. Tom dodged sideways, trying to see through the dark haze. He could just make out a twisted mass on the ground beyond, but he couldn't identify it.

Mr Armstrong moved too, stretching out an arm to bar his way.

'You can't take her,' he said, still in the same frozen, emotionless voice. 'You saw what happened to her last time. She can't exist outside this room. It's where she belongs.'

Tom's eyes had adjusted to the dim light now. He could see that the shape on the floor was a person, but he didn't recognize the pale, dirty face, or the cropped hair, or the contorted body, swathed in shiny brown tape.

She recognized him, though. 'Oh, Tom!' she said. 'You've been so *long*!'

Tom wanted to leap forward and rip off the tape that plastered her body. But he knew he wasn't strong enough to fight off Mr Armstrong. From somewhere, he managed to gather enough breath to speak calmly and reasonably.

'That's not Hope,' he said. 'It's not your daughter. That girl is Emma Doherty. You have to let her go.'

Mr Armstrong didn't even look round at Emma. 'She's my daughter now,' he said. 'And she stays here.'

'She doesn't even look like Hope,' Tom said desperately. 'Hope's *gone*.'

Mr Armstrong raised his head and looked straight at him. For one instant, Tom caught the full intensity of what was behind the ice wall. He felt a blast of anger and guilt stronger than anything he'd ever imagined. Only the ice walls held it in check. By sheer willpower, Mr Armstrong was shutting out the rest of the universe. He was insisting that reality should be exactly as he defined it.

But he couldn't keep it up.

Standing there between Emma and Tom, he was losing control of the world he'd made for himself and his family. It had ceased to make any kind of sense—and the ice walls around him were beginning to melt and disintegrate. When they collapsed, the forces inside his head would blow him to pieces.

And he might do anything.

Tom was swamped by the realization. Swamped by the misery and pain and desperation he could feel. *No. I don't want to understand him. I don't want to.*

But he couldn't help it. He'd lost the power to shut out what other people were suffering. Standing there, facing Mr Armstrong, he found himself wanting to reach out. Wanting to help. *But what can I do? There's nothing—*

'Are you all right, Daniel,' said a quick, nervous voice from behind him. 'What's happening down there?'

Tom turned, and saw Mrs Armstrong. She had wriggled out of Robert's arms and flung herself down on her knees beside the opening. She was peering frantically into the dark room and behind her was Warren, leaning over her shoulder.

Tom was caught in the centre of the tiny, suffocating world the Armstrongs had made for themselves. The world that imprisoned them as surely as they'd imprisoned Hope. He could feel the forces of fear and need and pity that held them together.

And he couldn't bear it. He felt as though he would die if it didn't stop. *I can't, I can't—*

And then he remembered Magee's voice. *You'll find it out for yourself. When the pressure's strong enough.*

The pressure couldn't get any stronger than this. Surely it couldn't get any stronger. But what was he supposed to find out? What had Magee told him?

Somewhere deep inside him, he felt a fierce anger beginning to grow. The pain was killing him, and it wasn't *his* pain. The anger gathered inside his head with a power he had never dreamed of, pushing the pressure away.

And, in that second, Magee's words sounded in his mind, as clear and sharp as if they'd been spoken in his ear. *All you have to do is visualize the place.*

He knew what place that was. The picture came into his mind immediately, almost unbidden, as sharp and remote as the image in a magnifying glass. He saw the hedge and the earth bank, the tunnel entrance and the tiny, intricate landscape of earth and stones shadowed by coarse, dying plants. *There,* said a voice in his mind. *There, not here.*

The real world was blurring in front of his eyes, pressing in harder and harder, but now he could sense the way out. He forced himself to look into the very centre of the pressure, where the pain was worst. The eyes that glared back at him were tortured and terrifying and he had to fight the appalling pity that hit him. If he gave in to that, he would be totally overwhelmed.

He didn't have to sympathize. Keeping the picture of the tunnel entrance steady in his mind, he pushed the pain away.

*That's not mine. It has nothing to do with me.* All his energy funnelled into that single thought, as he focused on the image of the cold, dark earth. *There, not here.*

And suddenly the pressure fell away.

His vision cleared and the pain evaporated completely. For a moment, he didn't understand what he'd done. Then the realization flooded in, raw and shocking. And with it came the knowledge that he had to go and find Magee, as fast as he could. He had to *make* him explain.

Because he was still looking into the same face as before, but the eyes looking back at him weren't tortured now. They were blank and empty.

Zombie's eyes.

In the cold space under the ground, Lorn was working frantically, without stopping. It was the only way to keep her mind still and her body warm. But it seemed like an impossible task. How could she make the shape of something that her mind refused to picture? How could she share a memory so frightening that her brain shied away when she tried to give it a form? She was attempting to conjure up a terror that came in the darkness—but gave substance to the whole world. An all-embracing fear, too big to see. At the beginning, she concentrated on the shape itself working at the great mountain of earth she had collected. But there was no way to make it *big enough*. Any shape her mind could hold was too weak, too trivial. In the end, she understood that she had to work in the space around it, carving out room for herself to move—pitiful little scraps of nothing—so that the great, ragged bulk in the centre took shape by itself, rising up behind her. When she hummed she could feel its huge mass, blocking the tunnel so that she had to make herself small to squeeze past it. It was there, sharing her tunnel, and it demanded to be seen. To be shown to the others.

But how could she make that happen?

Her brain knew how to make pictures out of smells and sounds and the movements of the air, but the others couldn't do that. They needed light. And if they brought the light with them, trooping down in a line, one behind the other, they would never see what she wanted them to see.

The people at the front of the line would arrive first and they would have time to get used to the shape she'd built. By the time the others got there, they would be peering and touching and chattering—maybe even laughing. The great darkness she had made would be diluted and lost before they could all feel the shock of it.

The impact had to be sudden. It had to appear out of nowhere, like a great monster rearing up ahead of them, seen and not seen. Terrifying because they couldn't understand it.

That moment was all she wanted. She wanted them to know what she meant when she said, *This is what it was like. That's why the story has to be told my way.*

If she had that, it wouldn't matter any more whether she was called 'Lorn' or 'Hope'. Because they would know who she was, deeper than any name.

If only she could make them see . . .

But how? She paced up and down the tunnel, fretting away at the problem. Now she had stopped digging, it was hard to keep warm. Even when she was walking briskly, she had to wrap both fur blankets round her body, very tightly, to stop the shivering.

But eventually, she realized what she had to do. Eyes were the key to the whole thing. *HE* had to have eyes. She wandered along the tunnels until she found a length of root that she could hack free with her blade. Carrying it back to the thing she was making, she clambered slowly up the side of the mass of earth, wedging her feet against the stones.

It was tricky work that took all her concentration. She sang a long clear note, to keep the shapes exact in her head as she drove the jagged root into the earth in front of her. Working it round slowly, she made a hole right through to the other side.

The second hole was harder. The earth was already loosened and it shifted as she tunnelled into it. There was no need for singing now. As she worked the root carefully round and round, she could tell exactly what was happening from the trickling sound of the soil.

She was almost through to the other side when she heard another sound. It was almost like an echo of the noise she was making—but it was coming from above her head. When she stopped moving to listen, the sound was unmistakable.

Outside, above the ground, someone was scratching at the earth with a stick. Someone was digging down towards her. Digging into the tunnel.

# IN MORTAL DANGERS

# 17

When he came round, everything had changed. He knew it before he opened his eyes, from the damp smell of the bare earth around him. From the clammy roughness against his bare skin.

He had no idea where he was, or how he could possibly have arrived there. The last thing he remembered was being down in Hope's secret room, struggling to save her from the marauders who had carried her off before. He'd been ready to defend her to the last drop of his blood.

What had happened?

He lay still, struggling to construct an explanation. He needed a theory which would offer him a clear and effective course of action. That was his usual way of proceeding. At every difficult point in his life he had made himself stop and

**FOCUS**

until he could be sure that he was in control once more. But this time it didn't work.

He was very, very cold. So cold that (unthinkably) his mind couldn't control his body. His eyes opened of their own accord, unbidden, and he saw—

(*It was important to remember that anything he saw might be a hallucination. Even a thing as simple as dehydration could cause severe confusion . . .* )

He was lying on a rough slope littered with boulders and huge clods of earth. Huge barbed branches arched overhead and beyond them, impossibly far above, were giant treetops, outlined against a darkening sky.

*This can't be real.* He tried to close his eyes again, but his will wasn't strong enough to control them. His shivering body clamoured for warmth and shelter, and there was nothing near him except a few heaps of dead leaves further down the slope.

He slithered down towards them, but there was no help there. The leaves on top were stiff and leathery and those underneath had decayed into a wet, stinking sludge.

**FOCUS**

**RELY ON YOURSELF**

His teeth were already clattering together. It was vital to get out of the wind and there was no suitable shelter above the ground. The only logical thing to do was dig down into the earth.

If he managed to dig some kind of trench, he could drag a few of the giant leaves across the top. That would expose the damp under-layer and give it a chance to dry in the wind.

Then he could use it as insulation inside the trench.

His brain was stirring now, getting a grip on the situation. He still had no way of explaining it, but that could come later, when his shelter was made. Now was the time for action.

He glanced around, making sure there was no one watching. Then he stood up, bracing himself against the icy wind. The clods of earth were heavier than he expected and he struggled to clear the surface of the ground in front of him.

(*That was hardly surprising, of course. He had sustained a serious shock. There was no reason to worry.*)

Things went faster when he found a dead branch to use as a tool. It doubled as a lever, for moving boulders, and a primitive spade, for scraping at the earth. If he'd had a proper spade, he would have dug down deep and lined the excavation with the boulders. As it was, all he could do was loosen the earth with his stick and then scoop it out with his bare hands.

His sense of power grew as he bent and lifted, bent and lifted. The work was warming and the trench was soon deep enough to shelter him from the worst of the wind.

**RELY ON YOURSELF**

As he wielded the spade, he could feel himself making sense out of chaos. Taking charge of the situation. Down and down and down—

And then everything gave way under his feet.

It happened without warning. One second he was pushing his stick into the soft, damp earth, trying to dislodge an embedded rock. The next second, he'd lost his footing. He was tumbling through empty space, with loose earth showering down all around him.

For the first instant, he could see it all—the flying clods, the crashing boulders, and the terrifying hole gaping underneath him. Then he hit the ground, hard, and a bigger fall of earth began, blocking out the light.

Instinctively, while he could still move, he rolled sideways, away from the collapsing ground. He seemed to be caught in some kind of air pocket, but it was impossible to see anything in the dark. All he could do was lie and listen to the slithering earth over his head as it settled into place. Knowing that he'd fallen too far to have any chance of digging himself out again.

Was this how he was going to die? Alone in the dark, with no family to take care of his food and clothes, nobody to lift him up and wash his body clean. After all he'd done to look after other people—all the care he'd taken—he was doomed to die on his own, suffering agonies of hunger and thirst. He lowered his forehead on to the cold ground.

* * *

And then a voice said, 'Who's there? Are you hurt?'

A second earlier—before he'd let himself think about death—he would have answered briskly, giving directions to the person who had spoken. But he'd allowed himself a fatal moment of self-pity—and the voice had asked a question that caught his weak spot. A question that no one had ever asked him before. *Are you hurt?*

The only manly answer was a quick denial. *No, I'm fine. Only a scratch.* But he couldn't make himself say it. He was bruised and battered and he'd given in to morbid thoughts of death. He had to clamp his lips shut to stop himself saying, *I hurt all over.*

'Please answer me,' the voice said earnestly. 'I can tell that you're alive. Are you injured?'

How did she know he was alive? He couldn't even work out which direction she was speaking from. Tightening his lips, he opened his mouth just enough to let out one unsteady word.

*'Cold.'*

It fell into a sudden, terrible stillness. He felt as though the sound of his voice had obliterated the only small part of the world that still remained. He was desperate to hear her speak again, but she didn't reply.

'I fell,' he said. Raising his voice this time, to make sure that she heard. He had to clench his teeth to stop himself from shaking. (*It was because he was cold. It had to be because he was cold.*)

Still no answer.

It was unbearable to think that she'd deserted him, that he was on his own again. He began to shout helplessly, panicking. 'Please don't leave me here! Come back! I can't bear it—'

He could hear himself sounding feeble. Pathetic. But what else could he do? She was his only hope of survival.

'Come back,' he yelled again. *'Come back!'*

'It's all right,' she said suddenly. Stiffly. She had been there all the time, in exactly the same place. Her voice sounded forced and cold now, but he crawled towards it, scrambling over the rough earth on all fours because he was afraid of falling. Reaching through the darkness with desperate hands, he tried to touch her.

'Where are you?' he called.

'There's . . . something between us,' she muttered. 'But I'll push a blanket through. Hold out your hand.'

He thrust it forward—and grazed his knuckles on a wall of earth and stones. It felt like a malicious trick and he drew his breath in sharply.

'You're in the right place,' she said. 'Just move your hand a little to the left.'

She seemed to know exactly where he was. How could she? For a moment he hesitated suspiciously. Then he walked his fingers slowly across the huge barrier in front of him. They came to a space and he pushed his hand into it.

And touched fur.

That was the last thing he was expecting. His fingers plunged into warm, silky fur, richer than anything he'd ever imagined. Clutching it firmly, he pulled it through the gap and it fell around his hands in thick, generous folds.

'Wrap yourself up.' Her voice was brisk now. 'Put the fur inside. It's warmer like that and the leather will keep you dry.'

It was a long while since anyone had given him orders. He ran his hands over the fur, trying to work out whether she was right.

'Don't waste time!' she snapped impatiently. 'Just *do* it! I can hear how cold you are.'

The fur was big enough to wrap his whole body (what kind of animal was *that*?) and it was already warm, as though she'd been wearing it herself. After a few seconds, he sat back on his heels, feeling his body relax.

But she hadn't finished with him. 'You need food too,' she said roughly. 'Hold your hand out again.'

Something else came at him through the gap. It was a thick, sticky slab, as big as the palm of his hand, without any kind of wrapping.

'What is it?' he said warily.

Her reply sounded impatient. 'Just eat it. It's what you need.'

**YOU CAN'T TRUST FOOD FROM STRANGERS,** said his brain. But an instinct older than rules made him push one corner of the slab straight into his mouth. It was a stiff, sweet paste, tasting of currants. It wasn't the kind of thing he would normally eat, but he found himself biting greedily at it, as though he was starving. The stickiness clung to his face and hands and he started to lick his fingers before he remembered how dirty they must be.

'What is this place?' he said.

There was a small sound from the other side of the barrier, like a wry laugh. 'You wouldn't believe me if I told you.'

'Don't be stupid,' he snapped. 'I'm not a child. I insist on being told.'

The only reply to that was another long silence. This time, she was the one to speak first.

'Don't you know who I am?' she said.

How could she be anyone he knew? It was impossible. He was about to point that out when he realized—just in time—that it might be wiser to play along with her. Maybe she'd made a mistake. Maybe she was only helping him because she thought he was someone else.

He answered very carefully, choosing his words. 'You sound . . . familiar,' he said. There was a shred of truth in that. By some odd coincidence, she sounded a little like his wife. Or, rather, as Lee *would* have sounded, if she'd had an ounce of energy and initiative. 'I'm afraid I can't quite place your voice. Maybe, if I could get through to where you are—'

'You want to come—here?' she said. With an abruptness that he didn't understand.

'I can't survive where I am. No one could live in a tiny space like this.'

'Oh no?' There was another one of her odd laughs.

'But the roof might fall in again,' he said. Trying not to picture the heavy layer of stifling earth above him. 'I have to get out of here.'

This time, the pause was so long that he called out again. 'Hello? Are you still there?'

'I was thinking.' Suddenly, she was crisp and practical. 'You can come through here—on one condition.'

'What's that?' he said quickly. (What was she after?)

'You must promise to obey my orders.' Her voice was firm and definite now. 'If there are two of us, we'll need more food and water. I know how to get them, but it won't be easy. If you don't do exactly what I tell you, you'll put us both in danger.'

That felt like agreeing to walk blindfold along a precipice. He hated losing control of what he did. But there didn't seem to be any other option.

'All . . . right,' he said, slowly and grudgingly.

That wasn't good enough. 'You promise? Absolutely?'

He shifted uncomfortably, pulling his blanket tighter. 'I promise. What do you want me to do?'

'Nothing yet. Just wait while I make a way through.'

He heard her hands beginning to scrabble at the earth. Scraping away at the barrier between them.

# 18

He waited impatiently while she widened the gap. She talked as though she could *see*—and that must mean, surely, that it was lighter on her side of the barrier. The light would be dim and shadowy, of course, but he visualized himself bursting through the barrier and out of his pitch-black prison.

When she said, 'You can come through now,' he scrambled forward eagerly, expecting her to catch hold of his hand and lead him through. But she didn't make any attempt to touch him. All she did was prompt with her voice.

'You'll have to stand up and squeeze through. Yes, like that. Just take a step to the right and then come forward. But *slowly*. Don't push at the earth.'

He inched between two damp, vertical surfaces, feeling the loose soil drag at his blanket. Because he was waiting to see light ahead, he assumed that he had a long way to go. It was a shock to emerge, quickly, into a space as dark as the one he'd left.

'What's happened?' he said. 'Where are you?' His arms flailed around, trying to catch hold of her, but she avoided him easily. He could hear the faint sound of her feet on the earth, but he couldn't work out where she was.

'Stop that!' she said sharply. 'Stand still and listen to me.'

Her voice was young, but she gave orders as though she was accustomed to being obeyed. (And she still sounded incongruously like a bossy, dynamic Lée. The coincidence—that was all it could be—was disconcerting.)

He wouldn't be able to take charge unless he worked out where she was, and seized her. And that was what he had to do. She was his only hope of survival, and he couldn't afford to let her get away.

**FOOLS RUSH STRAIGHT IN**
**WISE MEN PLAN AHEAD**

He stopped where he was, in the middle of what felt like a vast empty space. Pretending to play along with her. 'I'm listening,' he said meekly. 'What do you want me to do?'

'The first thing you have to do is *keep quiet,*' she said. 'If you make too much noise—'

The sound of her voice gave him the clue he needed. With both hands out, he darted forward to grab her. And he almost got it right. She was so near that he felt the warmth of her body in the cold air.

But she dodged away at the last moment. His hands closed on emptiness and he staggered forward, stumbling into some kind of wall. For an instant he heard the sound of her feet again, and then . . . silence.

She'd gone.

He called out, as loudly as he could. 'Where are you? I just stumbled, that's all. Don't play games with me.'

Nothing. No sound at all.

He held his breath until he thought his lungs would burst, listening for any tiny noise, however slight. But there was nothing. He seemed to be completely on his own.

He took a step forward, away from the wall he'd hit, but as soon as he lost contact with it he was swamped by panic. He scrambled back quickly, stumbling in his haste to feel its rough surface against his knuckles. It was the only solid, fixed point in the darkness around him.

For a second he simply stood where he was, feeling its reassuring solidity. Then he began to move again, but this time he followed the wall, running his fingers along the surface. As far as he could tell, he was walking away from the tiny space where he'd found himself at first. He headed into the unknown, trying to keep track of the distance by counting his steps.

*One, two, three . . . twenty-seven, twenty-eight . . .*

But as he reached *thirty*, the ground in front of him seemed to disappear. Just in time, he flung himself backwards, grabbing at the earth wall as his feet slid away. He would have slithered straight down what seemed like a precipice if his fingers hadn't clutched at a projecting root.

**FOOLS RUSH STRAIGHT IN**

He hauled himself back and huddled against the wall, with his blanket pulled tight round his body. He didn't mean to stay there. It was only intended as a short pause, until he stopped shivering. While he worked out what to do next.

**FOCUS**

**WISE MEN PLAN AHEAD**

An hour later, he was still there, unable to make himself move another step. *Focus*, he kept saying inside his head. *Focus, focus.*

But it had become a word without meaning.

He had no way of measuring exactly how long she left him there. After a time, he slept, because he was exhausted. When he woke, he didn't know whether he'd been asleep for hours or minutes. He drifted into a distracted, semi-conscious state.

Then, without warning, her voice spoke suddenly, almost in his ear.

'Have you had enough now?'

And he grabbed at her again. It was an instinctive action, a movement that happened before he could stop.

But this time he knew it was a mistake. Even as his arms went out, he was shouting.

'Please don't go! I don't mean it! I can't—'

Then his voice cracked and he realized—shockingly, unthinkably—that he was in danger of bursting into tears. It took his remaining strength to stop and shut down. He froze where he was, kneeling on the earth with his arms held out.

He'd lost her again. She was there somewhere—he could hear her breathing—but he knew now that she was too quick for him to catch. She had the upper hand and there was nothing he could do about it. Because he needed her help.

'I'm sorry,' he said at last. When he trusted himself to speak. 'That was stupid.'

He could never have admitted that in the light, to someone he could see. But the dark was different—and so was this unknown person who seemed to know exactly what he was doing, without seeing him. He was beginning to feel as though she knew everything.

'I'm sorry,' he muttered again. 'I'm afraid. Don't leave me here.'

'This is the last chance you have.' Her voice was clear and detached, but not unkind. 'I can take you to get food and more blankets. But only if you do exactly what I say. Otherwise it's too risky.'

'What kind of risk?' he said.

She hesitated. 'The food belongs to . . . other people. The only way we can get it is by stealing it. If we're caught, they'll drive us outside, into the cold, and we'll die.'

He had no trouble believing that last part. His memory of the cold outside was still sharp and real.

'All right,' he said. Understanding that it was the only sensible answer. 'I'll let you give the orders.'

'You promise?'

'I promise,' he said.

She touched the back of his left hand. When he turned it over to grasp her fingers, she didn't pull them away. 'I'll do what I can to help you,' she said. There was still no warmth in her voice, but it was steady and determined.

Pulling him to his feet, she began to move along the tunnel, walking so fast that he quickly lost track of the complicated, twisting route she followed. From time to time his free hand brushed against an earth wall, but there was nothing to distinguish one from another. If she'd let go, he would have been utterly lost, unable to do anything except stand and wait to be rescued.

But she didn't let go. She pulled him on, very fast, and then stopped suddenly, in a space that felt exactly like everywhere else they'd been.

But it wasn't.

'Reach out,' she said, dropping his hand. 'What can you feel?'

His fingertips made contact with something firm and hard. He ran his hand up and down the surface. 'A stone wall?'

'We have to get through it.' For the first time, her voice sounded unsteady.

He wondered whether she was afraid of the savages who lived on the other side of the wall. He guessed that they must be wild and uncivilized, but she didn't offer any information about them, and he was afraid to ask questions.

What she said was strictly practical. 'The stones we have to move are too big for me to shift, but you're stronger than I am. You can do it—but only when I tell you. You mustn't move *anything* unless I say it's all right. Do you understand?'

He nodded. 'You're giving the orders.'

'Good,' she said. 'Just as long as you remember that.'

* * *

She seemed to know the shape and position of every stone. Kneeling in front of the wall, she described each one he had to move. He worked them loose in turn, pulling them away from the base of the wall and placing them carefully to one side. Gradually, they were opening up a narrow passageway.

Once she stopped speaking for a moment and began to hum faintly instead.

'What are you doing?' he said.

'Ssh.' She tapped his arm to keep him quiet. 'I'm listening to the shapes ahead. Let me concentrate.'

He had no idea what she meant, but he waited obediently, rubbing his bruised knuckles. Now that he had worked his way deep into the wall, the stones were hard to move. And, all the time, he was nervously aware of the great weight of the wall above him. If she was mistaken about any of the stones, he would be crushed to death.

'OK,' she murmured at last. 'There's just one more stone. If you push that out of the way, we can go through.'

Carefully, he crawled towards it. It was a huge stone, wider than the space he was in. When he gave it a nudge, the other stones ground together above his head. The noise sent him wriggling backwards at top speed, out of the passage.

'It's too dangerous,' he said. 'The whole wall's resting on top of that stone.'

'No it's not.' Her voice was calm. 'It's just blocking the front of the passage. Go back and push it away.'

'It's mad to be tunnelling *underneath* the wall. We ought to be breaking down the top. I could lift you up—'

'Go back,' she said. 'Trust me. I know this wall.'

It was ridiculous for a young girl—clearly she *was* young—to be giving orders to a mature, experienced man. She hadn't even had the courtesy to listen to his idea. Why *should* he trust her?

His mind kept complaining, even while he went down on his knees and crawled back into the passage. But she was right. When he put his shoulder to the stone and heaved, it rocked gently for a second and then rolled away from him, into the open space beyond.

As soon as it moved, he felt a draught of warmer air. He squeezed through the gap that had opened and stood up unsteadily. The space around him was invisible in the dark, like the space he'd left behind, but it felt like a cave. And on the far side, twenty or thirty paces away, he could see a dim red glow coming down from above.

Light.

It shone through an opening in the roof, illuminating the top part of a steep ramp that ran down the far wall. That ramp was the way out of the terrible underground darkness. He took a step towards it.

'No,' her voice said softly. Close to his ear. She had crawled through the tunnel behind him and, before he could take another step, she caught at his hand and held him back. 'You *must* be quiet.'

He was so desperate for light that he almost shook her off. Her hand felt very small, and he could probably have sent her flying with one flick of his arm. But as she spoke, he caught the sound of other voices filtering down from whatever place it was above their heads.

*If we're caught, they'll drive us outside, into the cold. And we'll die.* Was that true? Should he trust her again?

Who were those people talking overhead? He could hear the rise and fall of their voices, but it was impossible to make sense of any words. He pictured a horde of uncontrollable savages, daubed with crude body paint and covered in ritual scars.

Her hand was flat across his mouth now, keeping him silent. 'We have to be quick,' she murmured. 'I'll fetch what we need.'

She began to move quickly around the space where they stood. Once or twice he glimpsed her shape against the red glow beyond. He was startled to see how narrow her body was, how small and slight her darting hands. She seemed to be flitting from one place to another, collecting things.

She went backwards and forwards, bringing armfuls of food. First it was a rough, bulging net, smelling of the sticky paste she'd given him to eat before. Then fur blankets, wrapped tightly around hard, heavy lumps that he couldn't identify.

'We need water too,' she muttered. 'I'll fill a shell—'

She broke off short, putting a hand on his arm. It was another second before he realized what she'd heard. There were new noises coming from overhead. Feet walking over the earth.

Then he saw shadows moving against the red light at the other end of the cave. They flickered across the back wall, and then loomed suddenly downwards, sharpening into long, distorted silhouettes.

There were people coming down the ramp.

# 19

There were two of them. They walked on to the ramp side by side, talking as they came down. Even though they were at the other end of the cave, he could hear their voices plainly.

And he could understand the words.

That took a second to register. The image of a crowd of alien savages had rooted so firmly in his mind all he was expecting was some kind of primitive mumbo jumbo. Instead, he heard a girl's voice that could have come straight from his ordinary—his *real*—life.

'Two shells, Bando,' she said. 'And no spilling.'

He had no idea what she was talking about, but that didn't matter, compared with the relief of knowing that he could *talk* to these people. He wouldn't be dragged off and butchered without a chance to explain himself.

'I never spill them.' The second voice was male. Sounding slightly injured. 'I can carry them both at once, without losing a drop.'

The girl came further down the ramp, holding a light above her head. It was a piece of wood, burning away very fast. (No electricity, then. So this wasn't civilization, in spite of the way they spoke.) 'Bando' moved ahead of her and his bulky shadow leapt across the wall, very black and sharp.

He was massive and terrifying, a brutal thug, with heavy shoulders and feet that thudded as they hit the ground. Suddenly, the darkness wasn't a good enough hiding place. It would only take one treacherous shaft of light for Bando to spot them. (But how can you find a hiding place in the dark? When you don't know where your enemy is heading?)

Watching Bando, he felt his throat tighten as he began to panic. But then a hand closed round his wrist. He was pulled gently sideways and down, into a small, close space, shielded by a heap that smelt of flour and dust.

She was there beside him, tapping her fingers on his hand. Warning him to keep still as Bando blundered closer. They heard the scrape of one hard surface against another and then . . . water, running into a hollow vessel.

Water.

He hadn't realized until then how desperately, agonizingly thirsty he was. He bent his head, bringing his hands up to cover his ears, so that he could shut out the tormenting, liquid sound.

**SELF-CONTROL IS ESSENTIAL**

But he hadn't remembered how close he was to the heap in front of him. He caught it with one hand, knocking against a hard, shiny globe, as big as a football. The globe slid out of place—and the heap began to disintegrate. His attempts to grab at it only made things worse. The shiny football shapes rolled down and away from him, spreading across the floor.

'Annet!' Bando shouted. 'Annet—the *grains*!'

The girl—Annet—came rushing down the ramp with the glowing torch held high above her head. It lit up her fierce, dirty face, and her bright eyes that peered ahead, into the shadows.

There was no hope of escaping back through the wall. She was near enough to see them while they were still crawling into the passageway. And it would be lunacy to push past her and run up the ramp. It sounded as though there were dozens more of them up there. There was only one sensible way to proceed.

## WHEN DANGER THREATENS TAKE PRE-EMPTIVE ACTION

He rose to his feet, pressing down lightly on the small, neat head next to him, to show her that she should stay hidden. There was no point in both of them getting captured. He was the one who'd given their hiding place away. He had to take responsibility.

He walked quickly forward, into the light, stumbling against the heavy globes that littered the ground. 'I'm the one you're looking for,' he said.

Bando took a step back. In a way that didn't match his appearance. 'Who is it, Annet?' he said nervously.

It seemed wise to answer quickly, making the words as reassuring as possible. 'My name is Daniel Armstrong. I apologize for causing a disturbance.'

'Bando—get him!' Annet said fiercely. 'I don't know who he is. We have to take him up into the cavern, for Cam and Zak to see.'

Tentatively, Bando moved forward. She followed him, holding her light high so that the whole cave was illuminated. Everything was visible now—and none of it made any sense. There were heaps of the globes that Bando had called *grains,* arranged in neat rows across the floor. Thick furs were stacked in piles along one wall, and huge nets hung from the ceiling, holding dark, wizened shapes, like monstrous raisins. It was all strange and unfamiliar, as though it came from an alien world.

He stared straight ahead, resisting the temptation to look down at the small, slight figure crouched by his feet. To do that would be to give her away. Instead, he watched Bando coming across the cave towards him. In a moment, he would have to go forward, to meet that terrifying figure. He had to make himself do it. He *had* to.

But he wasn't quick enough. Bando looked past him suddenly, into the shadows, drawing in his breath with a faint hiss. It was obvious that he'd seen the girl on the floor. For an instant he hesitated, as if he didn't know what to do.

'Hurry up!' Annet called from behind him. 'I can't hold this torch much longer. The flames are almost down to my fingers. Get him!'

It was like breaking a spell. Bando's great arms came out like a grab, latching on to him so tightly that he could feel the bruises forming. He was pulled away from the crouching figure, with no sign that anyone else was there. If it hadn't been for that hiss of breath, that slight hesitation, it would have been impossible to believe that she'd been seen at all.

As they moved away, he felt a quick, light touch on his ankle. *Thank you.* He had no way of responding without making Annet suspicious. All he could do was let Bando lead him away, towards the ramp.

Annet was there ahead of them. The glowing branch in her hand had burnt down to a stump. As the three of them stepped up on to the ramp, the fire touched her fingers and she winced. (*Surely it was unnatural for a log as thick as that to burn away so fast?*) He saw her toss the stump into a corner, leaving it to burn out harmlessly.

Then she led the way up the ramp, and with every step they took the air grew warmer. They came out into a small, hot space with a huge furnace at one end. The furnace was so tall that he had to tilt his head back to see the top of it. The air was dense with wood smoke and the heat was almost unbearable.

Walking round one side of the furnace, they emerged into a vast, high cave, much bigger than the cellar they had come from. The walls ran off into shadow and, way above them, huge ribs of wood zigzagged randomly over the ceiling. The whole space was red with firelight and crowded with wild, grimy people dressed in crude tunics.

'We found someone hiding!' Annet shouted. 'He was in the storeroom.'

The savages turned to gape at him. They shuffled to the sides of the cave, leaving a clear route down the centre, and he saw two people rise to their feet at the far end.

One was male and one seemed to be female. They were dressed as roughly as everyone else, but, in view of the way the others looked towards them, he assumed that they were the king and queen of the tribe. It was obviously a waste of time to attempt to discuss his situation with any of the others. Striding ahead of Annet and Bando, he headed down the cave towards the leaders.

Knowing nothing of the culture of these people, he had no idea whether he was supposed to approach the king and queen with some particular form of ceremony. Maybe it was prudent to wait for them to speak first. He stopped in front of them and stood silently, watching them and trying to work out who wielded the real power.

The king smiled questioningly, raising an eyebrow. But it was the queen who spoke. (*A matriarchy, then?*)

'Who are you?' she said abruptly. 'How did you get into our storeroom?'

He couldn't tell the exact truth without betraying his rescuer. He settled for the nearest safe approximation and answered quickly, looking her straight in the eye.

'I have no idea how I arrived. I just . . . found myself there, ma'am.'

'Cam,' she said.

Was that her name or some kind of title? He repeated the word, trying to match her accent precisely. 'Cam.'

She gave him an odd look. 'You say you just . . . appeared in the storeroom?'

He nodded. It was almost the truth (he had, after all, found himself in that peculiar forest with no idea of how he'd got there) but he couldn't help thinking that it sounded thin and unconvincing. He would hardly have been surprised if Cam had rejected it out of hand.

But she didn't. She glanced sideways at the king, uncertainly. 'Has it ever happened like that before, Zak?'

The king smiled his irritating, quizzical smile. 'Each time is different,' he said.

Maybe he wasn't the king after all. Maybe he was some kind of witch doctor or shaman, given to spouting senseless riddles. *Each time is different.* What was that supposed to mean? It was a pointless answer.

Unless—

The explanation jumped suddenly into his head and he blurted out a question. 'Are you telling me this kind of thing has happened *before*? Other people have suddenly found themselves here, without knowing how?'

'Unnerving, isn't it?' Zak said wryly.

There was a low murmur of agreement from all around the cavern. Was it possible that they'd *all* been through this strange experience? His mind raced wildly, filled with ideas about mass kidnapping and hallucinogenic drugs. 'Are you telling me that *none* of you knows where we are?'

Zak's eyes blanked suddenly, looking through him, and Bando made a low, unhappy noise in his throat. Behind them, people stirred restlessly, muttering words he couldn't hear.

They *did* know!

'Tell me!' he said fiercely. 'What is this place? You have to tell me.'

For a second, there was silence.

Then Zak said, 'That's something that people have to discover for themselves. We don't let them join us in the cavern until they've found out.'

Cam nodded vigorously. 'If they can't cope with *that*, then they're no use to us.'

He looked at her and then at Zak, trying to work out where this was leading. 'But I've joined you already. I'm here.'

'A most unusual situation.' Zak's smile had vanished now and his eyes were grave. 'Logically, we should send you out of here, to take your chance above the ground. Until you know.'

*But it's too cold. I'll die.* He realized, just in time, that he couldn't make that protest. He wasn't supposed to know anything about the world outside. Pulling the fur closer round his body, he stood firm, trying to appeal to their sympathy.

'Are you going to send me out like this? With nothing?'

What was this terrible secret that they couldn't just *tell* him? They must know what the temperature was like outside. Were they really going to send him out into that?

Cam's face was unrelenting. And when he glanced over his shoulder, the others avoided his eyes, staring down at the ground and scuffing the earth with their feet.

'He's got to go out,' someone muttered. 'He'll never believe it unless he sees for himself.'

They began to whisper to each other, gradually fixing on a single word. Almost under their breath, they began to chant, falling into a rhythm that hovered on the edge of his hearing.

'Out . . . out . . . out . . .'

Soon, Bando was the only one not chanting. He shook his head from side to side, looking wretched, as if he was trying to get rid of the sound. But the others ignored him, and the chant went on and on.

'. . . out . . . out . . .'

It was Zak who brought it to a stop. Lifting the little drum he was holding, he rapped on it twice, with his fingertips. Like magic, the murmuring subsided and everyone turned to face him, waiting for him to speak.

'This is a hard existence,' he said. 'We have to trust each other with our lives. We can do that because we all share the terrible knowledge of where we are. Because we've all been through the shock of finding out. Everyone must experience that.'

He nodded at Cam, and immediately she began to give orders. 'Ab—open up the tunnel. Dess and Shang—you take him through.'

Oh no. He wasn't having that. No one was going to drag him out, like a criminal. If he really had to go, he was going with his dignity intact. Lifting his head high, he turned his back on them all and started walking towards the entrance tunnel, holding the fur around himself, like a robe.

'That's our blanket,' Cam called after him. 'And we need it.'

At the same moment, Ab pulled a plug of branches out of the entrance tunnel and a swirl of icy air came billowing into the cave. Even through the blanket, he could feel how cold it was. He clenched his teeth, determined not to turn back and plead.

**SELF-CONTROL AND SELF-RESPECT GO HAND IN HAND**

But he knew he couldn't do it. It would be suicidal to go out into the cold without even a blanket to cover his body. He was about to give in, about to turn and beg, when something happened that altered the whole situation. From the far end of the cave, a voice shouted urgently.

'Fire!'

He did turn then, like everyone else. They all stared down towards the furnace and saw a cloud of smoke come billowing round one side of it, swelling out of the space behind.

# 20

He expected a mass panic, with all of them bolting past him, like the savages they were. Trampling him underfoot in their scramble to escape. But it didn't happen. No one moved except for Cam. She raced down the cavern, towards the smoke, and disappeared round the furnace. After a moment, she called out of the shadows.

'It's all right. There's no danger—it's almost burnt out already. But come and look at this.'

They all went together. If he'd wanted to run away from them, that would have been the ideal moment. But there was nowhere to go—except out into the cold air overhead. And that meant certain death. His only hope was to stick with them until he understood what had happened and where he was.

And that made the smoke important to him too.

He followed them, as unobtrusively as he could, into the cramped, crowded space behind the furnace. There was still smoke hanging in the hot, stale air, but the fire had gone. All that was left was a small heap of grey, fluffy ash, with a few stray sparks running through it.

And an arrow.

It was scratched into the earth ahead of them, pointing towards the ramp. Even in the dim light, the grooves were clearly visible. The shaft of the arrow was as long as his arm.

'What does it mean?' Ab said uncertainly. 'Is it a message?'

'Of course it is.' Cam bent down, moving forward as she traced the line. When she reached the point of the arrow, she stooped and lifted something off the ground. 'Look.'

The others pushed forward. Peering between their heads, he saw that Cam was holding the end of a primitive rope. The rest of it had been laid along the ground, so that it led down the ramp ahead of them and into the storeroom.

'It's . . . Lorn,' Annet said. 'That's what she did before, when she wanted us to come and save Bando. She's left us a trail to follow.'

'How can it be Lorn?' someone else said scornfully. 'We shut her in behind the wall. She could never have moved those stones on her own.'

Was that the name of the girl in the tunnels? Lorn? It looked as though she'd saved him again. But how long would it take these savages to work out who had moved the stones? And what would they do when they realized that he'd lied to them?

He was the one who almost panicked then. But a lifetime of self-control kept him from running. And it was justified. Clearly, no one was thinking about him at that moment. All their attention was on the rope.

Cam looked down at the end she was holding. 'So what do we do?' she said pensively. 'Are we going to do what she wants—after throwing her out of the cavern? How do we know this isn't some kind of trap?'

'Lorn wouldn't do that!' Bando said hotly. 'She wouldn't hurt us!'

Ab kicked at the pile of ashes. 'She tried to start a fire, didn't she? If she could do that—'

Zak shook his head firmly. 'That fire was never meant as a danger. It was just a signal, to draw our attention. Of course we must follow the rope. How else will we know the end of Lorn's story?'

That seemed like a completely ridiculous argument. Why go down into the darkness for something as trivial as a *story*? Surely even savages wouldn't be persuaded by such a triviality?

Clearly he didn't understand their primitive minds. They muttered to each other for a second and then Cam called out to someone called Perdew to fetch a torch. Guided by the unsteady light of a piece of glowing wood, they all began to move forward, picking up the rope and running it through their hands as they went down the ramp.

He watched them go, without any idea of following. But as the last person disappeared into the storeroom, Zak turned to him and held out the end of the rope.

'You too,' he said.

What had it got to do with him? He backed away, shaking his head. 'No thank you. I'm not interested in stories. I prefer real life.'

There was no reply. Just the rope end, held out to him, and Zak's steady blue stare. Something about that stare made him move forward, slowly and reluctantly, and take hold of the rope.

As his fingers touched it—as they felt the intricate, twisted pattern—he was hit by a shock of recognition. The rope was made of many separate strands (*he knew there were twelve, without counting*) intricately braided together into a neat, square plait. It was like . . . exactly like—

**NO. THIS IDEA IS NOT APPROPRIATE.**

Before his mind could make the comparison, some deeper part of his brain clamped tight, not letting him complete the thought. Recognition of the rope was clearly an impossibility. Smoothly, his mind produced a more correct idea.

**THIS IS A PRIMITIVE ROPE CLEVERLY PLAITED BY HAND THE DESIGN IS PRESUMABLY TRADITIONAL**

Zak watched him with a small, wry smile. 'This is your story too,' he said softly.

A flicker of fear danced at the edge of his mind. But he wasn't going to let himself be intimidated by a shabby, tinpot shaman. If it was necessary, he would follow the rope, but only on his own terms. As a detached observer.

Without wasting any breath on answering, he went down into the dark, after the others. And Zak came behind him, bringing up the rear.

The torch didn't last long. They were following not a single rope but half a dozen or more, knotted together in sequence. By the time his hands closed around the second knot, the wood had burnt away and Perdew tossed it to one side in a shower of sparks.

That sudden, dying brightness was gone within a few seconds. Now they were in pitch darkness, shuffling along one behind another. What were they expecting? What could there possibly be at the end of the rope that would justify this mindless procession?

In spite of his own precarious position, he almost took the risk of pointing out what an idiotic waste of energy the whole thing was. The words were actually forming in his mind, when Cam called out suddenly from in front.

'We've reached the end of the rope!'

Before anyone could react, a loud, clear voice shouted from ahead of them. 'And you've reached the next part of my story. Make a line across the tunnel, so that everyone can see.'

It was her, of course. The girl who'd saved him. Her voice was instantly recognizable—even though he had no idea what she was talking about. It seemed to make sense to the others though. They began to inch sideways, spreading out so that they stood side by side, staring forward.

He tried to squeeze in at one end, to watch without getting involved. But Zak seized his hand and pulled him right into the middle of the line. Wedged in between Zak and Bando, he had no chance of sneaking away.

The girl ahead of them didn't speak again until they'd stopped moving. When there was complete silence, her voice rang out again. This time, it seemed to be coming from somewhere higher up. She wasn't shouting now, but every word was clear.

'You've heard my story about three friends trying to rescue a prisoner. And Zak told you about the man whose daughter was stolen away from under the floor—'

(What? The words jerked him to attention. How had Zak come to be talking about that? *This is your story too,* he'd said. Did that actually mean something? Peering forward into the darkness, he tried to see the girl who was speaking, but he couldn't even work out exactly where she was. There was only her voice, continuing steadily.)

'You've listened to both of those—but no one has ever asked for the most important story of all. Have you even thought about it?'

No one attempted to answer her question. After a brief pause, her voice went on, uninterrupted.

'There's a story that goes right to the heart of what was happening, down in that black room. That's what I'm going to tell you now. I've brought you here to listen so that you can *see* and *feel* the truth of it. Are you ready?'

A small noise of assent, faint as a sigh, ran quickly along the line. He was the only one who didn't make a sound. He stood frozen, fighting the voice in his brain that told him to cover his ears and hang on to the truth he knew.

With a huge effort, he willed himself to hear what she was going to say.

And then she began. 'Once upon a time, there was a girl whose father kept her down in a hole in the ground . . . '

'Once upon a time, there was a girl whose father kept her down in a hole in the ground.'

From high on the shoulder of the great *THING* she'd built, Lorn listened to her words dropping into the silence. As she said them, she knew that she was telling the right story, at last. The one she knew and understood. Her voice grew stronger as the power came to her.

'Was the girl really precious and beautiful? What do you think? Down there, in the dark, she couldn't learn the things that other people do. She couldn't run or jump. She didn't know how to sing or argue—or even to speak properly. All she could do was make twisted patterns out of her own hair.'

She paused for a moment, controlling her anger. If she let it loose now, she would ruin everything. The story had to be quiet, right up to the moment of shock. The moment when she lit the fires. Until then, she must tell it softly, softly . . .

'Every day, for a few brief minutes, she was pulled up above the ground.' She closed her eyes, remembering the dazzling light and the terrible sickening fear. 'Her parents pushed food at her and forced her to try and walk. And her brother gibbered at her, calling her nonsense names.'

(*Prongo Hamster. H.Poor-garments. H.P.Strange-Room.*)

'No one ever told her she was meant to be special. She thought they kept her hidden because she was ugly. Stupid and clumsy and bad. Why else would they shut her away from the rest of the family, when they kept her brother up in the light with them?'

She could feel the warmth of the snail shell wedged next to her. Everything was ready now. The monstrous shape was made. Its two eyeholes were stuffed with white fluff. The embers in the shell would burst into flame when she blew on them. All she had to do was make sure the others understood.

That *he* understood.

'Maybe Zak was right,' she said. Sounding every word clearly. 'Maybe the man did put his daughter into the hole to protect her. In the beginning. But he never told her she was precious. And, in the end, he kept her there because he thought she was *his*, and he couldn't bear to set her free. That's what ruined and stunted and crippled her. And do you want to know what it did to *him*? Do you want to know what she saw, when the hole was opened and his arms reached down to drag her out? Do you want to see?'

She was shouting now, but it was all right, because she was there, at the right point. She'd told them everything she could—and now she was going to show them what it was like. Wrapping a blanket round her hands, she picked up the snail shell and blew on the glowing embers.

'He came like a *monster*!' she yelled. 'Like a terrible giant! Like *THIS*!'

Tipping the snail shell forward, she held it against the back of the great, hollow eyeholes. Instantly, the fibres inside burst into flame and, for the first time, the dark tunnel was filled with light. The fibres flared wildly, revealing the crowd of people and the hidden space that arched high above their heads. And in the very centre of the light, like a shape half-seen in a nightmare, loomed the great pillar of earth that she had built.

She knew how it must look to the dazzled eyes in front of her. Peering down from the shoulder of the monster she had made, she could see the others gazing up at it, awed by its size and terrified by the fire.

They understood at last. She could see them struggling to stay detached and calm, but they couldn't do it. The great earth shape compelled their attention, forcing them to see what she saw—a shadow that was too big to be seen clearly, because it dominated everything.

The wild fire flamed in the darkness, burning away Zak's cruel distortion of reality. Leaning forward into its light, she shouted down at them all.

'*Now* do you know which is the right story? Do you see why the robbers had to take the girl from under the floor?'

The heads below her turned towards her voice—and *his* head turned with them. She saw the shock on his face as he saw her for the first time. He took one step forward and then stopped, staring up in disbelief.

And she stared back at him. Looking down from the shoulder of her monstrous image.

# RIGHT: THE MAGEE MAN

# 21

'Magee,' said Tom. 'We have to go and find Magee.' He was shaking so much that he could hardly speak the words.

Emma had no idea what was going on. One moment Mr Armstrong had been standing over her, shouting at Tom and insisting that she was Hope. The next instant—for no reason that she could see—all the conflict had fizzled out. Mr Armstrong stepped aside, in a polite, bewildered way, leaving Tom staring down at her, like someone who'd just had an electric shock.

She didn't understand any of it. All she knew was that she was still a prisoner—and it was getting more and more frightening.

Her throat was already sore from yelling, but she opened her mouth and yelled again. 'Rob, are you there? *Rob!* I need you!'

Wonderfully, he appeared in the hatch, pushing Warren and Mrs Armstrong out of his way. Jumping down through the hole in the floor, he scuttled towards her, crouching under the low roof.

'What's going on? Are you all right, Em?' Then he saw Tom and Mr Armstrong. And Emma, with her cropped hair, lying parcelled up on the floor. Cautiously he stopped, trying to work out what was happening.

Tom looked round at him. 'We have to go and find Magee,' he said again.

'Untie me first!' Emma croaked. 'Please, Rob—'

'Of course we're going to untie you,' Robert said

fiercely. He pushed at Mr Armstrong's shoulder. 'Don't try and keep me away from my sister!'

Mr Armstrong stepped back, with a vaguely puzzled expression. 'So that's who she is. I wondered what she was doing down here.'

'What?' Robert was completely nonplussed. 'You know why she's here. You *kidnapped* her.'

'Oh dear,' Mr Armstrong said. 'I'm afraid that must have been my wife. Excuse me.' He squeezed past Robert and headed back to the hatch.

'What's going on?' Robert said wildly. 'What's happened?'

Tom shook his head, as though he was working out how to reply. But Emma interrupted, before he could say anything.

'Just get me out of here. *Please*. I can't bear any more. You've got to get me out.' Her voice cracked, as if she might start crying.

Instantly, Robert was on his knees on the ground beside her, fumbling at the knotted cords. 'Of course we're going to get you out. Hang on, Em. I'll get rid of these and then I'll get going on the tape. Don't just stand there, Tosh. Come and help.'

But before Tom could join them, there was a scraping noise overhead and a shadow fell across the hatch. Emma recognized what was happening straight away.

'They're trying to shut us in! Stop them! Don't let them fix the trapdoor down!'

Robert had never reacted so fast, not even on the basketball court. He was down at the other end while she was still shouting. Vaulting up through the opening, he hit the trapdoor with one shoulder, knocking it out of Mrs Armstrong's hands and sending her staggering backwards. Then he heaved himself out into the conservatory and sat on the door.

'I'll stay and keep the entrance open,' he called down to the others. 'Tosh—get Emma free as fast as you can.'

It had to be that way round. Tom would have been too light to stand up against Mrs Armstrong as she threw herself back towards the hole. Using all her weight, she charged at Robert, trying to knock him back into it.

She was completely hysterical. Robert pushed her away, but she came at him again, screaming to the other Armstrongs to come and help her. 'We mustn't let them get away! If they do, we've lost Hope for ever! We've got to keep them here!'

Warren was hovering wretchedly, just out of Robert's reach. He took a step forward and then jumped back when it looked as though he might get hit. But Mr Armstrong didn't move at all. He just stood by the door, with a faint, disapproving frown.

Down in the black room, Tom had undone the cords that tied Emma down. He'd started working at the parcel tape, using his keys to cut through it. It came off in untidy strips, leaving sticky patches on her clothes and pulling painfully at her skin. Once or twice she caught her breath with a small, involuntary moan, but she wouldn't let Tom slow down.

'I make a noise—ignore me. Just get this horrible stuff off, as fast as you can!'

She could hear the shouting overhead, and she was terrified that Robert wouldn't be able to keep the hatch open until she was free. As soon as her hands were loose, she began to help Tom, wrenching handfuls of sticky brown tape away from her legs.

That hurt even more. Her legs had gone numb, and when the feeling started to come back she had to bite her lips to stop herself crying out. But she went on pulling at the tape as fast as she could.

'We don't have to get it all off,' she muttered. 'Just enough for me to walk—'

Tom made an odd, doubtful noise in his throat. She didn't know what he meant—until she tried to stand up. Immediately, her legs buckled and she hit the ground.

'You probably need to wait a bit,' he said.

But Emma wasn't having any of that. 'If I can't walk—then I'll crawl. I'm not staying in here a moment longer.'

She dragged herself across to the hatch, calling out, 'Pull me up, Rob. Get me out!'

But before Robert could move, another voice intervened.

'Let me help you,' Mr Armstrong said politely. 'I've had many years of practice.' He came across to the trapdoor and knelt beside it, both arms reaching down into the hole.

Mrs Armstrong stopped screaming and stared at him. Gazing up from below, Emma could see the shock on her face. And she could see Warren too, frozen and terrified.

'What have you done?' Mrs Armstrong whispered. 'What have you done to my husband?'

Nobody answered. Mr Armstrong and Robert heaved Emma out of the hole and on to the only chair in the conservatory and she sat there, silently, rubbing her legs and blinking in the light.

It was the first time Robert had seen her properly. 'Your hair!' he said. 'Oh, Em—they've cut off your hair.'

'It'll grow back,' she muttered. 'Don't fuss. Just get me on my feet and take me home.'

With Tom and Robert supporting her, she managed to stand. As they started towards the front door, Robert looked back at Mrs Armstrong.

'Don't even think about following us,' he said. 'If we ever see you again, we'll go straight to the police.'

*Maybe we ought to have done that in the first place,* Emma wanted to say. But she had no breath to spare. She was concentrating on getting her legs to work. By the time they reached the bus stop, she could almost manage on her own.

'Better put on my coat,' Robert said, 'if we're going on the bus. You're covered in bits of tape. And what's that on your back?'

It was one of Warren's peculiar scraps of paper, caught on a sticky patch where the tape had been. Emma reached round to take it off, pushing it into a pocket as she took Robert's coat. Gratefully, she put on the coat and zipped it up, pulling the hood round her face.

Two minutes later, they were sitting on the bus, heading into the city centre. Emma leaned against the window, feeling the cold glass on her cheek. 'Do you think the Armstrongs will give up now?' she said. 'Do you think it's over?'

Robert frowned. 'How can we tell? They're so weird, aren't they? Look at Mr Armstrong just now. What was going on with him?'

'No idea.' Emma shook her head. 'When you came, he was in a frenzy, saying I was his daughter and he wasn't going to let me go. And then he just—changed. When he looked at Tom.'

'What did you do, Tosh?' Robert said lightly. 'Scare him witless?' Tom was in the seat in front. When he didn't answer, Robert leaned forward and prodded him in the back. 'Hey, what's the matter? Aren't you talking to us?'

'It's not that.' Slowly Tom turned round. 'It's just—I think I know what happened to Mr Armstrong. But I don't want to say anything. Not till I've talked to Magee.'

'What's it got to do with him?' That didn't make any sense to Emma.

'He—' Tom hesitated and then shook his head. 'No. I really need to talk to Magee. I'll go round to his flat as soon as we've taken you home.'

Emma sat up straight. 'Oh no you won't. Not on your own, anyway. If you've got to do it, then Rob and I are coming too.'

'You need to go home and recover,' Tom said. 'After what you've been through.'

'If I go home, I'm not going to get away in a hurry.' Emma grinned suddenly. 'Even Mum's going to ask questions when she sees me looking like this. If we're going to see Magee, it has to be now.'

Robert and Tom looked at each other, doubtfully.

'You don't have to come,' Robert said. 'Tosh will be fine with me. You need to have a rest, Em, and get back to normal.'

But Emma had no intention of being left out. She squared her shoulders and tossed her head, as though she still had hair to flourish. 'I'm in this up to the neck, as much as either of you. And if Magee can explain what's going on, I want to be there to hear him.'

# 22

*I must find Magee. He's the only one who can explain. I have to talk to him.*

That was the only thought in Tom's head. What had happened to Mr Armstrong—what *he'd done* to Mr Armstrong—was so frightening that he couldn't concentrate on anything else. And no one except Magee would understand. He had to get to Magee's flat as fast as he could.

When the bus reached the middle of town, the three of them got off and walked from there. By the time they reached Stepney Parade, Tom's heart was beating so fast that he could hardly breathe. As they went up the stairs from the street, he had to stop halfway, holding on to the wall. But his determination didn't waver.

*I'm not going away without seeing him. If he isn't in, I'll just sit on the landing and wait.*

There was no need for that. Magee was in. He opened the door immediately, as soon as Robert knocked. Tom drew a long breath and met his eyes, full on.

His head was full of words, but as soon as he saw Magee he realized that he didn't need to speak any of them out loud. Whatever had happened to him, Magee *knew*, just by looking at him.

'Welcome,' Magee said softly. 'It's time to talk at last.'

'It certainly is,' Robert said, impatiently, not giving Tom a chance to reply. 'We haven't got any more time for riddles. We need straight answers now.'

Magee's eyes flicked sideways, taking in Emma's filthy clothes and her ragged, cropped hair. 'I can see that,' he said. 'But don't worry. You'll get them.'

'Not out here, though.' Emma took a step forward. 'Can't we come inside?'

Her voice sounded brisk, as it always did, but Tom could feel the tension behind the words. She was tired and hungry, and the last twenty-four hours had shaken her badly. In spite of that, she didn't flinch under Magee's eyes. Lifting her head, she stared straight back at him.

After a second, he smiled and nodded. 'Glad to see you're all right—in spite of that thuggish hairstyle. Yes, you can come in.' And he stepped aside, waving them through the door.

The inside of the flat was completely unexpected. Tom was imagining a magician's den, full of candles and purple velvet drapes. But it was cool and bare, with very little furniture and blinds at the windows. The front door opened straight into a small living room with a glass table and two shabby armchairs. A ginger cat was curled up on one of the chairs and it lifted its head warily as they walked in.

'I'll fetch some stools from the kitchen,' said Magee. 'George doesn't care to be disturbed.'

He went through a door on the far side of the room and they heard him clattering around for a few moments. When he came back, he was carrying a stack of cheap plastic stools with a plate balanced on top of them.

'I thought we might have some shortbread,' he said easily, putting the plate down on the table. 'Don't wait for me. Help yourselves.'

Emma looked hungrily at the shortbread, but none of them bent to take a piece. They stood awkwardly, close together, while Magee arranged the stools in a semicircle, facing the empty chair. He took one of the stools himself and waved a hand, inviting them to sit down.

Emma sank quickly into the empty armchair. 'This feels like the most comfortable seat in the whole world.'

'You've obviously been somewhere very *un*comfortable,' said Magee.

'She was kidnapped,' Robert said roughly. 'Kept in a hole under a conservatory floor. I think you know the place.'

It was almost a question, but Magee didn't answer it. Instead, he asked one of his own. 'So how did she come to escape?'

'We guessed where she was,' Robert said. 'So we went to rescue her. And then Tom—and then Mr Armstrong—' He stopped.

Magee's head turned slowly. 'I thought it might be something like that,' he said. 'Can you tell me what happened, Tom?' His stare was so piercing that it hurt.

Tom looked down to avoid it. 'I didn't mean to do anything,' he muttered. 'I just meant to grab Emma and take her out of there. But when I saw all the Armstrongs together, I couldn't bear it. There was too much pressure. I just—' His voice died away.

Magee didn't let him stop there. 'You just—what?' he said.

'I—' Tom scrabbled for words to describe it. 'I looked at Mr Armstrong and I thought of the place. The way you told me to. And then I *pushed* with my mind, and suddenly—'

Faltering again, he lifted his head and saw everyone staring at him. Robert and Emma looked completely bewildered, but Magee was nodding.

'You found the power,' he said softly. 'You felt the trap they were in, with all its pain and anger. And you found out how to break through and set them free. Well done.'

'What do you mean?' Robert said irritably. 'What trap? *What* did he break?'

'He broke the pattern,' said Magee. 'The situation that was ruining all their lives. He tapped into the power of that pain and *used* it. To play the game.'

'The *game*?' Tom burst out. That was the last word he would have used. 'How can you call it that?'

Magee smiled. 'I call it the *Rescue Game*. Or sometimes *Magee's Cure*. Because it makes things better. And that's what you did. You saved them, Tom.'

Emma was still looking baffled. 'Who did he save—apart from me?'

'He saved all the Armstrongs,' said Magee. 'And especially Mr Armstrong.' He looked at Tom again. 'Isn't that right?'

*No, it's not,* Tom wanted to say. *It's WRONG. It must be wrong to interfere with someone's life like that.* But he wasn't sure any more. What he'd done, down in the black room, had broken the obsession that imprisoned all the Armstrongs. Wasn't that a good thing?

Robert was frowning, trying to understand what Magee was talking about. 'I don't get it,' he said. 'What does he mean? What did you *do*, Tosh?'

How could he be so obtuse? Wasn't it obvious by now? Tom was almost angry as he spelt it out. 'I did what Magee did to you. I *shrank* Mr Armstrong. Pushed him out of the life he was living and dumped him down on the ground, on his own. To live or die.'

As soon as he'd said the words, he saw that it hadn't been obvious at all. Robert and Emma looked horrified.

'That's impossible,' Emma said. 'You're not like that, Tom. You're good. You care about people.'

'Of course he cares about people,' Magee said wearily. 'That's the whole point. Why do you think he has headaches, and blurred vision, and bruises all over his body? That's what happens when you care too much—and you can't do anything to help.'

'I wasn't like that before I met you,' Tom said gruffly. 'Not the bruises and the headaches and everything. What have you done to me?'

'I *recognized* you,' said Magee. 'The first time I saw you, I knew you could be like me. All you needed was . . . sharpening up a bit. Once I'd done that, it was only a matter of time before you discovered the power.'

'I don't want power!' Tom said fiercely. 'Whatever you did, you've got to take it away. I just want to be an ordinary person.'

Magee shook his head. 'Your eyes are open now. You can see into people's lives. There's no going back on that. From now on, you have to live with the pain that brings. Or heal the pain by playing the Rescue Game.'

'You mean I'm going to be like this for ever?' Tom said. 'For the rest of my life?'

'It gets easier,' Magee said gently. 'Once you understand how much you're helping people.'

Robert almost exploded. '*Helping* people? How can you call it that? Don't you realize what it's like, down there in the cavern? They spend their whole lives struggling to protect themselves, and stay warm, and find enough to eat. And then—when it gets really cold—they die.'

'But everything they do has *meaning*,' said Magee. Suddenly his eyes were alight. 'What does it matter if their lives are short? Every single moment is significant and intense and vital. Isn't that better than what they've left behind?' His eyes sharpened, fixing on Robert's face. 'Are you trying to tell me it wasn't better for *you*?'

'I—' Robert hesitated and stopped.

Tom could feel his angry confusion. And he understood what was holding him back. Robert had changed, down in the cavern. He'd grown stronger and braver and more confident, shaking off the fears that had held him back before.

Wasn't that a good thing?

Emma was watching them both. Frowning, as though she was trying to puzzle things out. 'Let me get this straight,' she said slowly. 'Are you telling us Mr Armstrong is down in the wood, Tom? In the cavern?'

Tom nodded. 'I think so.'

'He's down there *now*?' Emma said. 'The way Robert was?'

What was the matter with her? Why couldn't she take it in? 'That's right,' Tom said. 'I know it's hard, but you've got to believe it, Em.'

Emma frowned again. 'So he's down there *with Hope*?'

The words hit Tom like a punch in the chest. He hadn't seen it. He hadn't thought, not for a moment, that he was doing *that*.

Robert obviously hadn't seen it either. Suddenly his face was white. 'He can't be in the cavern. He *can't*. They wouldn't let him in.'

'You've got to understand—' said Magee. But they never heard what it was they had to understand, because he broke off there. For a second he leaned forward intently, listening. Then he slid off his stool. 'Excuse me for a moment.'

As he strode across the room, there was a sound of scuttling feet outside. When he opened the front door the little landing was empty, but they could all hear the noises on the stairs. Someone was making a clumsy attempt to creep away without being caught.

Magee walked over to the top of the staircase. 'Ah,' he said, looking down. 'It's you. Why don't you come up and join us?'

The footsteps paused. Hesitated.

'It's perfectly safe,' Magee said. 'And we've got some shortbread.'

'What's he doing?' Robert muttered. 'We can't talk with some stranger here. We've got to find out—'

But it was too late to protest. The clumsy, blundering footsteps started again, but this time they were coming up. Tom saw Emma's face change suddenly, as though she recognized them. When they reached the landing, she turned round in her chair.

'Hello, Warren,' she said, as he appeared in the doorway.

Robert jumped to his feet. 'No,' he said. 'Not him, Magee. He can't come in here!'

'Sit down!' Magee said sharply. 'If you don't like the company I keep, you can go elsewhere.' He nodded at Warren. 'In you go.'

Warren stood frozen in the doorway, looking terrified. Tom could see the fear coming out of him, thick and suffocating, like stinking smoke.

'Go on.' Magee put a hand on his back and gave him a push. 'Have some shortbread.'

Warren lurched across the room and crouched down awkwardly to take a piece of shortbread. He crammed it into his mouth with both hands, peering at them over his fingers. The air pulsed in Tom's ears and when Robert spoke, the words thundered around his skull.

'You followed us here, didn't you?' Robert growled at Warren. 'You've been sneaking around, listening outside the door.'

Warren didn't answer. He just stared at Robert, as though he was too petrified to look away.

Robert glanced at Magee. 'He can't stay here. You've got to make him go.'

'We've heard a lot about what you want,' Magee said coldly. 'Maybe someone else should have a chance to speak.'

His voice was tenser than it had been. Through the black haze in his head, Tom thought, *He can feel it too. Warren's getting to him—and he doesn't like it.*

Warren had been following the conversation silently,

pushing shortbread into his mouth and looking from one face to another. He gulped down the mouthful he was chewing and rubbed his mouth with the back of his hand.

'Well?' said Magee, still in the same chilly, impatient voice. 'What have you got to say for yourself?'

For a second, Warren was struggling to speak. Then the words came in a rush. 'What's all that stuff about danger?' he blurted. 'And people freezing to death? Dad always said Hope would die, if anyone took her away. You've got to give her back. Where is she?'

'You wouldn't believe it if we told you,' Robert said bitterly.

But Warren wasn't going to be fobbed off like that. 'You think I'm stupid,' he said fiercely. 'But I'm *not*. I found out where you lived, didn't I? I scared you all. And I took your sister away—the same as you took mine.' His voice was rising, hysterically.

'Oh dear,' Magee said, under his breath. 'Oh *dear* . . .'

The stinking black fog thickened in front of Tom. He could still hear Warren's voice, but the pressure in his head was beginning to distort the words. He wasn't sure any more whether he was hearing right.

'I took your sister away,' said the hysterical voice, 'and I made her ***my other dame***, I made her ***tread my home***. I did it, and you couldn't stop me, even though you are ***the terror body***. You were just a ***red toy brother***—'

The words were incomprehensible nonsense, but the pain was real. More violent than ever before. And it was even worse because Tom knew, this time, that there was a way out. He couldn't—he mustn't—

But why not? If he didn't play the game, Magee would do it. What was the point in waiting for that? Why not do it himself? Now?

Dimly, through the fog, he saw Warren waving his hands about, talking faster and faster. '—you can't have

Hope as part of your ***rescue game***. She doesn't need ***Magee's cure***, whatever it is. ***Curse Magee—***'

Magee turned and looked straight at Tom, his blue eyes piercing the fog. His voice seemed to be speaking straight into Tom's brain. *What's stopping you? Can't you hear him? He's been driven mad. Completely ruined. Nothing's going to save him except a total change. That's what he needs . . .*

Almost without willing it, Tom began to picture the bank behind the hedge. The rough clods of earth and the tiny little stones . . . the great, gnarled trunks of the hawthorn bushes . . . the dead leaves, edged with frost . . .

Sending Warren there would plunge him into a new life, with a different name. It would shake everything up and give him another chance. How could that be wrong? Magee was right. He had to do it. He called up all the energy of his mind and felt the power come surging in.

But Emma was faster than he was. She leapt out of the chair and stood in front of Warren, facing the rest of them.

'Stop it!' she shouted. Her voice was clear and strong, cutting through the noise and the darkness inside Tom's head. 'I thought we were trying to help those poor people in the cavern. None of this is going to help *them*. And that's what we all want, isn't it? We've got to rescue them, before they freeze to death. We've got to rescue *Hope*—because she hasn't got any other body. If she dies down there, she's gone for ever.'

It was Magee's voice that answered her, thick with anger and frustration. 'You'd better give up on that. If she's down in the cavern completely—with no shell left behind—then that's the life she's chosen. You'll never get her back.'

# 23

'You'll never get her back,' said the man they called Magee.

That was the first thing Warren had really understood. When he was outside on the landing, he'd listened as hard as he could, but nothing he'd heard seemed to make any sense. Hope was obviously still alive, but why were they talking about caverns, and freezing? Was she in some kind of cellar?

Being hauled into the flat was the most terrifying thing that had ever happened to him. He would have refused to go if he hadn't needed to know what was going on. As it was, he'd gritted his teeth and made himself walk through the door.

And now he'd heard things he did understand. But he couldn't accept them. *You'll never get her back . . . that's the life she's chosen.*

How could that be true? Wherever they'd put her, it sounded like a horrible, dangerous place. He couldn't imagine her surviving for five minutes. He had to rescue her—somehow.

'Let me—let me talk to her,' he stammered. 'She—she can't really *want* to be there. Not Hope. I'm good at persuading her. When—when she wouldn't come out of her room before, I used to go down and talk to her. She likes that. Let me go and see her.' He looked desperately from Magee to the boy called Tom, not knowing which of them he was asking.

Neither of them answered, because Doherty stepped in

front of Warren and tugged at Tom's arm.

'If anyone's going into the cavern, it's me,' he said. 'You know it has to be me, Tosh. I'm her friend. Send me down there to fetch her.'

He sounded desperate. Almost pleading. Warren stared at him. Why would a bully like Doherty call Hope his friend? She didn't belong with him. She belonged in her own place, with her family. Wherever they'd put her now, she must be petrified. Warren could still see her small, bewildered face peering over Doherty's shoulder as he carried her off.

'Hope's nothing to do with you!' he said loudly. Standing up to Doherty made his whole body tremble, but he had to do it. 'She's *my* sister!'

'Why didn't you take care of her then?' Doherty whirled round in a fury. 'Why did you let your parents treat her worse than an animal?'

Confronting him was more terrifying than Warren's worst nightmares. He was taller than any boy ought to be, and his eyes were wild and menacing. But that didn't make him right about Hope.

'You—you don't understand,' Warren stammered. 'We had to protect her—otherwise she'd have died. That's what happened to Abigail. She was born first, and the social workers took her away. They put her in hospital—and she never came back. We had to stop that happening to Hope.'

Doherty and the others might not have seen the photo of Abigail on the sitting room mantelpiece, but they'd seen Hope. Why hadn't they realized that she needed protection?

'Hope can't manage on her own!' he said wildly. 'She's not like other people.'

'Did you never think,' Doherty said, and his voice was ice-cold now, 'that she was like that *because* they kept her under the floor?'

For a second, Warren couldn't speak. That had never occurred to him, not for a moment. But, now that Doherty said it, he had a sudden, devastating glimpse of what it would mean if he was right. If his parents had made a terrible mistake—if they'd ruined Hope by trying to keep her safe—then all the work and trouble and secrecy had been totally pointless.

And cruel.

The whole world of people and feelings and things shifted in his head, scrambling together like the letters in a name. Even the bones of his skull seemed to be shuffling themselves. His stomach lurched and he looked round frantically, knowing he was going to be sick.

Just in time, he felt Magee's hand on his back, pushing him towards the bathroom. He stumbled through the door and across to the toilet. Kneeling down in front of it, he vomited violently, over and over again. He felt as though he was turning inside out. Breaking into pieces.

The only steady thing was the pressure of Magee's hand on his back. It rested there until he sat back on his heels at last, empty and exhausted. Then Magee took a step back and watched, waiting for him to speak.

Warren looked down at the floor. 'It's not true,' he muttered. 'What Doherty said—it's not true.'

'You don't have to believe it,' said Magee. 'You can go home and forget all about it, if that's what you want.'

Yes. He could. For a moment, Warren saw the choice, quite clearly. All he had to do was stand up and walk out of the flat, clinging tightly to the world he knew. No one would stop him, if that was what he wanted. No one cared what he thought.

But he didn't stand up. The moment passed, and he was still kneeling on the bathroom floor, looking down at the carpet.

'How can I go away?' he said. 'Wherever Hope is, I have to find her. I need to know if she's safe.'

'Whatever happens,' said Magee, 'you won't get her back. Not the way she used to be.'

'It doesn't matter,' Warren said shakily. 'As long as she's all right. Please send me there.'

Magee's mouth twisted wryly. 'Ten minutes ago, I could have done it. But it's too late now. You've moved on. If you want to make anything happen you'll have to talk to the others.'

That meant Doherty and the other two. Warren could hear them muttering together in the living room. Normally, whispering made him sweat, because it meant he was going to be hurt, but this time that didn't seem to matter. When Magee held out a hand, he let himself be hauled to his feet. He let Magee lead him back through the kitchen and into the living room.

Doherty, Emma, and Tom were huddled together on the stools. As Warren came in, they looked up and he swallowed quickly, tasting the sourness in his mouth. He wished he'd remembered to rinse it out. He felt grubby and gross and repulsive.

'Sit down,' Magee said gently, pushing him towards the empty chair.

Warren sank down into the cushions without a word and the other three ignored him. It was Magee they'd been waiting for. They all began to talk at once, interrupting each other.

'There has to be a way of getting people out of the cavern,' Doherty said. 'If *I* came back—'

'—it *must* be possible for Hope!' That was Emma. She looked filthy and exhausted, but her voice was fierce. Why? Why did she care about Hope? Warren could hardly believe it.

The other boy—Tom—was leaning forward, frowning at Magee. '*How* did Robert come back from the cavern?' he said. 'What did you do?'

Magee perched on his stool, waiting for them to stop. Gradually their voices died away and he began to speak.

'I didn't do anything to bring Robert back. That was someone else. Someone down in the cavern.'

'Who?' Doherty said sharply. 'Who was it?'

Magee hesitated for a second. 'It was . . . a person with a different kind of power from mine. I thought I'd got rid of him a long time ago, when I first found out how to play the game. But he learnt another kind of strength, down on the dark ground—the strength that comes from choosing to be there completely, like Hope. To stay for ever.'

Doherty drew a long, slow breath. 'You mean Zak, don't you?' he said.

Magee nodded, watching his face. 'Yes, I mean Zak. My brother.'

For a moment, no one spoke. Doherty was staring at Magee, totally stunned, and Emma and Tom were looking at each other, uneasily. It was Tom who broke the silence in the end.

'Then why can't Zak do the same thing for all the others? Why can't he help *them* escape him?'

'Most of them don't want it enough,' Magee said wryly. 'Zak senses what people are feeling, even more than I do. He'll help anyone who really wants to make the journey—and believes that it's possible.'

'Robert's *shown* them it's possible,' Emma said quickly. 'So why don't they all—?'

She stopped. Magee was shaking his head at her.

'Too late,' he said. 'It's already too cold for travelling. And by the time the winter's over, Zak will be dead.'

Emma stared at him. 'How can you possibly know that?'

'He's my brother.' Magee shrugged. 'I can see you don't understand the strength of that—yet. But you will. And when you do, imagine what it's like for two brothers who can both feel what people are thinking. The way Tom can.'

Tom shivered, but he didn't say anything. It was Doherty who spoke, very slowly, as though the words were hard to say. 'So you mean—no one else is going to escape from the cavern the way I did? They've missed their chance?'

Magee nodded. 'They have. Unless—' He looked up, meeting Robert's eyes full on. 'A person who decides to stay in the cavern for ever—like Zak—has the power to help everyone else escape. If that's what she chooses . . . '

He let his voice fade away. There was no need to finish the sentence out loud. Even Warren knew he was talking about Hope.

*But—*

Warren waited for the others to argue, to say the thing that seemed obvious to him. But no one said a word. In the end, he blurted it out himself, stumbling and stuttering because he was so frightened.

'B-but that's not *fair*! How could Hope make a choice like that? She—she's not *like* other people. She doesn't know anything about the world. How could she choose without understanding anything?'

Magee shrugged. 'All she needed to do was recognize the place where she belonged. The place where she could be most herself. Are you surprised she chose the cavern?'

Half an hour ago, Warren would have disagreed, blindly, contradicting everything Magee had said. Now he forced himself to think. What would Hope be like, if she was free to be *most herself*? What would she want then?

'Suppose she's changed her mind?' he said slowly. 'If she's different, she might want to make a different choice.'

Magee raised his eyebrows. 'You can go and call her, if you like. If you call hard enough, she *might* choose again. But I think you'll be disappointed. And what about the others? As things are, she could take over from Zak when he dies—and give them a chance of escaping. If she leaves, they'll lose that chance.'

Doherty looked up sharply, but Warren didn't care about any *others*. 'Hope should have a proper chance too,' he said doggedly. 'Where do we have to go to call her?' Magee didn't answer and he looked round at Doherty and Tom.

Doherty's face was wretched. 'Calling's no use,' he said miserably. 'She won't hear us properly. Down in the cavern, our voices just make a kind of rumbling sound.'

'That's it then,' said Magee. 'There's nothing else I can tell you.' He stood up to open the front door.

'No,' said Warren. '*Please*.'

He still had no idea where Hope was. The more they talked, the weirder it sounded. But he had something to cling on to at last, and he wasn't going to let it go.

Magee stopped, with his hand on the door handle. 'Please what?' he said.

'Please tell me where Hope is,' Warren said nervously. 'I don't understand what's going on, but I have to go and call her, if that's the way to get her back. Only I don't know where—'

'Don't tell him!' Doherty rounded on Magee. 'If you do, he'll tell his parents. And they'll try—they'll go and—and—' He stopped, shaking his head in frustration.

'I'm afraid you need him,' Magee said smoothly. 'If you're offering Hope the chance to choose again, you can't shut out any part of her life.'

Doherty looked uncertainly at the other two. 'We can't tell him. It would be like sending Hope back to that horrible hole in the ground.'

'No, it wouldn't,' Tom muttered. 'It was Mr Armstrong who made that happen, and now he's—not there. Don't you understand? That changes everything. If we do manage to get Hope back, she'll be able to go home.'

'Can we trust you?' Emma said. 'If we tell you, will you promise to keep the secret?'

Warren felt as though he was jumping blindfold off a cliff. How could he promise without knowing what it was? *No,* said his brain. *Don't do it.*

Only—what would happen if he didn't?

He turned round, wildly, to look at Magee, remembering that steady hand on his back. 'What should I do?' he said. 'What's the right thing?'

'It's your choice,' said Magee. 'No one can make it for you.'

There was nothing reliable any more. No list of regulations, to tell him how to act. Warren closed his eyes and took a leap in the dark.

'All right,' he said. 'I promise.'

'Let's get going then,' said Emma. She glanced at Magee. 'What is it we have to do?'

'I told you,' said Magee. 'You have to go there and call her. That's all. Except—wait a moment.'

He went quickly into the bedroom and came out with an old grey blanket, pulled straight off the bed. Rolling it up, he held it out to Emma.

'You'd better have this. Just in case something does happen.'

Emma looked at the blanket for a moment and then tucked it under her arm. 'All right,' she said. 'But I still don't really know what we're doing. *How* do we call her?'

Magee gave another of his strange little smiles. 'You just call her name,' he said. 'That's all. If you need anything else, you'll have to ask Warren. He knows all about it. Only—he doesn't *know* that he knows. You'll have to help him work it out.' He opened the door and stood back, to let them through.

Emma went first, with Doherty close behind. Tom signalled to Warren to follow them. Stepping into the hallway, Warren heard Tom mutter to Magee.

'What *are* you? You're not like me.'

'No, I'm not,' Magee said softly. 'But you might be like me, one day. If that's what you want.'

And then he let Tom out and shut the door.

# 24

Without Warren, they wouldn't even have got there. They'd used up most of their money already, catching the bus to Magee's flat. When Robert put his hand in his pocket, at the bus stop, all he found was a handful of copper coins. Tom was no better off, and Emma had nothing at all. Mrs Armstrong had taken her backpack, with everything in it.

'No—no it's all right,' Warren said quickly. 'I can pay for everyone.' He pulled out a note and flapped it in front of them. 'That's enough for us all.'

Robert looked at the money in that fat, pale hand and wished he didn't have to take it. But it was their only chance of getting there before it was completely dark.

'Thank you,' he said gruffly. He wished Warren would stop looking at him in that wide-eyed way, as if he was some kind of freak.

He'd want to know everything now, of course. As soon as they were on the bus, he would expect them to explain where Hope was, and why. Robert didn't know where to begin.

*Your sister's in another hole in the ground. She chose it instead of coming back to the one in your house, even though it's smaller. Much, much smaller.*

Warren was never going to believe that. He probably wouldn't even believe when they showed him. He wasn't clever enough to understand—you only had to look at his face to see that.

As soon as the bus came, Robert jumped on. He went

straight down the bus, leaving Warren to buy the tickets, and sat next to a fat woman with a screaming toddler on her lap. At least he could avoid the questions until they were actually there. He didn't want to talk to Warren. He wanted to think.

All the others were focused on getting Hope out of the cavern, because she was the only person they knew down there. But it was different for him. He couldn't help thinking about Bando and Cam. About Annet and Shang and—and every single person who had helped him and shared with him and been his friend. Was he going to take away their chance to be saved?

What was right? How could he possibly choose?

He saw Emma come down the bus to sit next to Warren. How could she bear to be near him, after what he'd done to her? Warren sat with his head down, frowning, and Emma didn't speak to him. But when they reached the stop at the side of the park, she touched his arm.

Warren jumped. 'We're getting off here?' He looked round, startled, as if it was the last kind of place he had expected.

'That's where we lost Hope,' Emma said. 'Didn't your father tell you?'

Warren shook his head, staring apprehensively into the wood. For a moment, Robert wondered what Mr Armstrong *had* said to make him so frightened. But he wasn't going to ask. He walked briskly down the bus and stepped out on to the pavement.

As the bus pulled away, they went into the wood, following the path in single file, with Robert leading the way. When they reached the hedge, he stepped off the path and turned along the ditch. It was almost dark now, and the sky was completely clear. It was going to be a very cold night.

If they didn't rescue Lorn now, the winter was likely to kill her too. Then she wouldn't be able to help anyone.

They *had* to call her.

When they were level with the tunnel entrance, he stopped, looking across the ditch. 'We're here,' he said in a flat voice.

The hedge bank was a shadow in front of them, with the black, twisted bushes of the hedge rising out of it, almost completely leafless now. Warren stared ahead for a second and then looked round wildly.

'Where?' he said. 'I don't understand. Where is she?'

'Hang on,' said Tom. 'I've got a torch.'

They never did that. They never used torches in case people came to see what was happening. But they'd taken so many risks already that one more didn't seem to matter. Robert didn't protest as Tom took out his little torch and switched it on.

The beam was weak and narrow. Tom had to hunt for a few moments, shining it up and down, before he found the right hole in the bank, among all the other almost identical holes. When he'd worked out where it was, he held the light steady on the entrance.

'There you are,' he said evenly. 'That's where she is.'

For a second, Warren looked bewildered. Then an expression of horror came over his face. 'You've *killed* her,' he whispered. 'You've killed her—and buried her in the park.' He sounded terrified.

'Of course we haven't killed her,' Robert said impatiently. 'Why would we be bothering to do this if we thought she was dead? She's alive, under the earth, but she's very, very small.'

'How small?' Warren whispered. He could hardly get the words out.

Robert lifted his right hand into the torchlight, holding the thumb and forefinger a couple of centimetres apart.

'You don't have to believe it,' he said. 'But I've been there. I *know* it's true.'

Warren stared at the fingers without moving, as though he'd turned to stone. After a moment, Emma touched his arm.

'It's all unbelievable,' she said gently. 'When Robert and Tom first told me you had a room under your conservatory, I thought they were being ridiculous. But that was true. And so is this.'

'And anyway,' said Tom, 'what have you got to lose? We're only asking you to call Hope's name. Nothing difficult.'

*But it* is *difficult,* Robert thought. Were they meant to make a loud noise or call softly? One after another, or all at once? Who was going to begin? He glanced at the others, feeling stupid and embarrassed. And afraid too, in an odd, irrational way.

'I suppose we've just got to . . . go for it,' Emma said awkwardly. She knelt down carefully and called in a low voice. 'Hope? Are you there?'

Nothing happened. She called again, repeating the name for almost a minute, but when she stopped, nothing had changed. The dark wood was still, except for the noise of cars beyond the trees.

'Let's do it together,' said Tom. 'That's what Magee said.'

He knelt beside her and the two of them called in unison. 'Hope! Please come. Hope!'

The sound sank into the earth and disappeared among the dark intertwined branches of the hedge.

*Of course nothing's happening,* Robert thought bitterly. *It was never going to work. We can't save Lorn, and she won't be alive to save the others either. Magee just wanted to get rid of us, so he sent us here to make fools of ourselves.*

He shook his head angrily, trying to blot out the mocking, cynical voices in his head. To stop himself thinking about them, he crouched down quickly on Emma's other side. Without waiting for the others, he called into the darkness.

'Hope!'

As soon as he'd said it, he knew that he'd used the wrong name. Because it wasn't Hope he wanted—that pathetic, stunted girl with her matted hair. He wanted Lorn, his friend. Lorn, who'd risked her life to save him.

Leaning forward, over the ditch, he called again. 'Lorn! You can't stay there. You'll freeze to death. Please come out. *Lorn!*'

And it still didn't work. Of course not. How could it be that simple? *He'd* had to make a long, dangerous journey to get back to his full size. He'd seen Nate die and risked his own life crossing the road. Wasn't that how it had to be? Wasn't the suffering the price you had to pay?

'Lorn!' he called into the shadows, again and again. Hearing his voice start to crack.

What was Warren doing? Glancing over his shoulder, Robert saw that he was still standing behind them, like a lump of lard. Probably laughing like crazy inside his head. The three of them must look ridiculous, kneeling in the mud and talking to a hedge.

'Magee said you had to do this too,' Robert hissed savagely. 'Come on.'

Warren stumbled forward and lurched down on to his knees next to Robert. 'What do I do?' he muttered.

What had Magee said? *Warren knows all about it. Only—he doesn't know that he knows.* Huh! That made about as much sense as the rest of it. Robert turned his head slightly, just enough to see Warren's fat face. 'You heard what we were doing. Just join in and *call.*'

'Oh. Yes.' Warren cleared his throat nervously. Then he looked sideways at Robert, waiting for him to start.

*This is farcical. How can it change anything? Let's just get it over, so we can say that we've done it.* Robert tried to ignore the heavy sound of Warren's breathing as he called again. 'Lorn! Where are you?'

Tom and Emma joined in. 'Hope! Hope—come out.'

And after a second, Warren added his voice to theirs, sounding stiff and unconvincing. 'Hope. Hope, we're calling you. Come here, Hope.'

Nothing. They waited, holding their breath and staring at the hedge bank, but nothing had changed. Except that the bank had grown darker while they knelt there. The air around them was colder and the little circle of light from Tom's torch looked more and more feeble and pale. Robert could feel the chill of the earth seeping into his body.

'How long are we going on with this?' he muttered. 'We've done what Magee said, and it hasn't worked. I can't bear much more.'

'Let's give it one more try,' said Emma. 'Just so we know we did the best we could.' She gave Warren an encouraging smile. 'Give it all you've got.' Sinking back on to her heels, she called in a low, intense voice. 'Hope! Please come.'

Obediently, Warren joined in. 'Hope? Are you there? Hope—'

Tom was on the verge of calling too. But he stopped suddenly, catching his breath. 'There's something wrong,' he said abruptly. 'I can feel—'

'Someone watching?' Robert looked round sharply.

'No. Nothing like that.' Tom hunted for words. 'It's more . . . a sort of obstacle. As if—'

'Yes?' said Robert. And then, when he didn't answer, 'Oh, go *on,* Tosh. Don't fool around. What kind of obstacle?'

'Someone's holding something back,' Tom said hesitantly. 'When we call Hope, someone's not really doing it.'

'But that's silly.' Emma shook her head. 'You've heard us all. How else can we do it?'

*'Warren knows,'* Robert said. Speaking the words that kept going round and round in his mind. *'Warren knows all about that—but he doesn't know that he knows.* He's the one who's holding back.'

'But I'm not—I can't—what do you want me to do?' Warren said frantically. 'I called her, just like everyone else. I called—'

'—just like everyone else,' Emma said slowly. 'But you're not like the rest of us, are you? You're her brother. And you like *playing with names.* You like—wait a minute.' She was still wearing Robert's coat and she began to hunt in the pockets, feeling for something.

'What is it?' said Robert. 'What have you got?'

Emma took out a crumpled piece of paper and pulled it straight. 'Quick, Tom. Shine the torch so I can see if I'm right.'

Robert leaned closer, trying to read what was written on the paper. It looked like a list of nonsense to him. *MY OTHER DAME . . . MARY THE DEMO . . . MEMORY DEATH . . .* But Emma ran her finger down it and then turned on Warren.

'They're all *me,* aren't they? All anagrams of my name.'

'I—I—' Warren was stuttering so much that he couldn't speak.

'Hope likes patterns,' Emma said excitedly. 'And so do you—but you make yours out of letters. When she gave you a braid for your bag, did you give her something back? Did you jumble her ordinary name and make her a new one?'

*'That's* the one you should be using,' said Tom. 'Because that's what you call her in your mind. Come on. What is it?'

'No,' Warren said. Very fast. 'No, it's nothing. I can't—'

'Of course you can,' Robert said impatiently. He reached across and took the torch out of Tom's hand. 'Come on. If you don't tell us—'

He twisted round and pointed the torch at Warren. He didn't really mean to threaten him. He just wanted him to know that he had to tell them his private name for Hope. That there was no chance of keeping it secret. So he pointed the torch straight at Warren's face.

And he saw—terror.

Warren's mouth was frozen open and his eyes were staring. He couldn't have spoken if he'd wanted to.

*He can't be afraid of* me, Robert thought. *Not like that. He can't.*

But he was. There was no escaping it. Robert recognized the fear he'd felt himself when he saw his friend Nate in the hedge-tiger's jaws. The fear that had paralysed him when he lay flat on the road, tiny and defenceless, as a gigantic car roared over him in the dark. To Warren, *he* was like that. A monster too huge to escape from, too big to fight.

*That's not fair. That's not how I am.*

But it was a waste of time to think like that. There was only one way to stop frightening Warren. It felt like the hardest thing he'd ever done, but he made himself turn the torch, to show his own face.

'I'm sorry,' he said. Trying to look as though he meant it. Trying to *mean* it. 'I shouldn't have bullied you. I just—' The words were true, but saying them to Warren made them as bitter as ashes in his mouth, 'I just can't bear the idea of losing her. But I will, unless you help me. Please, Warren. Please call her properly.'

'I—I—' They could hear Warren breathing hard in the dark. Struggling to speak. 'They're all stupid,' he said at last. 'I just can't—'

*I'll do anything to get her back.* Robert had thought it

inside his head a million times. But he hadn't thought it would be so hard when it happened. He hadn't expected it to be so painful. *'Please,'* he said again. He reached out and touched Warren's arm, turning the torch just enough to see him.

Warren still looked afraid. But now his mouth was trembling. 'Her name isn't very good for patterns,' he said. 'Not like Emma's. I kept making new ones, and she liked that, but they're all stupid. You'll laugh.'

'No we won't,' Emma said gently. 'I promise we won't.'

Robert tried to imagine what it must be like to be so afraid of something like that. 'We won't laugh,' he said. 'Just tell us. What do you call her?'

Warren took a long deep breath and looked down at the ground. 'I call her *H. Poor-Garments,'* he mumbled. *'Hoprag Monster, H.P. Strange-Room, Prongo Hamster, Honest Program, Graphomonster . . .'*

Long before he finished, he was in tears.

# 25

From the shoulder of the great earthen pillar, Lorn looked down at her father and knew that she was safe. He was smaller than the image she had made—and too clumsy and heavy to climb its steep, high sides.

When she leaned forward, to see him better, the flaming eyes threw her shadow long and dark across his face. He knew who she was. She could see that in his eyes. And she could see that he understood the image, too. That it had shocked him.

He'd heard her story.

The others were shocked too. Annet was gazing up at the monster, white with disbelief, and Perdew's mouth was tight and twisted, as if the sight was painful. All along the line, the faces Lorn knew so well—the faces of her friends—showed that they were seeing what she meant them to see.

Except for Bando, of course. He was frowning angrily and clenching his fists, but he didn't really understand. 'I would have rescued that girl!' he said fiercely. 'If I'd been with the robbers, I would have broken the door down and saved her! I would have *killed* her father!'

It was true. He would. And if that was the kind of justice she wanted, all she had to do was point a finger and shout. *He's there! He's standing next to you!* Still caught up in the story she'd told, Bando would have turned and seen—what she wanted him to see. He would have lashed out, using all his massive, simple strength, confident that what he was doing was right.

All she had to do was point.

But she knew, at once, that she wasn't going to do it. If she used Bando like that, she would have to spend the rest of her life clinging to her own version of the story, to justify what she'd done. And maybe she didn't understand it all yet. Maybe there was more to discover.

The white fluff burnt brightly, but very fast. For a few seconds, she let everyone stare at it, while she watched her father's face. It looked the same as it had all her life. Cold and stiff. Almost expressionless. But now she sensed that he was afraid. Perhaps he'd always been afraid.

Before the others had recovered from their shock, the flames died down, leaving only a few sparks chasing each other through the ashes. Lorn slipped off the shoulder of the image and began climbing down towards the tunnel floor.

She was only halfway down when the rumbling started.

In the cavern, they heard noises like that all the time. They were made by the huge figures that walked through the wood, shaking the earth and talking together like thunder. The sound was part of the ordinary fabric of their lives and they'd all learnt how to ignore it.

But this time it was much closer than usual—low over the tunnel entrance—and it had an odd, repetitive beat. Lorn could feel the vibrations all through her body. She slid the rest of the way to the ground and caught at Zak's hand.

'What is it?' she whispered. 'What's happening?'

'Hope?' said her father's voice. 'Are you there?'

She sensed his hands fumbling towards her and she sidestepped instinctively, to avoid him. 'Zak! What is it?' she asked again.

Zak didn't answer. She could feel him listening as the rumbling stopped for a moment and then began again, more insistently. It was starting to unsettle the others now.

'Let's get back to the cavern,' muttered Dess. 'Everything's weird down here.'

'Don't be such a coward.' That was Cam, speaking briskly to keep them all calm. 'That noise hasn't got anything to do with us. Has it, Zak?'

Zak ignored that question too. 'Lorn,' he murmured. 'Can you find a faster route than the way you brought us?'

Lorn smiled to herself in the darkness. She'd made sure that the journey there was as long as possible, to give their torches time to burn out. Trust Zak to realize that. The straight way home would only take a few minutes.

The flames had gone completely now, and people were beginning to blunder around in the dark. Raising her voice, she said, 'Hold hands in a line and I'll take you back.'

She took Bando's hand very quickly—to avoid her father's—and waited while the others shuffled into place. Cam made them call out their names, all the way down the line, to check that no one was left behind. Then Lorn started forward, leading the way.

And all the time they could hear the strange, staccato rumbling.

It was very close and with every step it seemed to get closer. By the time they reached the wall, it was almost directly over their heads. Lorn led Bando right up to the opening in the secret passage and then slid her hand away.

'Here you are,' she said. 'All you have to do now is crawl through to the storeroom.'

'Aren't you going first?' said Bando.

Lorn shook her head at him, even though he couldn't see. 'You've forgotten,' she said gently. 'I'm not allowed to come. I have to stay down here.'

They'd all forgotten. She felt the shock go down the line as they remembered.

'You mustn't stay.' Bando caught hold of her hand again. 'Come on, Lorn. I'm not letting anyone through before you.'

'Stop it, Bando,' Cam said unhappily. 'You know we have to keep the rules. If Lorn comes through—'

'Lorn *must* come through,' said Zak, interrupting her. His voice was loud and forceful. 'Don't worry—the rules will all be kept in the end. But she has to come up to the cavern.'

He hardly ever spoke like that, but when he did, no one argued. Bando stepped aside and Lorn went down on her knees and crawled into the passage, lying on her stomach and dragging herself along with her elbows.

She was expecting Bando to follow her, but somehow her father managed to slip in before him. As she scrambled out into the storeroom, she could hear him scrabbling behind her, dragging at the stones as he squeezed through the narrowest part of the passage.

The rumbling voices sounded much louder once she was through the wall. It was impossible to understand them—impossible to make out any words at all—but she couldn't stop listening. The noise nagged at her mind and she knew there was something about the rhythm that she ought to understand. Some kind of pattern. But she couldn't work out what it was.

Her father heaved himself out of the tunnel and began to feel around for her. 'Hope?' he muttered. 'Are you there?'

Silently she sidled away, towards the foot of the ramp. She could hear Bando blundering through the passage now, but she didn't wait for him. She walked straight up the ramp, as fast as she could. As she came out into the space behind the brazier, she heard her father stumbling between the heaps of grain in the storeroom.

It was as she stepped into the main cavern that the pattern of the rumbling suddenly changed. Until then, it had been a steady, simple rhythm, worked out in single beats. Now, suddenly, there was another strand. A pattering, intricate, polysyllabic thread that wove its way in and out of the others.

The noise drummed in her ears, shaking every cell of her body. It was more than a sound. It belonged to her, in some way that she couldn't quite grasp. Why not? Why couldn't she remember? She began to walk down the cavern, towards the entrance tunnel.

By the time the others arrived, she was crouching by the entrance, reaching in to pull out the clump of branches that blocked it. Annet ran towards her and caught at her arm.

'What are you *doing*?' she scolded. 'Come away from there! It would be crazy to go outside now.'

'That's for Lorn to decide,' said Zak. He was still at the other end of the cavern, but his voice carried clearly. 'What can you hear, Lorn? What are the voices saying?'

Lorn stood up, knowing and not knowing. 'They . . . want me,' she said slowly. 'They want me to go out there. To go back.'

Her father moved suddenly, appearing round the brazier. 'You mustn't go!' he shouted. 'You'll freeze to death out there!'

He started towards her as though he meant to grab her and pull her away from the entrance by force. But he was only halfway when Zak bellowed after him.

'Stay where you are! Don't meddle with things you don't understand!'

Lorn saw her father pause for a second, turning round to bellow back. 'I can't let her go! *She's my daughter!*'

As soon as the words were spoken, he realized what he'd said. There was a long, horrified gasp from Annet, and another from Perdew. Lorn could see the revulsion on their faces as they looked at her father.

And she saw his face too, as she'd never seen it before. He looked hesitant and uncertain, as though his own words had shaken him.

'She's not yours,' Zak said. Almost gently. 'She's bound to us. She chose this life in the cavern in preference to everything else.'

He began walking towards Lorn, down the length of the cavern. She felt as though his eyes were seeing right into her head, as though he could hear what she was thinking. *But suppose I don't want to stay after all? Suppose I've changed my mind?* She turned her face away, to stop him picking up the other voice, that sounded even deeper in her mind. The voice that said, *Robert* . . .

But Zak wouldn't leave her even that much privacy. He caught her chin in his hand and made her turn towards him. 'You chose this place,' he said. And his blue eyes were relentless now. 'You chose the cavern—and all of us—and that makes you special. We can't let you go, unless you give us something in exchange.'

'But I haven't got anything,' Lorn said. 'You know I've never had anything, outside this cavern.'

She heard her father catch his breath, as though he'd been hit, but she had no time to work out what that meant. Pulling away from Zak's hand, she stepped nearer to the entrance.

'Don't even think of going,' Zak said implacably. 'Not like that. You'd just be going back to the misery you left before. To the underground prison and the poor stunted Hope who couldn't walk or talk. Is that what you want?'

'But they're *calling* me—'

'So what are you going to give us?'

Zak didn't move his eyes from her face—but Lorn had a curious sense that he wasn't looking at her any more. She could feel him listening for a sound from somewhere else in the cavern. But when she glanced over his shoulder, everything was very still, except the flickering light from the brazier.

'I haven't got anything,' she said desperately. 'But I *must* go. Please—'

There was no softening of Zak's expression. She could see that he wasn't going to change his mind and allow her to leave. A wave of despair surged up in her mind, so black and vast that it almost blotted out everything else. *They'll never let me go—*

And then it happened. The last thing she was expecting. Her father came walking down the cavern towards her, brushing past Zak as though he hadn't seen him.

'You do have something,' he muttered. 'You have me.'

'What?' Lorn couldn't take in the words. 'What do you mean?'

'I'll stay here in your place. If they'll have me.' He looked over his shoulder, at Zak. 'Is that a fair exchange?'

For a second, Zak watched him, not answering. Then he said, 'Is that your choice? Made of your own free will?'

Lorn wanted to hear her father say yes. Wanted it so much that she could hardly breathe. But she knew it wouldn't be right. She made herself speak, forcing the words out quickly, while she still had the courage.

'He can't make that choice. He has no idea what it would mean. He doesn't even know where we are—or *what he is.*'

'Perhaps that doesn't matter to him,' Zak said softly. 'Maybe he wants to stay in your place whatever that means. It all depends on his reason. Why don't you ask him?'

Lorn lifted her head and made herself look full into her father's face. He looked awkward and uncertain, and the idea of asking the question filled her with revulsion. She didn't want to know what he felt. Didn't want to be that close.

But Zak wasn't going to let her escape. '*Tell* her, Daniel,' he said. 'Tell her why you want to stay in her place.'

Lorn saw her father's eyes slide away, as though Zak had embarrassed him. 'She saved my life,' he said stiffly. 'Without her, I would have died down in those tunnels. I owe her something in return.'

It wasn't enough. Lorn didn't know what she wanted, but it wasn't that. Zak clicked his tongue disapprovingly.

'*I owe you something* won't do,' he said. 'Lorn needs the truth. Your real reason.'

'She's my daughter. I have a duty to protect her—'

This time the words were defensive and hasty. And they didn't please Zak any more than the first answer. He shook his head sternly.

'Duty has no place in this. Anything we take in Lorn's place must be freely given. If you're not doing that, then the exchange fails.'

Lorn felt her father waver, holding back from giving a third answer. She could still hear the voices rumbling overhead, calling out to her, but she was suddenly afraid that they were tiring and fading away. It was that fear that pushed her into speech at last.

'Please,' she said. 'If you have a reason, please tell me—'

Her father raised his head and looked at her. When he spoke, his voice was harsh and low, as if every word was painful. 'I want you to be happy,' he said. 'Because you're the most precious thing in my life. And I love you. You have to believe that.'

She couldn't bear it, just as she'd known she wouldn't be able to bear it. But she knew that she couldn't refuse what he was offering, because refusal now would be the worst, the unkindest thing of all. There had to be a way of accepting what he'd said. And acknowledging how much it had cost him to say it.

Shakily, she took a single step towards him, coming so close that she could see her reflection in the centre of his eyes. Her arm trembled as she reached out towards him.

'I'm not sure I understand,' she said—and her voice was as raw and rough as his had been, 'but, yes, I believe you. Thank you—'

*Thank you, father,* was what she meant to say. But her mouth wouldn't make the sound. She reached for a name that she was able to speak instead.

'Thank you . . . Daniel,' she said. 'Thank you for what you're doing.' And, reaching a little further, she brushed the back of his hand very lightly, with the tips of her fingers.

He gave her a long look, staring into her face as if he was trying to learn it. Then he stepped back, glancing towards Zak.

'Is that good enough?' he said. 'Can she go?'

Zak met his eyes. 'There won't be another chance for you,' he said. 'Is this really what you want? Are you sure?'

'I'm sure,' Daniel said.

Zak turned quickly to Lorn. 'Then hurry,' he said. '*Hurry*—before they stop calling you.'

She looked down the cavern. At Perdew and Annet and Dess. At Cam—and all the others who'd been her friends and her family for so long. 'What about everyone else?' she said. 'Am I the only one who's going to get away? Has no one else got a chance?'

Zak's reaction startled everyone. He threw his head back and gave a joyful shout of laughter. 'That's a question for my brother,' he said. 'When you find him, say, *Zak has found someone to take over after the winter*. Make him tell you what that means. Now *go*! Before those people outside lose hope and stop calling you.'

For one last second, Lorn stared down the cavern, trying to fix everything in her mind. Then she threw herself on to her hands and knees and began crawling through the entrance tunnel as fast as she could. Crawling into the huge, cold world outside . . .

They couldn't keep it up any longer. It was never going to work. Robert could hear Emma's voice wavering, could hear Warren starting to cry again, this time with disappointment.

'One last call!' he said fiercely. 'Tom, Emma, Warren—give it all you've got. Don't worry about the noise. Just shout.'

And they did, every one of them. They called her names into the empty air, with no idea of what could possibly happen. Just calling, calling, calling for the person they wanted.

Until—unbelievably—Robert saw the thing he wanted most in all the world. One moment the mouth of the entrance tunnel was empty, and the next—

'Look!' he shouted. 'Look! It's her!'

Without being told, Emma stepped forward, holding the blanket wide, calling a gibberish of names. 'Oh, Hope, oh, Lorn—oh, it's you, it's you, it's *you*!'

And suddenly she was with them, swelling up into the blanket, solid and real and *there*. Laughing at them over the fringed edge so that they could see that she was more than Hope had ever been, because she was there and free and herself.

When Tom went back to tell Magee what had happened, the flat was completely empty. The door swung open on to bare boards and windows without curtains. When he stepped inside, the living room felt cold and damp, as though no one had been there for weeks.

He searched every room, thinking that there must be some message from Magee. But the whole flat was picked clean, like a skeleton on a hillside. For all he could see, Magee might never have existed. They might have imagined him.

When he was sure there was nothing, he went out and turned to close the door behind him. As he pulled at it, he saw a piece of paper caught in the hinge. He tugged it free and spread it out eagerly. That had to be what Magee had left for him. A clue to the rest of his life.

The paper was totally blank.

That was when he understood that no one was going to write a script for him. He had to work things out for himself, as he went along.